sammy KEYES

and the ART of DECEPTION

sammy KEYES

and the ART of DECEPTION

WENDELIN VAN DRAANEN

A DELL YEARLING BOOK

Published by Dell Yearling
an imprint of Random House Children's Books
a division of Random House, Inc.
New York

Visit us on the Web! www.randomhouse.com/kids

Educators and librarians, for a variety of teaching tools,
visit us at www.randomhouse.com/teachers

ISBN: 0-440-41992-1

Reprinted by arrangement with Alfred A. Knopf

Printed in the United States of America

May 2005

10 9 8 7 6 5 4 3 2 1

Dedicated to my darling sister Nanine—may your artistic talents continue to blossom!

A chromatic palette of thanks to my excellent editor, Nancy Siscoe, and my ever-creative husband, Mark Parsons. Also, thanks to the mysterious H. Bizot, whose painting continues to inspire.

PROLOGUE

Marissa says I'm a magnet for mayhem. That wherever I go, so goes trouble.

Some friend, huh?

But I do have to admit it's a little strange. I mean, how can you go someplace as boring as an art gallery and wind up *attacking* someone?

And you'd think it would all have ended right there, but no. I got crushed in a pileup. A pileup of jealousy and lies. And the harder I tried to get up, to get *out*, the more pinned down I became.

Who knew art could be so dangerous?

ONE

March is windy in Santa Martina. And my theory is, it does something wicked to the air. Maybe it whooshes up devil dust and pixie pollen, I don't know. What I do know is, if you're a quiet, in-your-seat-when-you're-supposed-to-be kind of person in February, by the middle of March you'll be antsy. *Hyper.* Like all you want is to get outside and tear it up in nature's big gust bowl.

Which I guess is why I wasn't completely flattened when Marissa charged me out of nowhere between classes, practically swung around my neck, and cried, "Guess what!"

It's the kind of thing you learn to expect in the middle of March.

So I just hitched my backpack back on my shoulder and said, "What?"

"Danny wants to meet me at the Faire!" she says, whirling around with her arms spread wide.

"The Renaissance Faire?" I ask her, because Ms. Pilson's been talking it up all week in English class, saying it'll "tune our tympanic membranes" for some play her Drama Club is putting on next week.

Hop-hop, hippity-hop Marissa goes, like a manic March hare. "Yeah! Can you believe it? Can you even *believe* it?"

Well, no, I couldn't. Danny's one of those cool dudes, you know? The kind who walks cool and talks cool and even puts his jacket on cool. And since Marissa's a sucker for guys who put their jackets on cool, well, she's been sizzling for Danny Urbanski since elementary school. But since he's an eighth grader and we're only in seventh, I just figured it would never happen. Even if he did like Marissa. It would be too, you know, uncool to go out with a seventh grader.

I guess my eyebrows were stretched up pretty good, because Marissa giggles like you wouldn't believe, then runs off, saying, "Maybe Casey will ask you!"

I yell after her, "Shut *up!* He's Psycho-Heather's *brother,* remember?"

She just laughs over her shoulder and waves, and that's when I realize I'd yelled really loud. I mean, kids all around are looking at me, and I can tell—like lightning to a rod, this is going to find its way back to Heather.

I hurried off to class thinking, when, *when* am I ever going to learn to watch what I say? Especially at school, where gossip is king, and Heather Acosta is queen.

At least that's what she's angling for. Right now she's more like the evil step-princess or something, wearing her crown jewels all up and down her earlobes. But there's no doubt about it—that girl wants to reign supreme.

Anyhow, I blasted over to art class, and the minute I blew through the door, I could tell that our teacher Miss Kuzkowski had been outside, mixing it up with nature.

Now, Miss Kuzkowski is not real tidy looking to begin with. I think her hands are permanently stained with paint—especially her cuticles and under her nails. And even though she wears a smock and a *beret* when she's showing off, mixing up colors on her fancy wooden palette, she still manages to get paint in her hair and on her clothes, too.

But today she looked even messier than usual. Her hair was ratted around everywhere and falling over one eye—it was wild! She was all out of breath, too, rosy-cheeked and smiling. "Hi, guys!" she says when the tardy bell rings. "Glorious day, isn't it?"

Everyone peels off their backpacks and sort of eyes each other.

She notices some green paint on the heel of her hand and starts rubbing it away as she says, "Guys, I've been thinking . . ."

Half the class groans, because we know that when Miss Kuzkowski thinks, the rest of us suffer.

"Hang on! You're going to like what I have to say." She gives up on the paint and straightens her posture. Her hair, though, is still totally shock-waved. "I do think our section on art history was a good idea, only I've decided you're bored by it because you're not *experiencing* it. You don't *feel* it, ergo, you don't *get* it."

No one argued with that. For *days* she'd been putting us to sleep with endless names of painters and their different styles. You know—Gothic and Renaissance and neoclassicism and impressionism and *post*-impressionism and who-knows-what-else-ism. It was worse than regular history with Mr. Holgartner, and that's saying something.

It was also the opposite of what I'd wanted when I'd signed up for art. I was looking for a class where I could *do* something, not just sit like a brick, taking notes.

Anyway, Miss Kuzkowski's up front, pacing away, saying, "So I've decided . . . I've got to give you an assignment that will make you experience art. *Feel* art." She whips the hair out of her eyes, then clamps on to her podium with both hands and says, "Talking about art is like talking about the weather. What makes it come alive is actually experiencing it."

Tony Rozwell interrupts her with, "Does that mean we're finally gonna get a new project?"

"Yes," she says, shooting a finger up in the air. "But first I want you to walk with art, *be* with art, listen to your heart and spend time *feeling* art."

"Are you talking like at a gallery or something?" Emma Links next to me asks.

"Yes! Now, I know Santa Martina doesn't exactly have a fine art museum, but there *is* a gallery, and there just so happens to be an artist reception at—"

"*Aaaarp!*"

It was the loudest burp I'd ever heard. I swear the windows shook. *Snap* went twenty-seven heads. *Gasp* went twenty-seven mouths. And when we spotted little Trinity Jackson at the back table with her hand over her mouth and her cheeks on fire, twenty-seven kids all busted up.

Miss Kuzkowski stares at us a minute as we try to quit laughing, then she closes her eyes, shakes her head, and says, "Scratch that idea."

"Scratch what idea, Miz K?" Tony asks her.

"Never mind," she grumbles. "I don't need you embarrassing me in front of people I admire." Then she takes a big breath, and it's like she's putting the winds of March right back in her sails. "My other idea is probably much more in keeping with your level of appreciation anyway."

We all look at her like, Well?

"My *other* idea is that you should all go to the Renaissance Faire this weekend."

"The *Renaissance* Faire?" Matilda Grey asks.

"Yes!" She was definitely reinflating. She starts breezing around the room, saying, "Have you guys ever been? It's fabulous! The food, the atmosphere, the entertainment . . . you could have fun *and* learn about art."

"How art?" Emma asks her.

"There's an amazing amount of art, and the fabulous thing for you is, a lot of the artists are right there, in the booths! Think of the questions you could ask . . . think of the insight you could gain . . ."

"Think of the money you could lose," Tony says. "Last year it was like ten bucks to get in."

"Well, that's true," Miss Kuzkowski says. "So of course I can't *make* you go. But I would highly recommend it as a fun way to do your assignment."

We all look at her like, What assignment?

She smiles at us. A wicked, oh-it's-so-much-fun-to-torture-you smile. "Go to the Faire or check out a gallery. Choose an artist and either research them or interview them. Your marks will be higher for an interview with details about their process. Classify the art, then tell me how it affects you and *why* you like it or don't like it."

Tony interrupts again with, "Does it have to be a painting? What about all that clay stuff or those wooden jobbies—do those count?"

"Aha!" she says, smiling wickeder than ever. "Jolly good point!"

Jolly good point? We were in some sticky deep doo-doo now.

"What *is* art? That's the other thing I want you to do for me—define art. I want *your* definition of art. Is photography art? Are crafts art? Why? Why not? Give me your thoughts and definitions, and be prepared to defend them in front of a panel of your peers."

This was going from bad to worse in a hurry. And I could tell—she hadn't thought this out, she was just winging it! Demon dust was stuck in her lungs and it was making her zoom around, faster and faster, while she added more and more things to the assignment. By the end of class, I felt like I'd been through Hurricane Kuzkowski.

When I met up with Marissa at the bike racks after school, she was still flying high, too. Only she wasn't swooping around wildly like Miss Kuzkowski had been. No, she was floating on cloud nine.

Danny, Danny, Danny. That's all she could talk about. And yeah, Danny's cute, but he's not *that* cute. And who cares if he's got a blue backpack some days and a brown one other days? What's it *matter*? I tried to tell her about Miss Kuzkowski and her wicked assignment, but she was only tuned in to one thing—Danny, Danny, Danny. The walk over to the mall never seemed so long.

So I was relieved when she didn't even mention going inside the mall to play video games like she always does. We crossed Broadway, and when I turned off to go to the Senior Highrise, where I live with my grams, she just waved and zoomed off on her bike, calling, "Bye!" For the first time ever, I was glad to see her go.

Now, I *did* start for home, but then I plopped down on one of the mall benches and just sat there, thinking. And the more I thought, the more upset I got. I mean, Marissa has been my best friend since the third grade, and even though she's been zany about Danny Urbanski for years, she's always been able to talk about stuff besides Danny Urbanski. Like softball and what's happening at school and what we're going to do on the weekend. And even though it had only been one afternoon, I could already tell—Danny Urbanski was going to start dominating conversations. More than Heather Acosta *ever* had.

And it's not like I felt jealous because she was meeting a guy at the Faire and I wasn't. I mean, Marissa keeps telling me Casey likes me, but that whole situation is too weird. Sure, he *seems* really nice, and he *has* stuck up for me around his sister—even put his neck out for me in a big way—but I don't know. It's like he's playing some complicated game with me and I'm not sure what the rules are. For instance, he still has my skateboard. That's a long story, but the bottom line is, I can have it back any time—I just have to "ask nice." Or go over to his house and get it.

See? Is that stupid, or what? It's *my* skateboard. Why should I have to ask nice? Or go clear out to his dad's house in Sisquane? Maybe if he lived in town at his mom's I'd go. It's a whole lot closer.

Then again, Heather lives at his mom's, so probably not.

Anyway, the point is, why can't he just bring it to school? It's a game, I tell you. A stupid game. And I'm not playing. Period. And if that means I have to walk everywhere, well fine. That's what I'll do.

So, I guess I was feeling kinda lonely because after sitting on the bench for a while, I didn't go home. Instead, I headed back into the wind, back along the mall, past the fire department and police station, over to Cypress Street. And before you know it I'm waving at my favorite old guy in the whole wide world, calling, "Hiya, Hudson!" as I turn up his walkway.

"Sammy!" He swings his boots down from the porch railing and anchors his newspaper on the table with a brick. "How are you, my friend?"

All of a sudden I'm all choked up. I mean, *I* think of *him* as a friend—a great friend. But I'm thirteen and he's seventy-two, and, well, sometimes I think I'm more trouble to him than anything. Like he's the river and I'm the bear, and I get to fish and drink and wash off bugs, and all he gets is churned up and muddied.

So I'm just standing there in the middle of his walkway, blinking away the sting in my eyes, when he asks me, "You okay, Samantha?"

"Yeah," I tell him. "I'm fine."

He studies me a minute, then says, "Come on up and have a seat. I'll fetch us some cinnamon cake and tea." He smiles at me. "Sound good?"

"Sounds great."

Hudson's porch is the best. Nice and shady in the summertime, dry and woody smelling when it's raining. And in the wacky winds of March, it's like a quiet breezy harbor.

It's also a great place to think. Or watch the stars. Or just look at the world go by. To me, it's a magical spot. A place where even the most confusing things start to make sense.

A lot of that's thanks to Hudson, but the porch works all by itself, too. It's just an amazing place, and if you told me right now that I had to pick one place to spend the rest of my life, I'd say Hudson's porch.

Definitely Hudson's porch.

So when he came back out with a tray of cake and tea and said, "Okay, Sammy, what's got your feathers ruffled, huh?" I didn't even bother to make him coax it out of me. I jumped right in, telling him all about Marissa and Danny and the stupid Renaissance Faire and how I was afraid my best friend was turning into a boy-crazy bore.

And when I'm all done baring my soul about losing Marissa to the nefarious black hole of love, you know what he does?

He throws back his head and laughs.

"You're laughing at this?" I ask him. "It's like good-bye, Marissa—hello, Blather Brain."

"Blather Brain?" He shakes his head. "Aren't you being a little hard on her?"

"You should've heard her! She said his eyes sparkle like *diamonds*. His chin juts like *granite*." I lean in. "Hudson, she said his teeth are like little glaciers rising through a sea of minty freshness!" I stop right there and just look at him. I mean, if he doesn't get it after hearing about the Sea of Minty Freshness, he's never going to get it.

"Hmmm," he says, then chuckles and takes a big bite of cake.

"What?"

"She's got it bad, Sammy."

"No kidding!"

He chewed for the longest time, then washed the cake down with some iced tea. "Just let her be infatuated, Sammy."

"Well, it's not like I can *stop* her."

"That's true." He was quiet for a minute, then smiled at me. "Just try to be patient with her. Relationships at this age don't last. Friendships do."

We were both quiet for a minute, and it's funny—all of a sudden I felt better. A lot better. This blather-brain stuff was temporary. A phase. I'd just have to hang in there until she came back to earth. Besides, even though I'd never gone blather-brained on her, she had stuck by me through some pretty tough spots. Some *really* tough spots.

"Feeling better?" Hudson asked.

I dug into my cake and nodded. "Thanks."

"So how's the rest of school going?"

"It was crazy! It's the wind, Hudson. I swear it's the wind. Everyone's kinda wacky. Even the teachers! You should have seen Miss Kuzkowski today. She was . . . she was *wild*."

"How so?"

So I told him all about her electric hair and her insane assignment and how she's telling everyone they should go to the Renaissance Faire to look at art.

"The Renaissance Faire? For *art*? Sammy, everything you'll see there is going to be . . . how do I say this politely . . . B-grade, at best. You're not going to get any sense of true art at the Renaissance Faire." He shook his head and said, "I'm surprised she didn't encourage you to go to L'Artiste or the Vault or someplace like that."

"Never heard of them."

"They're local galleries, Sammy."

"The only gallery I've ever heard of is the one in the mall."

"That's not a gallery. That's mass-market junk."

"They have van Goghs and stuff there."

"Those are not van Goghs, Sammy."

"Yes, they are."

"They're reproductions."

"So?"

"*So?*"

His eyebrows are flying high, let me tell you. But before he can bend my ear about why van Goghs aren't van Goghs, I cut him off. "Well, she started to say something about some kind of artist reception, but then Trinity Jackson let out an earth-shaking burp, so she switched to talking about the Faire instead."

"A burp, huh?" Hudson yanked the *Santa Martina Times* from underneath the brick and started rustling through the Lifestyle section. "Was your classmate sent to the office?"

"For *burping*?"

He sighed, then shook his head and kept turning pages. "I think I read that . . . yes! Here it is!" He folded back the paper and stuck it in front of me. "I'll bet this is what your teacher was going to tell you about."

We both read the ad:

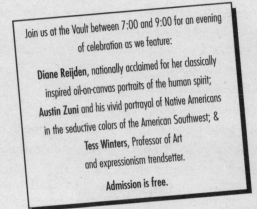

Join us at the Vault between 7:00 and 9:00 for an evening of celebration as we feature:

Diane Reijden, nationally acclaimed for her classically inspired oil-on-canvas portraits of the human spirit;

Austin Zuni and his vivid portrayal of Native Americans in the seductive colors of the American Southwest; &

Tess Winters, Professor of Art and expressionism trendsetter.

Admission is free.

Hudson slapped the paper with the back of his hand and said, "Forget the Faire. Forget the mall. I'm taking you to see some real art."

"But—"

"Go home, have some dinner, change your clothes, and—"

"My clothes? Hudson, I'm not going if I have to dress up."

He frowned. "That attire is not appropriate for an artist reception."

"But Hudson—"

"Neither is burping, in case your teacher didn't make that clear." He practically yanked me out of my seat.

"Meet me in front of your building at seven sharp. And tell your grandmother I'd love for her to join us, okay?"

"But Hudson . . ."

"No ifs, ands, *or* buts. This will be way better for your art education than the Renaissance Faire, believe me."

I grabbed the rest of my cake and wolfed it down, then glugged some tea. And as I was jetting down his steps, I grinned at him over my shoulder and let out a burp that would have made Trinity Jackson proud.

Then I headed straight for home.

What I didn't know was that in about three hours we'd all be headed straight for trouble.

TWO

An artist reception may be no place for high-tops, but I wore mine anyway. Grams had switched out of her usual A-line skirt-and-blouse into a longer A-line skirt-and-blouse. Not a drastic difference, believe me. And even though she grumbled plenty about the way I looked, getting me out of my sweatshirt and into a pink angora sweater was not going to happen. Nuh-uh. "Better to be cultured than look cultured, I suppose," she sighed as we met up at Hudson's car. "But once, just *once,* I'd like to see you in something a little more feminine."

Hudson was wearing some peach-and-black snakeskin boots and a little black bow tie. Not one of those stiff jobbies—this was a thin black ribbon, tied in a bow. "Nice boots," I told him. "Cool tie."

"Thank you," he said, but from the way he was checking me over, I could tell what he was thinking. So I said, "Better to *be* cultured than look cultured," and climbed in back.

I tried to pretend I still believed that when we walked into the reception. Heels were clicking. Jewelry was dripping. Perfume polluted the air.

Hudson knew I was about to bail, because he grabbed

me by the arm and pulled me along. "I tried to warn you," he whispered. "But you are here for an education, so let's consider this the first lesson learned."

Yeah. Next time, stay home.

We weren't actually even *in* the Vault yet. To get to the gallery, you have to go through a coffee shop called—get this—the Bean Goddess. The Bean Goddess is decorated in faux-funky Bohemian. It's too clean to actually *be* funky Bohemian, plus the furniture's some hybrid of wood and resin and the Roman columns are some wimpy whitewashed fiberglass. I know. I knocked on one and it made a real hollow *thonk-thonk-thonk* sound.

The plants are all fake, too, and they're everywhere—in big pots, little pots, hanging from shelves, winding around columns—everywhere, faux. At the counter there's a newspaper rack with about twenty different papers poking out of it and a long cooler with quiches and cheesecakes that look like *they're* plastic, too.

I guess the three of us were acting a little lost, because a man in super-shiny brown-and-white platform shoes dashes up to us and says, "Helloooo there! I'm Jojo Lorenzo, your host. And may I say, welcome, welcome!" He shakes Hudson's hand and then Grams', and it's the weirdest handshake I've ever seen. It's a *horizontal* handshake. Like instead of shaking hands so the thumbs are up, he twists everything so his hand is on top, then kind of flaps like a seal.

When he gets to me, his eyebrows go up as he checks me over. Then he giggles and gives me a horizontal handshake. "New to art, are we?"

I pulled my hand free. "Uh, this kind, yeah."

"Maaaarvelous. Please, please, sign in at the reception table, then go on through to the gallery." He makes a grand sweep of his horizontal hand toward an archway with THE VAULT painted over the top of it, then gives me a wink and says, "We don't have milk and cookies, but there's complimentary champagne for adults, and of course help yourself to our fine assortment of pungent cheeses and earth-stone crackers." Then off he goes to greet a couple coming in behind us.

"Yum," I grumbled. "Stinky cheese and rocky crackers."

"It's an acquired taste," Hudson whispers. "And no one's requiring you to eat."

Now, from the way Grams and Hudson are looking at each other, I can tell they're thinking that maybe I'm not ready for this. Not *mature* enough for this. So I whisper back, "Okay, okay . . . I'll try to keep an open mind," because that's what Hudson's always coaching me to do.

"Thatta girl," Hudson says. "After all, you're here to learn, not criticize."

We passed through the arch and into the gallery, where there were lots of people with little paper plates of stinky cheese milling around. The paintings were mounted on three walls, and to our left there was a big wooden table with a cash register and one of those old-fashioned gold-and-white phones. You know, the kind that scoops around under your chin when you talk and sits on a big stand with a couple of mini-goalposts when you're done with it?

Anyway, seeing one of those was nothing new, but what I hadn't ever seen before was a table like the one it was sitting on. It was really dark, with spiraling legs and big clawed feet, and had fierce looking bat heads popping out at the corners.

It was the scariest piece of furniture I'd ever seen.

Hudson must've noticed me gawking because he whispered, "It's an antique, Sammy. Probably out of an old English castle."

I shivered.

"Probably meant to keep away evil spirits." He guided me along, saying, "Why don't we start here and work our way around?"

When I finally tore my eyes away from the table, I found myself face to face with something even scarier.

A big orange splot.

I jumped back a little, then tried to figure out what it was. Or, at least, why it was hanging on the wall. I mean, if you saw a five-foot splot like that on the floor, you'd say, Whoa, now! Get me a mop! But here they'd framed it and named it and . . . I noticed the price tag. "Eight *thousand* dollars? That's crazy!"

Grams elbowed me. "Shhh!"

"Well it is!" I whispered.

"*Citrus Sun,* by Tess Winters," Hudson said, reading the plaque. He took a step back and shook his head. "Well, I must agree with Sammy. I don't see—"

"Shhh!" Grams said again, practically jabbing Hudson, too. "I think that's the artist, right over there!"

The woman was small, with pouty red lips and long stringy hair. She was wearing black from head to toe and holding a champagne glass with both hands. And she did seem to be listening to the people gathered around her, but she also kept glancing through the archway into the Bean Goddess.

I shut my mouth and moved over to *Renewal,* a four-foot gash of green on a jet-black background, with "Tess Winters" scrawled in big white letters across the bottom right corner. The green gash had a raggedy thickness to it, and I recognized the smell of linseed oil from art class. It was sweet. Kind of . . . vapory. Like some sort of industrial perfume.

"This one is *nine* thousand?" I whispered. *"Why?"*

"Shall we move on?" Grams whispered to Hudson. "This really isn't my cup of tea, either."

But just as we were passing by the pouty-lipped painter, the group that had been talking to her moved on, too. So all of a sudden there she is, you know, *available.* So Hudson sticks out his hand and says, "You're Tess Winters?"

She doesn't shake his hand. She just dips her nose a fraction of an inch and stares at him.

Hudson drops his hand and says, "These are done in oils? Or is that acrylic?"

Her nose goes up a few clicks. "Oils."

He clears his throat a little and says, "Ms. Winters, we're trying to give my young friend here a little exposure to art. Would you be so kind as to give her some insight into your paintings?"

She just stares at him with her lips clamped tight, then gives me the once-over like I'm polluting the place with my looks. And when she's all done condemning me with her eyes, she sticks her nose in the air and looks over at the coffee shop area.

Not a word.

So Hudson tries again, "Maybe you could tell her a little about expressionism and how you came to—"

"Excuse me, sir," she says, her eyes flaring at him. "This is a *reception,* not a classroom. If your little *friend* is truly interested in art, I suggest she spend some time at the library." Then she looks away. Like he isn't even there.

Now, Hudson Graham is the King of Cool. I have never seen him get flustered over *any*thing. So it didn't register right off that his lips turning thin and white and his eyes squeezing sharp and tight meant he was mad. But Grams did. She grabbed him by the arm and pulled him away before he could figure out what to say to the Snotty Splotter.

And I did follow along, only I was pretty heated, too. I mean, how snotty could a person be? Hudson had been nothing but nice to her!

So, at the last minute I turned back and said, "I may not know much about art, but I can tell you this—you are one *ugly* excuse for a human being." I said it like I was cool, too. All full of sass and attitude.

And you know what she did?

She put up a hand like a claw and *hissed* at me.

I laughed at her. I mean, come on. How seriously can you take a woman who thinks she ought to get eight grand for a five-foot splot and *hisses*?

Please.

There were people around who heard, too. And even though they were pretending they hadn't, I could tell by their popping eyes and nudging elbows that they'd seen the whole thing. So I caught up to Grams and Hudson before anyone went to have me tossed.

Grams was still trying to calm Hudson down, but he was steamed, boy. Under that thick white hair of his, even his *scalp* was mad. I could see it, pink as could be.

"Hudson, it's okay," I told him.

"No," he said. "It's not!"

"Hey, you know how you're always telling me not to let Heather get the better of me? Well, that Tess Winters is just like Heather . . . only not as sneaky."

"Impossible."

"Seriously, Hudson. As you would say, she's her own worst enemy."

He was still frowning.

"Are *you* gonna buy any of her paintings?"

"No."

"You think anyone *else* is?"

His nostrils flared. "How can a teacher behave that way?"

"What do you mean?"

"Isn't she some kind of professor? How can she possibly behave that way?"

"*Psst*, Hudson?"

"What."

"I don't care who she is—that's not art."

"But—"

"It's not. And I don't need a Ph.D. in Painting to tell you what it *is*."

He's still frowning, but not as bad.

I lean in a little and whisper, "It's absolute penguin poop is what it is!"

All of a sudden he busts up. Just throws his head back and *laughs*. And pretty soon my grams is laughing, too. And every time one of us looks over our shoulder at the Splotter's wall, we start busting up all over again.

Then a guy with a patch of black fuzz under his lip and a tray of plastic glasses on his hand stops in front of us, saying, "Champagne?"

Hudson says, "Thank you," then snags two glasses and hands one off to Grams. "Here's to a child's perspective." They both take sips, then he says, "Well. Shall we move on?"

The next group of paintings were mostly desert scenes. Ones with pueblos and buffaloes and very serious looking Indians. Not a smile in the whole bunch. But the prices were way lower than the Snotty Splotter's. They ranged from a few hundred dollars to fifteen hundred dollars. The fifteen-hundred-dollar ones were big portraits of Indian chiefs or braves, and there were little pin lights hanging from the frames, shining right into their eyeballs.

"That's a bit eerie, don't you think?" Grams whispered to Hudson, and I added, "And the pupils are way too big. They'd be all constricted in that kind of light."

"Here," Hudson says. "Stand back a little. And don't go for the technical . . . see if it evokes some mood in you."

So I stand there, trying to *feel* something, but the more I look at this Indian chief with the oversized pupils, the more it seems like one of those paintings of Elvis on velvet.

Then a man with white cowboy boots, a white cowboy hat, and the orangest tan I'd ever seen comes up to Hudson with a lopsided grin, saying, "Hey, partner. Love those skins."

Hudson looks down at his feet. "Picked them up in Ecuador. Soft as kid gloves."

"I'll bet." He sticks his hand out and says, "Say, I'm Austin Zuni. This is my work. Glad you could come out tonight."

So Hudson introduces us, then says, "Samantha here is interested in knowing more about art, and we thought it would be a good experience for her to—" but all of a sudden Super-Tan Man puts up a finger and says, "Excuse me," and hurries away.

Now we're all just standing there blinking at each other, when we notice that the Snotty Splotter has abandoned her post, too. And both she and Super-Tan Man are heading straight for the scary table where Jojo is giving a very enthusiastic horizontal handshake to a guy with a big black shoulder bag.

"Well," Hudson says. "So far, this has been most disappointing."

"But interesting," Grams says with a smile. Then she adds, "Why don't we get a little something to eat?"

So we head over to a round table full of stinky cheese and stony crackers, and one whiff tells me I'm not having any. Pee-yew! But Grams and Hudson put little chunks of this and that on little plates and then we snag a group of folding chairs and sit down. And while they nibble and sip and make polite conversation, I watch the action over by the scary table.

First it's just the guy with the big black bag, Jojo, the Snotty Splotter, and Super-Tan Man. And get this—the Splotter is *smiling*. Her pouty red lips are flying up and down, whipping around all over the place! And Super-Tan Man's acting all chummy and jovial, too, tilting back his hat and looking like, ee-haw!

But pretty soon lots of people are gathering around. And I'm just realizing that this one lady in a tight knit dress and slicked-back hair standing near Tess Winters is Miss Kuz*kow*ski, when a soft voice in my ear says, "Did you really tell her she was an ugly excuse for a human being?"

I jerk around, and standing right beside me is a woman with soft fluffy ringlets of reddish-brown hair. And I guess I was looking a little worried, because she pats my shoulder and says, "It's all right. I haven't had such a good laugh in ages."

Now, this woman has the most amazing eyes I've ever seen. They're blue, but not a regular blue. There's a definite tint of *purple* to them. And her posture is very regal. You know—straight up and down, but in a relaxed way. And she smells powdery—soft and sweet and . . . nice.

She puts out her hand and smiles. "I'm Diane Reijden, and you are . . . ?"

"Sammy," I tell her. "Sammy Keyes."

"Sammy," she says with a little twinkle. "Short for Samantha?"

I nod.

"And these are your grandparents?" she asks, smiling at Grams and Hudson.

"Yeah. I mean, well, this is my grandmother and this is our friend Hudson."

Grams shakes her hand and says, "Rita Keyes," then adds, "Pronounce your last name for me again, would you?"

"Reijden," she says, then laughs. "Like 'ridin' a bus.' But please, call me Diane."

Hudson stands and shakes her hand, saying, "Hudson Graham. It's a pleasure to meet you, Ms. Reijden. We haven't had the chance yet, but we're looking forward to viewing your installation."

So, ding-dong. It's finally sinking in that this woman with the purple eyes is the third painter, when I notice that Hudson is *still* shaking her hand. Like he's having trouble letting go.

Grams has noticed, too. She's looking from Hudson to Diane with a drooping smile, and let me tell you, the air is suddenly charged with all sorts of confusing signals.

Finally Grams clears her throat and says, "Could we offer you a plate?"

"Oh my, no! We had plenty while setting up. And I certainly didn't mean to intrude, I just wanted to share a smile with Samantha." Then she whispers to me, "It's not every day someone dares to put Tess Winters in her place."

"What's her problem, anyway?" I whisper back.

"Oh, well, we certainly don't want to get into *that*." Then she gives Grams a warm smile and says, "Thank you for coming out tonight. If you have any questions about my work, by all means ask."

"I have a question," I say, then add, "Uh, but it's not about your work."

She smiles. "That's all right. What is it?"

I nod over at the scary table. "Why is everyone over there? Who's the guy with the big black bag?"

"Ah," she says. "Well, we were told that a correspondent from the *Los Angeles Times* promised to show up tonight. I didn't believe he actually would, but it seems I've been proven wrong."

Hudson says, "The *Los Angeles Times*? Why, that's enormous exposure!"

"Yes," she says with a smile.

"Shouldn't you be over there? Certainly your work deserves the attention and exposure more than the other two."

She winks at Hudson and says, "Thank you, but I don't fawn well. I find it . . . distasteful. Besides, I'm sure he'll make his way over here soon enough." She smiles at us and says, "Excuse me now, won't you? I should go attend to my guests," then glides over to where a couple is standing, discussing one of her paintings.

When she's gone, Grams smoothes a nonexistent wrinkle from her skirt and says to Hudson, "I thought you weren't familiar with Ms. Reijden's work."

"I'm not."

She levels a look at him. "Yet you think she deserves the exposure more than the other two?"

Her lips are tight.

Her face is flushed.

And believe me, I *do* recognize this look—Grams is *steamed.*

Hudson clears his throat. "Well . . . Just look, Rita. Even from here you can see her work is something real."

"Hrmph."

He grabs Grams' hand and pulls her up. "Let's take a look and see if I'm right."

Now for a minute there I thought Hudson was going to keep right on holding her hand, but Grams shook free, then sniffed and marched over to the installation on her own.

There were only eight paintings on Diane's wall. And they weren't huge. Or trendy. And the signature in the bottom left of every one didn't jump out at you like, Notice ME! They were worked into the painting and, I don't know, quiet.

I went from one painting to the next, to the next. And I found myself moving slower and slower, because the more I looked at them, the more I liked them. They weren't flashy or stunning, they were more moody. And the longer I stood in front of them, the more their mood sort of replaced *my* mood. Kind of edged it out and left itself behind.

One painting titled *Pool of Gold* was of a woman gazing at her hands in her lap. That was it. But the way the light fell across her face and sort of collected in her palms, it looked like she was holding a little dish of liquid gold.

Then there was one that Hudson seemed to like called *Resurrection*. It was a painting of autumn leaves being stirred high in the air—the wind lifting them up, up, up. One tattered leaf was separate from the rest. Higher than the rest. And it seemed to glow orange and gold with two points like arms, spreading up and out, reaching for the sky.

Another, called *Awakening*, was just a sunlit field of young wild grass with a small tree off to one side. But it made me want to find that place. To sit and listen to the breeze rustle the grass.

But the painting I kept coming back to was of a little girl on her tiptoes, stretching up to whisper in someone's ear. The painting is mostly shadows, so you can't see the face of the person she's whispering to. All you really see is the girl's face and her sparkling brown eyes, lit up by the moon shining through a window.

"*Whispers,* is it?" Hudson said, reading the plaque. "Who do you suppose she's telling secrets to?"

"Her mother," I answered without thinking, and suddenly there were tears in my eyes.

Now honestly, I was embarrassed. I mean, this was nothing to start *crying* over. So I hadn't seen my mom in a while. So the days of me telling her secrets were long gone. This painting wasn't me *or* my mom. As far as I knew it wasn't anybody real. It was just paint.

But Hudson put his hand on my shoulder and said, "I find them to be very moving, too. It's amazing what she does with light."

And that's when everything kind of happened at once. I noticed Grams coming toward us from one side, Diane was moving toward us from the other, but just as they're about to reach us, a side door blasts open and the air petrifies with, "FREEZE!"

And standing there, twenty feet from me with the door

wide open and the night sky behind him, is a *bandit*. He's wearing a black mask across his eyes, a faded blue bandana tight across his nose and mouth, a brown cowboy hat crammed down on his head, and jeans that make mine look dressy.

'Course he's also wearing a nylon jacket and running shoes, so he looks a little . . . goofy. Like he's part Zorro, part Jesse James, and part . . . Bill Gates?

And everyone in the Vault is sort of going, "Huh?" until he jabs the left pocket of his jacket forward and screams, "I said, FREEZE!"

And this time everyone does, because now it's easy to see—

This bandito's got a gun.

THREE

"Oh, lord," Hudson whispers. "Let's just stay calm—see what he wants."

The Bandit edges our way, shouting, "One move out of any of you and it's curtains, you hear me?" He keeps the gun in his pocket poked up and forward, and when he gets near us he locks eyes with Diane.

Diane wobbles for a moment, then her eyes roll up in her head and down she goes. And while Hudson's busy catching her and easing her to the ground, the Bandit gets busy yanking her paintings off the wall with one hand while he practically jabs a hole in his pocket with his gun hand. "Sit down! All of you! Right where you are! NOW!" Everyone drops to the floor, including me and Grams.

So while the Bandit's yanking down pictures and Hudson's cradling Diane's head in his lap, trying to get her to come to, Grams is flashing between Hudson and the Bandit like she's not sure who's committing the worse crime.

Me, I'm keeping one eye on the Bandit and one on ol' Jojo. He hasn't exactly pounced on his goalpost phone to call 9-1-1, so I'm hoping he's got a hot button for the police. But either Jojo's a really good actor or he *doesn't* have a hot button, because all he's doing is sitting on the floor, shaking in his platform shoes.

So I'm crouched down, thinking *someone's* got to make a move to stop this guy, when I notice a dark spot in the corner of the Bandit's gun pocket.

A dark spot that wasn't there before.

At least I *think* it wasn't there before.

By now the Bandit's got four of Diane's paintings stacked and crammed under his arm, and he's screaming, "I said, SIT DOWN!" across the room. And he's sounding really jacked up and desperate, and I know I shouldn't even be thinking about it, but my mind can't stop asking, Can it be?

Then he starts backing away, poking his pocket across the room, shouting, "Don't move. None of you!" and that's when I know it's true.

I mean, it *must* be true.

Why else would the dark spot on his jacket be *growing*?

I didn't have time to talk myself out of it. He was making his getaway and I had to do *some*thing. So before Grams could finish shouting, "Samantha, NO!!!" I was tackling the guy like I played for the 49ers.

I grabbed him around the legs, and the paintings spilled out from under his arm and crashed onto the floor. Trouble is, as he was coming down, his shoe whacked my jaw and snapped my tongue between my teeth. And since it really, really, *really* hurt, well, I let go.

The Bandit rolled away from me and jumped to his feet. His mask stayed on. His bandana stayed on. Even his hat didn't really come off. It came loose, but the minute he landed he crammed it right back on his head.

But the paintings were scattered, and since he knew I was on to him, he didn't even bother trying to reach them. He just turned around and ran.

I tried yelling, but it came out, "As sas a swurcun!" because my tongue hurt so bad. And everyone was either shrieking or frozen, and no one was understanding me. "A swurcun! As jus a swurcun!" I yelled, but he got away. Just giddy-upped out the side door and into the night.

And *then,* after he's totally gone, someone finally says, "Did she say *squirt* gun?"

I nod my head like crazy and yell, "Id was jusd a squird gun!"

All of a sudden, everyone starts charging everywhere. Miss Kuzkowski and a bunch of other people dash for the exit. Some men go tearing out the side door after the Bandit. Jojo does sort of a flying stumble halfway across the gallery, before fluttering around in a circle and clip-clopping through the archway and out of sight. And Grams, well, she charges me.

And does she say, "Samantha! Are you all right?"

No. She lays into me with, "Child, are you out of your *mind*?"

I flex my tongue from side to side, trying to make it work right. "He only had a squirt gun, Grams."

"How do you know that? Did you *see* it? Samantha, he could have killed you!"

"It was dripping, Grams."

She hesitates. "Dripping? Are you sure?"

"Uh-huh." I look over at Hudson, who's helping Diane into a chair. "I see she's come to."

"Hrmph."

"Give him a break, Grams. He's just being chivalrous."

All of a sudden Jojo's all over me. "Oh! Oh! You plucky little *tiger*. You're all right, aren't you? Please, please, tell me you're all right."

I laugh and tell him, "I'm fine."

"And the paintings?" He swoops down on them and checks them over quickly. "Oh, thank heaven! Oh, thank God. It's only the frames. The art is fine. Fine!" He races over to Diane and skids to a halt on one knee in front of her. "Di, darling! Di, they're fine. Perfect! Not a scratch."

"Joseph, *what* did I tell you about security?"

"But Di, in my wildest *dreams* . . . !"

All of a sudden the man with the big black bag is there, too, and now he's got a camera with a lens the size of a salad plate hanging around his neck.

Diane asks him, "Did you manage to . . . did you get any pictures of what just happened?"

"Only one as he was fleeing."

Diane takes a deep breath, closes her eyes, and says, "I don't suppose that'll show us much, do you?"

"No, but it'll still be dynamite in the article!"

"The . . . the article?" Diane asks.

He puts out a hand and says, "T. William Huffer, *Los Angeles Times*. I'm sorry I didn't get the chance to introduce myself before the . . . well, that *was* a holdup, wasn't it?" He turns to Jojo. "What's the condition of the paintings? Were they damaged?"

"No," Jojo says. "They're perfect. Perfect! One or two may need new frames, but the canvases are fine!"

"Very good. I'll need access to them—I want to photograph the whole collection." He looks at Diane. "With your permission, of course." He turns back to Jojo. "And a time to interview her. Can we set that up?"

"Certainly, certainly!"

By now everyone has pretty much congregated around us, including Austin Zuni and Tess Winters. And when Tess hears ol' T. William Huffer say all that about Diane's collection, her big red lips push way out for a minute, and then she says, "So this is how it works, huh?"

Everyone turns to her, and from the look on her face it's easy to see—she's as ticked off as a whacked wasp.

Jojo puts his arm around her and says, "There, there."

She throws his arm off. "Don't there-there me, Jojo! Can't you see what's happened here?"

No one says a word.

Tess points a bony finger at Diane and screeches, "She set this up!"

"Set this up? Are you *mad*, woman?" All heads whip around to see who's just called the Splotter mad, only I don't need to. I'd recognize Hudson's voice anywhere.

I check Grams, and sure enough, she's steaming like a baked potato.

"You!" Tess snaps at Hudson. "You and that . . . that ragamuffin girl!" She points at me. "You're part of this whole performance!"

"Plucky tiger" was bad enough, but "ragamuffin girl"? I looked at her and shook my head. "What are you, *jealous*?"

"Of *you*? Ha!"

"No, you sloppy splotter! Of the fact that someone wanted to steal her stuff and not yours!"

"Sloppy splotter? Sloppy *splotter*? Jojo, did you hear what that insolent little brat just called me?"

Jojo just stands there with half a smile plastered on, his eyes big and kind of roving around the crowd like, Tell me this is not happening . . . Tell me this is *not* happening . . .

"Throw her *out*," she screeches. "No, have her arrested!"

Jojo cringes. "Arrested? For calling you a . . . splotter?"

"No! For being part of this charade!"

Diane says, "There is no 'charade' or conspiracy or anything else involved here, Tess. That man tried to heist my paintings, this girl stopped him. That's all there is to it."

Tess looks around the crowd. "Doesn't *any*one else find this a little bit coincidental? Think about it! A reporter from the *Los Angeles Times* actually comes to this wretched town with the promise to do a piece on one of us . . . what better way to make a media event of it than stage your own robbery? Of course he wants to cover *her* now! It's got everything he could want in a story . . . even though none of it has a thing to do with art!"

Austin Zuni steps forward and says, "Now that you mention it, it is a bit convenient to have a robbery—"

"I didn't *have* a robbery!" Diane turns to Jojo. "What utter nonsense *is* this?"

"Yeah," I tell ol' Splotty. "If anyone hired that guy, it was probably you."

"*What?*"

"Well, you can't exactly put paintings in the *L.A. Times* if they aren't around, right?" I shrug. "It's one way to cut down on the competition."

"Saaaay," Austin Zuni says. "I hadn't thought of that . . . !"

Tess snaps, "Oh, shut up, Austin. That's ridiculous."

"I don't know," I tell her. "You seem pretty desperate to me."

"Jojo," she says through her teeth. "Get her *out* of here."

And yeah, it probably would have been polite for me to keep my mouth shut, but I was mad at her. Mad because she'd been so rude to Hudson. Mad because she'd looked down her nose at me. Mad because that's how I get when I hear glass scraping glass, and that's exactly what she sounded like to me.

So I tell her, "Well, you do. I mean how can your paintings possibly compete with hers? Anybody can dump a bucket of paint on a canvas. Anybody can take a big ol' fat brush and slash it across something and frame it. You don't need a Ph.D. to know it's ugly."

"GET HER OUT OF HERE!"

"I'm goin', I'm goin'!" I tell her. "Just next time watch who you call a ragamuffin."

Grams is hurrying along beside me as I make for the door, only Jojo runs in front of us and blocks our path. "Wait, wait! You can't go! The police are going to want to talk to you!"

Well, I didn't exactly want to talk to them, so I said, "Look. You know everything I know. The guy tried to rob the place with a squirt gun. He didn't get anything, and now he's gone. End of report."

"But . . ."

Just then some men come shuffling in, all out of breath and windblown. They shake their heads when they see Jojo. "Couldn't find him. We searched blocks in all directions. He's just gone." Then one of them adds, "What's taking the police? How long's it been since you called?"

"Oh!" Jojo cries, and holds his cheeks. Then he turns beet red and runs toward the scary table.

"Brother," I grumble, and head for the door. And Grams is right there beside me, only she keeps looking over her shoulder at Hudson, who's hanging on Diane's every word.

"You want to walk home, don't you?" I ask her when we get outside.

"I most certainly do," she says.

"Well, at least let me leave a note on his windshield."

"He doesn't deserve a note."

"Grams," I say, digging through her purse for a scrap of paper and a pencil, "he's just being attentive to a damsel in distress."

"And what were *you* in there?"

I look up at her. "Me? A damsel?" I get back to digging. "Never!"

"He's being an old fool," she says with a scowl. "It's those Liz Taylor eyes."

"Who?"

"Elizabeth Taylor. The actress? Don't tell me you've never heard of her?"

"Nu-uh."

"Well she had eyes just like those. Brought men to their knees just as quickly, too." She *hrmphs* and then waits for me as I snap a "We walked home" note under Hudson's windshield wiper.

I put my arm around Grams, and as we start down the street she looks from her feet to mine, saying, "I guess it was a good night to wear high-tops after all."

I grin at her. "Every night's a good night, Grams."

She laughs, then says, "I'm glad you didn't want to stick around and talk to the police. I was more than ready to get away from those people. What a wretched bunch!"

We turn the corner toward Broadway, and suddenly the wind gusts up and whirls around us. Like it's dancing with us for a minute before moving on.

Grams starts walking a little faster, saying, "I just love this weather, don't you, Samantha? It makes me feel . . . electric."

"Electric?" I laugh and say, "I would've guessed you *wouldn't* like it."

"Oh, no. I've always loved the wind. Mind you, not the steady ones—they're draining. But gusty winds? Oh, I adore them."

Now it's funny. I'd never seen my grams act like this before. She was practically skipping along the sidewalk, practically flinging her arms around in the air. She *wasn't* actually skipping or flinging, but I could tell that in her heart she was feeling young and happy and defiant. Like she was as free as the wind and no starstruck senior citizen was going to get her down. She was going to *fly* instead.

Then Grams says, "That Tess Winters may be a real pill, but I have a hunch she's right."

"About . . . ?"

"I'll bet she set the whole thing up."

"Who? Purple Eyes? You really think so?"

"I do."

"But Grams—"

"There's something about her I don't trust, don't like, don't . . . *believe*."

"But—"

"I swear that fellow smiled at her."

"The Bandit did?"

"Well, he had that whole getup on, but just for a moment, I swear he did." She seemed to think about this a minute, then nodded. "I think that whole fainting routine was just to draw attention away from him."

"But Grams, why?"

"For the publicity! It's all about publicity." She kicks a stone and says, "Oh, I would love to prove it. It would serve him right, for being such a fool."

I grin at her and say, "Grams!" because really, even though I'd seen her mad about things before, I'd never seen her on fire like this. I mean, for the first time in my life I could see *her* using binoculars and hiding in bushes, chasing after bad guys.

This was a brand-new side of Grams.

One I'd soon learn a whole lot more about.

FOUR

I'm not supposed to be living in the Senior Highrise. It's illegal. But I'm there anyway, on what I call a permanently temporary basis, while my mother gets her act together in Hollywood.

Don't get me started.

So since I had to sneak up the fire escape while Grams could just waltz inside and use the elevator, she was already in the apartment when I slipped through the door. I found her sitting stiff in a chair with her arms crossed, watching the phone ring off the hook.

"You're not going to answer it?" I whispered.

She shook her head.

"Ever?"

Shake, shake, shake.

"What if it's not him?"

"It is."

"What if he's worried?"

"*Hrmph.*"

"Grams . . . !"

"I'm not in the mood to hear that I'm overreacting."

I scowled at her and picked up the phone.

She crossed her arms tighter.

"Hello?"

"Sammy?"

"Hi, Hudson."

"Why on earth did you two leave? *When* did you leave? One minute you're arguing with that Winters woman, then next thing I know you're nowhere to be found."

"Well, neither of us felt like sticking around. And you were, uh . . . a little preoccupied."

"Listen, let me talk to your grandmother. I feel horrible that she walked home."

I held the phone out to Grams, but she just shook her head and dug in deeper.

"Hudson? She doesn't want to talk to you right now."

"She's . . . mad?"

I eye her and say, "You betcha. Where are you, anyway? You don't sound like you're at home."

"I'm not. I'm still at the Vault. The police have been taking statements . . . it's quite an ordeal."

"How's the damsel?"

"Who?"

"Your damsel in distress."

Now Hudson Graham is probably the smartest guy I know, but until that moment, I swear he was clueless about why Grams and I had walked home. And I could almost hear the click in his brain as he said, "Ah . . . oh, dear."

"Um-hmm. So why don't you call back in the morning?"

Grams' head goes into hyper-shake, and across the line I hear, "But—"

"You know how she gets."

Grams' jaw drops, so I give her a little shrug and smile like, Well it's *true* . . .

"Okay," he says. "I'll do that. But in the meantime, would you try to convince her that I'm not a dog?"

"Aaarrroooo!"

"I'll talk to you in the morning."

"Good night," I told him, and hung up the phone.

Of course Grams wanted to know every little thing he said. And then we had to go and beat the whole evening to death. So when I finally got to hit the couch, well, Zzzzz, I was out.

So I'm seriously snoozing away, in the middle of a really great flying dream—one where I'm sailing over the rooftops of Santa Martina with my arms out, and the bad guys who are chasing me can't fly as high as I can. And I'm getting away, going up, up, over trees and St. Mary's steeple, laughing *heh-heh-heh* over my shoulder at them— when the phone rings.

One eye snaps open, but the rest of me tries to keep on flying. But what the one eye sees is the little clock on the end table next to me.

Seven-thirty?

On a Saturday?

What kind of moron would . . . and then I remember— Hudson.

Boy! I thought as I rolled the pillow over my head. He's getting dumber by the minute.

Grams didn't pick up the phone, either. And when it finally quit ringing, she took it off the hook and laid it on the counter. Then when it made a beeping noise and a mechanical lady told us to hang it up, Grams told her to shut her prerecorded mouth and unplugged the phone from the wall.

I never did get back to my flying dream. I got up and had some oatmeal instead.

Now, five-grain oatmeal may not seem like much of a Saturday morning treat to you, but really, it's all in the approach. Grams makes me eat it practically every morning, so I've learned how to love it. All you need is some brown sugar, some maple syrup, and walnuts. Lots of crushed walnuts. Mix it all together, add a little milk, and *yum*. You'll want seconds every time.

Which is exactly what I was having when all of a sudden there's a knock on the door. At first it's just a tap-tap-tap, but on the third try, it turns into a whack-whack-whack! And I say to Grams, "You've got to answer the door!"

"The *nerve* of that man! How dare he invade our . . . personal space!"

"Grams, just answer it, would you? You can't avoid him forever."

She crosses her arms. "Watch me."

I get up and say, "Okay, then I'll answer it."

"Samantha, you can't do that! What if it's *not* him?"

Whack-whack-whack.

"I guess that's a risk I'm willing to take."

At the last minute, Grams cuts me off and shoos me away to hide in her closet, which is where I always have to go when someone unexpected comes over. But for once I don't dive into Grams' pile of pumps. I just duck behind the bedroom door and peek out the crack as Grams opens the apartment door.

And who comes barging into the apartment all flustery and blustery and out of breath?

Marissa, carrying two bulging tote bags.

"Marissa?" Grams gasps as she snaps the door locked behind her.

"Don't worry!" she whispers. "I came up the fire escape. And I did try to call you, but first no one answered, then the phone was busy!"

"Did you . . . did you try very early this morning?" Grams asks her.

Marissa's face scrunches up into a cringe. "Did I wake you up? I'm so, so sorry! I just wanted to find out if Sammy could go before she took off somewhere else."

"Go?" I ask her, coming out from behind Grams' door. "Go where?"

"To the Faire!" she says, then starts yanking clothes out of a tote bag. "Look at this! Check these *out.*"

"Marissa, stop right there."

She looks at me, one arm up, a dark red velvet dress with puffy sleeves and some kind of white lace-up contraption of a blouse draping clear to the floor.

"I hope you're not thinking what I think you're thinking, because you can just quit thinking it."

"But my mom told me kids under fifteen don't have to pay if they're in costume. And since I know you won't let me pay *for* you, I figure—"

"It's a dress, Marissa."

"And hel-*lo*, you're a girl . . . ?"

"Not *that* kind of a girl," I say, pointing to the ruffles and frills. "You can't ride a skateboard in something like that. You'd *kill* yourself."

"Well you don't *have* a skateboard to ride, now do you?"

She was giving me an evil little grin, so I told her, "Shut up."

"Samantha!" Grams says, looking all stern at me.

"You have no idea what she's implying, Grams, so don't start sticking up for her."

It's like Grams didn't even hear me. She just spreads the skirt of the red dress Marissa's holding and says, "This is quite lovely."

Marissa hands the dress over to Grams, then out of the other tote bag she yanks a royal purple dress that's even frillier than the red one. "Look at the bodice on this," she says to Grams. "Isn't it gorgeous?"

"Oh, my!" Grams says. "Where on earth did you get these?"

Marissa grins. "Yolanda's closet, of course."

"That cinches it," I tell her. "I am not wearing that thing!" 'Cause the last time I borrowed something from her mother's closet, it turned out to be a designer sweater that I, well, destroyed.

"She's the one who brought it up. She says it's fine!"

"But—"

"Just don't put out any fires with it, okay?"

"But—"

"She doesn't *care*, Sammy. It's been in the closet for,

46

like, twenty years. Here!" she says, and tosses me the red one.

"That's all beside the point anyway! I don't *want* to go to the Faire."

"Sure you do! Everyone says it's loads of fun."

"You must be talking about the Renaissance Faire?" Grams asks Marissa, and when Marissa nods, Grams turns to me and says, "Samantha, you'll love the Faire. Why, I remember I went to one years ago . . . it was delightful. And I was *wishing* I'd had a costume to dress in. Everyone was in period outfits, talking in Old English, singing, dancing . . . I felt like a wet rag in regular clothes. You certainly should go. It's like taking a trip back in time!"

"Grams, you don't get it. Marissa doesn't want to go because she wants to be transported to a bygone era. She wants to go because Danny Urbanski is going to be there."

Marissa crosses her eyebrows at me, while Grams' fly up at *her*. And she asks Marissa, "Do your parents know this?"

"It's not *like* that! And I don't need a chaperone, I need a friend!"

We're all quiet a minute, looking back and forth at each other, and finally Grams says, "Well, Samantha, I think you should be a friend and go."

I mutter, "Doesn't anyone care that I don't *want* to go?"

Marissa comes right up to me and whispers, "Please? *Please?*"

I look down and say, "What about Dot? Or Holly?"

She shrugs. "They wouldn't understand. They haven't known me since the third grade." She scoops up my eyes with hers. "The third grade! Please, Sammy. I don't want to go without you."

"I don't want to hang around when you're with Danny . . . !"

"I'm not going to run *off* with him or anything. Besides, he said he's going with some friends. There'll be lots of people you know. Let's just go together and have fun, okay?"

I crinkle my nose at the dress and say, "Would I really have to wear that thing?"

"Yolanda gave me thirty dollars. We can spend twenty getting in, which will leave us ten for food—and that means we won't eat much. Or we can wear these and get in for free and have thirty dollars to spend."

"I'd rather pack peanut butter and jelly."

"Peanut butter and . . . Samantha!" Grams says, shaking her head. "Get into the spirit of it, would you? They didn't have peanut butter and jelly in merry old England. If you can save ten dollars wearing that dress, wear the dress!"

Grams' fixed income didn't leave me much to argue with. She wasn't forking over any cash, and even if she had money to spare, I don't think she would've offered.

She was finally going to see me in a dress.

I scowled at Marissa, then Grams, then the dress. And finally I said, "Okay, but I'm wearing my high-tops."

"Yes!" Marissa cried, pumping the air with her fist. Then she gave me a giant hug and said, "I owe you! I owe you big time!"

It's hard enough sneaking down five flights of fire escape stairs in broad daylight in jeans and a sweatshirt. But in our pouffy purple and red dresses, we must've looked like a couple of hot-air balloons descending on Santa Martina. And the whole hike over to the fairgrounds, people honked and whistled and yelled stuff out their car windows at us. They weren't really making fun of us—and Marissa didn't really seem to mind, waving back and even *curtsying* once—but I kept worrying that someone from school would see us.

Someone like Heather.

Then we got to the fairgrounds, and all of a sudden *everyone* was wearing weird clothes. There was a man right ahead of us at the turnstile who had on yellow-and-black knickers and tall black boots. His shirt was green and gold, broad at the shoulders and belted around the waist. He had a really wide accordion collar, a dagger hanging from his belt, and on his head was a hat with a plume. I'm talking the biggest, puffiest white feather I had ever seen.

The woman he was with was wearing a gold dress that was way fancier than ours. The skirt was really full and flared way out, and the top was laced on so tight, she looked like some sort of giant dinner bell waiting to be rung.

So by the time we went inside, I was already feeling a lot less geeky. And talk about being transported to a bygone era! It didn't take long to forget I was in Santa Martina. There were tents up everywhere. Not the camping kind, either. These were white canopies with bright little pennant flags perched on top. And everywhere you looked there was straw. Spread out on the ground, wrapped in bales, stacked as walls—everywhere. And the air was full of *voices*. Not like the buzz of people talking, but of individual voices. Loud ones. Calling to each other in a language I recognized, but then didn't.

"Good morrow, rennie! From where comest thou?"

"South Bay, good lord."

"Ah, the fair shire of South Bay, yes! I know that area well! Pray, what bringst thee to our Chipping-Under-Oakwood?"

"The blood of John Barleycorn, o'course!"

"Aye! To John Barleycorn, then!"

"Cheers!"

Then off they went in different directions, calling out to other people. And as we wandered deeper and deeper into the fairgrounds, past jugglers and minstrels, dancers and *goats*, I started feeling like some sort of bit player in the middle of a huge production that had the whole fairgrounds as its stage.

When we passed by a banner that said TOURNAMENT FYLD, Marissa suddenly pointed and cried, "Look, they're jousting!"

Sure enough, inside the arena there were jousters on horses all dressed up in armor and shields, charging each other with poles. "Wow," I said. "You don't think they're really going to . . . ," and then down one of the jousters fell. Just *thump, clank, ka-plunk*, he was on the ground, rolling away from his horse while the crowd cheered for the winner.

Marissa said, "Cool!" And since she wanted to go inside and see the next round, that's what we did.

I have to admit—it *was* cool. I'd never seen actual jousting before. And these "knights," as all the people around us kept calling them, were very intense about knocking each other over. They'd set up at opposite ends of the field, a man dressed like Robin Hood would drop a flag, and then the horses would charge, their hooves thundering and their tails flying. Then the jousting poles would tangle and a knight would fall, or they'd miss each other entirely and turn around and charge again. And right before the jousters rammed each other, everyone would hold their breath, so all you'd hear was the pounding of hooves.

And after each round, the winning knight took off his helmet and got a kiss from a lady with long curly blond hair, all dressed up like Guinevere.

"Wow," Marissa says as we're leaving the field. "Isn't this whole place . . . romantic?"

"Hmmm," I tell her. "So, where are you supposed to meet Danny?"

"It's not like that."

"Well . . . what *is* it like?"

She shrugs. "He just said maybe he'd see me here."

I grab her arm. "Wait a minute. You're telling me that you made me put on this ridiculous dress and dragged me clear across town because he said *maybe* he'd see you here?"

"Well he didn't say it like *that*. It was more like, 'I'll be looking out for you there,' or, 'It'd be really great if we'd run into each other there.' "

"But what he *said* was, 'Maybe I'll see you there'?"

She shrugs again, looking around. "You had to be there." She skips a few steps, then smiles and says, "But aren't you having a great time? I mean isn't this the coolest?"

From a small stage across the way, a man in a belted poet's shirt and a feathered black hat holds up a pewter mug and starts singing:

"Well, I'll tell you a story that happened to me,
One day as I went out to Cork by the sea.
The day it was hot, the sun it was warm;
Says I, 'A quick pint wouldn't do me no harm.'
I went in and ordered a bottle of stout.
Says the barman, 'I'm sorry, the beer's all sold out.
Try whiskey, young Paddy, ten years in the wood.'
Says I, 'I'll have cider; I've heard that it's good.' "

Then a fat man in brown tights hops next to him on-stage and they both clink mugs and sing together,

"But I'll never, no never, no never again,
If I live to a hundred or a hundred and ten.
Well, I fell to the ground and I could not get up
After drinking a quart of the Johnny-Jump-Up."

Then a third man joins them and they start up on the next verse, mugs held high, voices booming.

"After downing the third, I went out to the yard,
Where I walked into Brofie, the big civic guard;
'Come 'ere to me boy. Don't you know I'm the law?'

I let loose me fist and I shattered his jaw.
Well, he fell to the ground with his knees doubled up
'Twas not I what hit him, but the Johnny-Jump-Up."

The man in the black hat calls into the crowd that's gathered around, "Oh-hoy there, lad! Come join us!" And up on the stage jumps a boy in a Robin Hood cap, pirate pants, and a swashbuckler's vest. And as he raises a beer mug and starts singing, *"But I'll never, no never, no never again, if I live to a hundred or a hundred and ten . . . ,"* well, my jaw drops and my eyes pop because I know this guy.

He's an eighth grader at our school.

One with "cute freckles" and a tint of red in his hair.

And from the twinkle in his eye, I can tell—it's too late to duck and hide.

He's spotted me, too.

FIVE

Marissa, of course, grabs my arm and says, "Sammy, look! Isn't that Casey?"

"Let's go," I tell her.

"But he's singing to you!"

"Oh, great," I tell her. "He's serenading me with a song about being drunk."

"What?"

"Haven't you been listening?"

By now they're in the middle of another verse.

"*. . . Well, about twelve o'clock and the beer it was high.*
The corpse sits up and says he with a sigh,
'I can't get to heaven, they won't let me up,
'Til I bring 'em a quart of the Johnny-Jump-Up.'"

"Ohmygod," Marissa says as the whole crowd joins in with, "*But I'll never, no never, no never again, if I live to a hundred or a hundred and ten; well, I fell to the ground and I could not get up after drinking a quart of the Johnny-Jump-Up!*"

"Let's go, okay?"

"No, look! He's grinning at you."

"All the more reason to get *out* of here."

Then all of a sudden the man with the black hat stumbles backward and falls down on the stage. And he yells, "Ya beslumbering beef-witted barnacle! Watch what 'cher doin'!"

"Me?" yells the big man in brown tights. "Ya dare call me a beef-witted barnacle? Yer naught but a bawdy beetle-headed bum-bailey!"

"Ay!" calls the third man. "'Tis true!"

"Nay!" calls ol' Black Hat. "I'm a gent. But you! Yer but a churlish common-kissing clotpole!"

"Common kissing? A pox on thee for saying so! I've kissed the hand of Queen Lizzy herself, you loggerheaded knotty-pated malt-worm!"

And with that they all start fighting, with Casey in the middle trying to break them apart. And between punches, the insults fly fast and furious—"Ya gleeking hedge-born hugger-mugger!" "Ya paunchy, elf-skinned measle!" "Ya reeky, onion-eyed pigeon egg!" "Ya villainous, urchin-snouted wagtail!"—until finally Casey shoves them apart, crying, "God's blood! Yer but a band o' gorbellied, sheep-biting skainsmates!"

The three men freeze, then begin rubbing their jaws, muttering, "Ay. 'Tis true. We are!" And the next thing you know, they're all shoving their mugs in the air again, singing, *"But I'll never, no never, no never again, if I live to a hundred or a hundred and ten; 'cause I fell to the ground and I could not get up after drinking a quart of the Johnny-Jump-Up!"* Then they all link arms and take a great big bow while everyone claps and cheers. And Marissa joins right in, whistling real loud between her fingers, saying to me, "Wasn't that great! That was really *fun.*"

Now, I'm not hot to stick around whistling and clapping. I want to leave before . . . but it's too late. Casey's already hopped off the stage and is heading straight for us, calling, "Hey, Sammy! Sammy, wait up!"

"Hold, lad!" Black Hat bellows after him.

"What, Dad?" Casey says, turning around.

"Mind yer tongue! You'll be tossed from the Guild for such language."

Casey rolls his eyes and calls over his shoulder, "Aye, sir," then gives me the biggest smile I've ever seen. "How'd you know I'd be here?"

"I . . . ," and I'm about to say, I didn't! but then *he* says, "You look great in maidenwear."

"Maidenwear?"

"You know . . . that whole getup," he says with a whisk of the hand. Then he takes off his cap and sweeps it in front of himself grandly as he makes a bow. "A gent should doff his cap for a lady, nay?"

Well, Marissa positively giggles while my cheeks turn pink as petunias. But I hike up my skirt and stick out my high-top. "Don't be fooled, okay?"

He laughs, but keeps talking like I'm some "lady." "Willst thou attend the next performance? 'Tis funnier than the last."

"No!" I tell him. "I mean . . . we're just going to walk around and, you know, look around."

Then Marissa says, "I didn't know you were an actor, Casey."

"Casey? Thou mistaketh me for another. I am Sir Lucan, Knight of the Holy Blade of York."

Marissa giggles again, so he says, "But I must away, fair lass. Duty calls." Then before I realize what's happening, he grabs my hand, puts it to his lips, and says, " 'Til we meet again," and dashes off.

"Oh!" Marissa gasps. "Oh!"

I knew my face was completely bugged out, so I turned my back on the stage and wiped my hand against the skirt of my dress. I don't know why I was trying to wipe it off. It wasn't wet or anything. It just tingled. Soft, shivery tingles. All up and down my arm.

Marissa was grabbing on to me, giggling away. "Sammy! Ohmygod, Sammy!"

"He was *acting*, Marissa, you get it? That was Sir Lucan, Knight of the . . ."

"Holy Blade of York!"

"Yeah, whatever. The point is, that was not Casey." I was rubbing the back of my hand like crazy.

It still tingled.

"Ha!" she says. Just, Ha!

She kept in step with me as I hurried away, and finally she says, "I have never seen your cheeks this red, you know that?"

"You better not tell anybody about this, you hear me? Not Dot, not Holly . . . nobody!"

"About what?" she says, looking at me all innocent-like. And I'm just thinking, Phew! when she adds, "Love's first kiss?"

"Marissa!" I lay into her with both hands. "That was *not* love's first kiss! It was a meaningless little brush of the lips against my hand. He was *acting*."

She smiles and kind of shimmies from head to toe. "Ha!"

I rub my hand against my skirt, then shake it off like crazy, grumbling, "Let's go find Danny or something. Get your mind off of Sir Kiss-a-lot."

She laughs and skips along beside me, saying, "Slow down! Slow down!" Then she spreads her arms wide and takes in a deep breath. "Isn't it glorious out?"

"Glorious? Marissa, it is not—"

"Smell. Just *smell*. It smells like . . ."

"Hay. Or straw. Or whatever all those bales of stuff are."

She yanks me back. "Where are you going?"

"I don't know. Away from . . . there," I tell her, hitching a thumb over my shoulder.

"Well, stop, would you?" She points to a post with flat wooden arrow signs, saying, "That way's Goose Hill, Gypsys, Merrie Merchants, and the Tavern Walk. *That* way's the Village Green, Friar Tuck's Forest, and Food Mongers Row." Then she cries, "Oh! It's kettle corn! That's what I smell! Come on!" and drags me along to Food Mongers Row.

Now I am not hungry. Not at all. So while she's getting herself a nice fat sack of kettle corn, I'm trying to get my mind off my hand, checking out the tent-booth next door. One half of it has swords and armor and chain-mail vests, the other half has sundials and telescopes and other old-looking gadgets. And there's one gizmo with zodiac signs all around the edge that catches my eye, so I pick it up.

"Good morrow, m'lady. Hast thou interest in an astrolabe?"

I put the zodiac thing back down and ask, "Does everyone around here talk like that?"

"Ah, thou arst a traveler, then?"

"Uh . . ."

"Mayhap from the Isle of Rose? And pray, is something amiss with thy hand?"

"Huh? Oh. No." I didn't even know I was still rubbing it.

Marissa comes dancing up and shoves the bag of kettle corn under my nose. "This is so good. It's the best I have ever had! Try some. Try some!" Shake, shake, shake.

I push the bag away and say to the guy, "Uh . . . bye . . . or, later, or however you say see-ya around here."

"Anon!" he says with a smile. "We say, Anon!"

"Anon," I tell him, and follow Marissa down the lane.

"This place is so cool! Everyone is *into* it. Isn't it fun?"

I take a handful of kettle corn because she's shoving it under my nose again. "Yeah, but don't you feel . . . you know . . . like you're part of some weird play or something?"

"Exactly!" she laughs. "It's living theater!"

Now, she says this with a grand sweeping gesture and an English accent. And I'm thinking, Oh, no! when she darts over to a tent with dangling pewter necklaces. She points to one and says to the man behind the table, "How many pence is this, good sir?"

"'Tis twenty even," he tells her.

She gives a little curtsy and says, "Gramercy," then scurries back over to me.

"Where in the world . . . ?" I ask her.

She giggles and wiggles, and her eyes are twinkling. "A man in front of me over at the kettle corn." She spins completely around, holding out her skirt with one hand. "You've got to give it a try, Sammy. It's fun!" Then she points to a tent we're passing by and whispers, "Go on! Go try it!"

"But Marissa, I don't want a bedpan!" because that's exactly what they're selling at that booth.

"Bedpan, schmed-pan. It doesn't matter . . . you just ask!"

"Seriously?"

"And with a straight face, Sammy."

So I tried to compose myself, but I kept cracking up. And finally I said, "I cannot ask how much a bedpan costs with a straight face, Marissa."

She rolls her eyes and drags me along, and when we come to a booth selling dragon mugs and dragon bowls, she stops and says, "Okay, here. Just do what I did, all right?"

"I'm not gonna curtsy."

"Fine." She shoves me. "Just go!"

So up I went, feeling like a real doofus. But Marissa was breathing down my neck, so I cleared my throat, picked up a dragon cup, and asked a big hairy guy on a stool, "How many pence is this, good sir?"

He stood up, and that's when I realized that this big hairy guy was a big hairy *giant*. I swear he was eight feet tall, and his voice was about ten feet deep. "'Tis forty-five, lass. Forged and fired by me own hands. 'Tis but one in all the land. Truly a work of art."

I blinked at him, then put the mug down veeeeeery carefully. "Gramercy," I squeaked, and started to walk away.

"Thirty, then!" he bellowed, then dropped his voice. "But not a word to anyone!"

I swallowed hard and said, "Gramercy, good sir," and hurried away.

"Fie!" he grumbled after me. "Fie!"

"See?" Marissa said when we were far enough away. "Wasn't that fun?"

Now I'm about to tell her that no, having a big hairy giant growl, Fie! at me is not my idea of fun, when I see a small group of people coming our way. And what I notice first is that they look out of place. They're wearing tight jeans and tight tops, and they're looking down their noses at everything. Like, Oh, isn't this *lame*.

And *then* I realize that I know these people. Way better than I want to.

And at that moment they spot us and I can tell—trouble's going to break out on Food Mongers Row.

SIX

"Oh, I don't *believe* it," Marissa whispers, freezing in her tracks.

"Believe it," I tell her, because if there's one thing I've learned, it's that Heather Acosta is not a bad dream.

That girl's a living nightmare.

And no matter where I go she seems to haunt me, coming out of nowhere going, *"Bwaa-ha-ha-ha-ha,"* when I least expect it.

The second she spots us, the rest of Mongers Row falls back like a gunfight scene in an old Western movie. It's only Heather and her wanna-bes Monet Jarlsberg and Tenille Toolee on one end, and Marissa and me on the other.

And as they're approaching, Marissa starts to do a little of the McKenze dance, squirming from side to side, biting a nail, saying, "Oh god. We're never going to live this down. She's going to make fun of us from here to . . . to *high* school."

"And beyond," I muttered, keeping my eyes locked on Heather and her growing smirk.

And that's when it happened. In a flash, I went from feeling ridiculous in red velvet and a lace-up blouse to

62

feeling like *she* looked ridiculous in her trendy clothes and too-cool-for-all-of-you sneer.

So when Marissa whispers, "I'm sorry, Sammy. I know what you're thinking, okay? I'm sorry, I'm sorry, I'm sorry!" I turn to her and say, "Don't be. You're right, she's wrong."

"But—"

I grin at her. "When in Rome . . ."

"You're kidding, right?"

"Nay, lass. 'Tis no time to falter, come!" I held my head high, smiled at no one in particular, and started walking.

Marissa fell into step beside me, saying through her teeth, "We're just going to walk right past them like this?"

"Aye. 'Tis the plan."

She choked back a laugh. "You're cracking me up, you know that?"

Now, I knew Heather was not going to let us just walk by. I think she's got some kind of a kink in her brain that makes her *have* to say something snide. But I figured we'd act like we didn't care—maybe toss a few fun Old English words back at her and just keep on keepin' on.

And sure enough, she says, "Hey, *Guin*evere, looking for *Lan*celot?" and right on cue the other two snicker. Then Monet says, "That'll be the *day*, won't it? When Sammy lands a *knight*," and they all start laughing real loud, with Tenille and Heather telling Monet, "Hey, good one!"

So I just smile at them and say in my best Old English

63

accent, "Aye, 'tis a funny one, that! But thou mistaketh me for another. Anon!"

And I'm just smiling and walking on while they're looking at me like, What? when Marissa, *Marissa,* says, "Yeah, and besides, she's just been *kissed* by a knight."

Well, you better believe I spun on Marissa with a look that's screaming, "Shut *up!*" but it's too late. She's already saying, "Perhaps you've heard of him. Sir Lucan? Knight of the Holy Blade of York?"

Now Tenille and Monet are looking about as sharp as Play-Doh. But Heather's eyes bug out and she yanks me by the arm. "Liar!" she says, but there's doubt in her eyes.

I level a look at her and say, "Pray, traveler, touch me not!"

"He couldn't have!" she says, still holding on tight. "He *wouldn't* have!"

"I sayeth, touch me not!" This time I manage to twist my arm free, but she holds on to my sleeve, and I'm afraid with the way she's yanking that she's going to rip it.

"Who couldn't have?" Monet asks her. "Who's Sir Lucan, Knight of . . . whatever?"

Heather shakes me by the sleeve. "Did my brother kiss you or not?"

All of a sudden this short pudgy woman with a floppy hat, an apron, and a big *fish* comes up and says, "Unhand her, y'wench!" Heather just totally ignores her, so she says it louder, "Unhand her, I say!"

Now, *I'm* thinking, Who in the world is this woman, and what's she doing holding that big ol' ugly *fish* by the tail, when all of a sudden she takes a step back and *ker-splat,* she smacks Heather across the back with the broad side of the fish.

Heather cries, "Oooohhhh!" but I think she was way more grossed out than hurt. She lets go of my sleeve and shrieks at the pudgy woman, "You hit me with a *fish?* I'm gonna sue! I'm gonna sue you for—"

"Aw, flush it, ye saucy pin-hearted strumpet!" Then she calls out into the crowd that's gathered, "Sheriff!"

No one steps forward.

She calls to the other side, "Sher*riiiiiiff*!" and all of a sudden a man comes crashing through, calling, "What is it, washerwoman?"

The fish lady points to Heather and says, "This wench hath commenced to brawling in our row."

"Ah," says the sheriff, rubbing his goatee as he looks Heather over. "Well, traveler, I'll have ye know that the Crown has issued an edict that no violence take place upon penalty of lands and titles of those involved being stripped. It would appear there are no titles in danger here, but I advise thee well—be on thy way, or we'll have no choice but to set the privy monster loose upon thee." He bends a little closer to her, but says so the crowd can hear, "A common fish doth smell like a rose next to the likes of Harvey the Privy Monster!"

That makes a lot of people around us laugh, but Heather blinks at him like, *What?* and I'm still kind of stunned, too.

But in a flash it's all over. Heather's saying to Monet and Tenille, "God, let's get *out* of here," and as they leave, the washerwoman and sheriff take bows all around and the crowd claps and cheers.

Marissa and I tell the sheriff and the fish lady, "Gramercy!" and "Anon!" and then hurry off in the opposite direction from Heather.

The minute we're safely away, Marissa says, "That was too bizarre! And did you see Heather's face when she got clobbered with that fish?"

"She wouldn't have *had* to get clobbered with a fish if *some*one hadn't made her short-circuit in the first place!" I turn on her and say, "*Why* did you tell her Casey kissed me?"

She cringes. "I'm sorry! But she was being so, you know, snotty. That crack about Guinevere and Lancelot. I . . . I couldn't help it."

"This is going to get back to Casey, you know. And you made it sound like he kissed *me*, not my hand!"

"Aw, c'mon, Sammy. She deserved it. But I'm sorry, okay?"

So we walked for a little ways, saying a whole lot of nothing to each other until Marissa points and says, "Hey, check it out! Live chess!"

So we watched a bunch of grown men and two "queens" move around a giant grid of squares for a while, then went on to see a show where you could buy tomatoes and throw them at the players onstage. At first it was really strange, throwing mushy tomatoes at people, but everyone in the crowd was doing it, so we got into it, too. And Marissa—ace pitcher that she is—managed to get one of the players smack-dab in the middle of his forehead. He stopped and turned toward the audience, tomato goop just running down his face, while the crowd went wild, applauding and cheering.

After that we had fish on a stick and vinegar potatoes for lunch. And you know what we washed it down with?

Dragon piss.

Well, that's what everyone called it, anyway. No one would admit that it was really just lemonade.

Anyway, after lunch we watched some guys with heavy gloves launching falcons to snag pieces of food from the air and then the Mud Bumblers show, which was a funny pirate skit. Then we wound past some merchant booths, and people called, "How now, good ladies, welcome!" to us to try to get us to stop in and see their wares.

And actually, I *was* stopping and looking at a lot of things, because these were mostly arts and crafts booths, and even though I had been to a *real* art gallery, I was remembering what Miss Kuzkowski had said about checking out the art at the Faire and how we were supposed to decide what we thought was and wasn't art.

And I was in the middle of looking over some drawings of knights on horses when the man behind the booth cries, "You!"

I jumped. I mean, his "You!" was directed right at *me* and seemed to shoot straight through my heart. And before I could catch my breath, he reaches across the table, grabs me by the shoulders, and says, "My plucky little tiger?"

This guy's got a patch over one eye, scarves everywhere, a large plumed hat on his head, and a beard that's been charcoaled on. And I don't really recognize him, but from his voice I know who it has to be. So I peel up his patch and look him in both eyes. "Jojo?"

"It *is* you! Sweet Pea, you are simply stunning in a dress! And forgive me, but after last night's wardrobe display I would've thought you didn't *own* one." He hurries to add, "Not that that's a *bad* thing. My, my, no! Could you imagine tackling that criminal in a dress? He would've gotten away. Clean away!"

Now Marissa's heard every word of this, and she's looking at me like, What? so I tell her, "There was a little, uh, *incident* at the art gallery last night."

"The art gallery? You found trouble in an *art* gallery?" Then before I can say anything, she asks, "What art gallery?"

"Uh, it's called the Vault. I went there with Grams and Hudson." I motion to Jojo and say, "This is Jojo Lorenzo. He, uh . . ." I look at him and ask, "Do you own that place or run it or what?"

"I'm the agent-slash-proprietor-slash-grunt. I do it all!"

I turn back to Marissa. "Well some guy came in and tried to steal a bunch of paintings and . . . you know."

Marissa rolls her eyes. "Why you?"

I shrugged. "Well, *some*one had to stop him. He was holding the place up with a squirt gun!"

"A squirt gun? Who fell for that?"

Jojo's eyes get all big. "All of us did! He had it in his pocket and he was so . . . rugged-looking. None of us suspected!"

"So what's going on with all of that?" I ask him. "Did they catch the guy?"

"Oh my, no! He vanished! *Poof,* into thin air. And since the paintings are all accounted for and Di doesn't seem to have the emotional fortitude to press an investigation . . ."

"Wait a minute. She doesn't want to find the guy?"

"Oh sure she does, sure she does! She's just very . . . delicate. Moody, if you must know. And she does put on a good front, but underneath there's darkness. Pain. Conflict." He smiles. "Which is why she is such a brilliant artist."

"But . . . well, do you think that maybe the Splott . . . I mean that Tess Winters lady . . . is right? Do you think Diane Reijden set it all up so she would be the one in the *L.A. Times*?"

"My pet, it makes no sense! No sense a'tall. Unless you're her accomplice?"

"No!"

"Well there you go! If you hadn't stopped that ruffian, he would've gotten clean away. Clean away!"

"Well, it did feel kind of . . . desperate. Do you think maybe Tess set it up? You know, to remove the competition?"

He gives me a really prim look. "Watch me, darling. I'm biting my tongue." He sticks it out and clamps down on it. But then he leans forward and whispers, "She's haughty and hateful . . . but she's too mentally *boxed* to orchestrate a heist." He straightens a little and says, "But you didn't hear that from me!"

"So who do you think he was? A friend of Austin Zuni's?"

"Oh heavens no!" Jojo sucks in air through his nose, holds it, then lets it out all at once, saying, "He was simply someone who knows. Or maybe he *works* for someone who knows."

"Knows? Knows what?"

"That it's only a matter of time before you won't be able to touch a Reijden for under thirty, thirty-five grand a pop."

"Seriously?"

He nods. "She just got a stunning review in *Artist World* magazine. It's only a matter of time before she shoots to the stars."

"So why did the whole thing feel so . . . staged?"

"More like dramatic, if you ask me." Then he says, "Ahhhhh," and you can tell he's having a wonderful thought.

"What?"

"There's a *movie* in here somewhere. . . ." He claps his hands and says, "Oh. Oh-oh-oh!"

So while he's writing, casting, and directing in his mind, I'm looking around at his booth. And finally I ask him, "Is this your art, Jojo? It's not signed or anything."

He laughs. "Mine? Darling, I draw like a two-year-old."

Before I can bite *my* tongue, it's wagging away, saying, "Hey, there's big money in that. Frame it, call it something 'deep,' and charge ten grand!"

"*Tsk-tsk-tsk,*" he goes, but he's smiling. "Do I detect a jab at one of my clients?"

I shrug. "I just don't get it, that's all. And Tess sure wouldn't explain it to me."

"One shouldn't have to explain one's art." He leans in. "You insulted her."

"But . . . I was just trying to learn. I mean, can *you* explain it?"

He shrugs. "To each his own, I say."

"Well, do you get it? Do you *like* it?"

He shrugs again. "It sells, and that's what matters to me."

"At nearly ten grand a pop?"

"Hmm. That's yet to be seen. I had an installation of hers in when I first opened which sold very well, but since Di was asking so much for her paintings, Tess felt she would be giving the impression that her work was *worth* less if she didn't price in the same ballpark."

"But—"

"Ah-ah-ah! Don't be catty. Tess is simply projecting a value onto her work." He laughs. "And if they do move, you won't hear me complaining! Fifty percent of a few of those babies would keep me from enduring gigs like this." He rolls his eyes around the booth, then whispers, "I've had it up to here with all these rennies and their phony Faire accents, bragging and brawling and spitting . . . it's repugnant!"

Now I'm listening to him, all right, but my brain is pretty much stuck on his cut of the sale. "You get fifty percent? *Why?*"

He puts his nose in the air a little and says, "Darling,

rent's not free. And frankly, they'd be lost without me. How else would the buying public get to know their work? They certainly don't want people traipsing through their homes. And artists do not make good business-people. Most of them, anyway." He scowls. "Austin's the exception."

"His paintings were cheap compared to the other two."

Jojo nods. "It's a numbers game to that boy. He moves as much as he can, as fast as he can. And," he grumbles, "he's not going to let anyone slow him down."

Now, the way he said it was sort of . . . bitter. So I ask, "Why do you say that?"

He waves me off. "Never mind, darlin'. It's much, *much* too deep to get into." Then he spread his hands over the pictures on the table and says, "In the market? Please-please-please?"

I laugh and shake my head, because it's just a little weird hearing a swashbuckler go, Please-please-please. Then I ask him, "But if you hate being here, why are you here?"

"Because," he says, "I can make more on lithographs of dragons and knights in a weekend than I make some months at the gallery." He gives me a little scowl and whispers, "I'm trying to run an art gallery in Santa *Martina,* Sweet Pea. I have to make a living somehow!"

I think about this a minute, then ask, "What's a litho-graph, anyhow?"

"Mostly production-line art. They take a scan or make a photograph of the artwork and then just crank 'em out. Stamp-stamp-stamp! Thousands upon thousands." He reaches under the skirt of the table and pulls up a fat stack of copies of the knight on the horse I'd been looking at. "When I sell one, I've got one waiting down here to replace it."

"So . . . do you think it's art?"

He shrugs. "Actually, I think these were done on a computer."

"You're kidding! They look like pencil sketchings."

He smiles a sly little smile. "Exactly."

I take a closer look, but I sure can't tell. What I *can* tell is that Marissa's getting antsy. So I say, "Well, we'd better get going. It was nice talking to you."

"You too, princess!"

I cringe at him. *"Princess?"* Then I show him a shoe, to set the record straight.

He laughs, then adds, "But a clever disguise, nonetheless."

As we left his booth and walked around the Faire, I kept hearing Jojo's voice saying, "But a clever disguise, nonetheless." And I started getting this strange feeling. Like I was in one of those cartoons where one character is spying on another, popping in and out, up and down, hiding behind fences and in trash cans and trees.

I checked around for Heather and her wanna-bes.

No "travelers" in sight.

And it didn't feel like I was being followed, exactly. More like I was being set up.

Tricked.

Everywhere I turned, people were in costumes, pretending. Pretending they were someone they weren't. Someplace they weren't. Some *time* they weren't.

And I started thinking about the Squirt Gun Bandit and what was hidden behind his whole getup.

And the more I thought about him and what had happened at the Vault, the more it seemed like that whole scene had been living theater, too.

An act.

Where some people were actors and some were just there.

Me, I'd been like the washerwoman.

Only I hadn't exactly used a fish.

And the truth is, I didn't like being a part of the act. My mother's into acting, I'm not. What did I care who the Squirt Gun Bandit was or why he'd crashed in on the reception? I felt like I'd been dropped into the middle of a soap opera.

I just wanted to get off the stage.

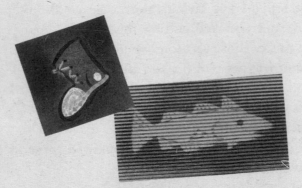

SEVEN

I didn't run into Casey again at the Faire. Or Heather.
And Marissa looked for Danny all afternoon, but she
never saw him, either.

What we *did* see a lot of was art. No sloppy splotters or
modern stuff like that, but there were a few booths selling
Southwest art, sort of like Austin Zuni's. Indians and buffaloes at a Renaissance Faire seemed pretty out of place
though. Even more so than the Star Trek booth we saw.

Marissa found a picture of a princess at a wishing well
that she really liked, but I didn't see anything that did
anything for me. Not like *Whispers* had, anyway.

I tried to talk to some of the artists about their work,
but mostly they told me about *how* they painted or
sculpted or cut things out of wood. When I asked what
masters they'd studied or admired or what they were
thinking about when they made a certain piece, they
didn't seem to have much to say. It was weird—like they
were bored. Miss Kuzkowski had told us to go out and
feel art, but how was I supposed to do that when the
artists were acting like they didn't really feel it themselves?

Anyway, we spent so much time at the Faire that it was
pretty late by the time Marissa and I got back to where

she'd locked her bike near the Senior Highrise. And since I didn't think it was too hot of an idea for us both to go back up the fire escape, I asked how she wanted to work getting her stuff back.

"Can you bring the costume and my other clothes to school on Monday?"

"Yeah, but how are you going to ride your bike in that dress?"

"Watch me," she said, swinging her leg over.

Now, she was trying to sound cheerful, but I could tell that she was feeling pretty bummed. So I said, "I'm sorry you didn't meet up with Danny."

She shrugged. "No big deal."

"Liar."

She shook her head and said, "I was being an idiot, huh?"

Now, what I was thinking was, No kidding! but what I *said* was, "You were just excited."

She scowled at me. "You have no idea how lucky you are."

I knew where she was going with this, so I said, "Don't even start with that again, okay?"

"Guys like Casey don't come around every day, you know."

"I *said*—"

"I know, I know." She crammed big folds of the skirt under her legs. "And no, I won't tell anyone about . . . ," she leans over and whispers, "the kiss!"

Before I can punch her, she laughs, "Hee-hee!" and pedals off with a wave.

I watched her until she was out of sight, then headed for home. And when I slipped through the apartment door, the first thing I noticed was a great big bouquet of flowers on the coffee table, and a great big frown on my grams' face.

"Wow!" I whispered, because I don't think our apartment had ever seen fresh flowers before.

Grams was on the couch with her arms crossed, just staring at them. "They refuse to take them back."

"Uh-oh," I said, sitting beside her. "I take it they're from Hudson?"

"What a ridiculous waste of money!"

"Is that why you're mad? Because he spent a lot of money?"

"Yes!" She crossed her arms tighter. "No! I'm mad because he thinks he can bribe me into *not* feeling mad."

I put my arm around her. "Grams, you're being kinda stubborn, don't you think?"

"No! No, I am not!" She looked at me, her eyes all big and flashing. "I didn't *want* to meet him for lunch, but I did. I didn't *want* to hear him out, but again, I did. Do you call that being stubborn?"

"Noooo."

"But just when I was starting to think he was truly remorseful, he calls here and informs me that he's managed to get you an interview at two o'clock tomorrow with the queen herself."

"Who?"

"Diane Reijden!"

"He . . . he did?"

"He says you need it for some art paper." Her eyes come zooming in on me. "Is that true?"

"Well, yeah . . ."

"But does it have to be an interview with a famous artist? No teacher could possibly assign that, right?"

"She's not famous, is she?"

"According to Hudson she is! Or will be, soon enough."

"Well, whatever. It just has to be an artist. Miss Kuzkowski didn't say what, you know, *caliber.*"

She throws her head back. "Ha! Just as I suspected."

"But Grams, interviewing a good artist is way better than interviewing a rotten one. I actually tried that at the Renaissance Faire today and got a whole lot of nowhere. Hudson's just doing me a favor."

Her nostrils flare and she says, "You, child, don't understand men." She crosses her arms again and mutters, "He almost had me convinced that he was impressed with her art, not her, and then he goes and stirs the stew with a rat tail!"

"A rat tail? Grams, that's gross!"

"Don't you see? He contacted her *after* he sweet-talked me, and then had the nerve to send me flowers." She kind of burrows into herself, scrunching into a little ball of arms and shoulders. "My original impression of Hudson Graham was right—the man's an insufferable flirt."

I sat beside her for a few minutes, just thinking. And finally I said real quiet-like, "Are you upset because you like Hudson more than you want to admit? Or is it because Diane Reijden's a . . . you know . . . younger woman?"

Grams looks at me for a minute. Then she takes off her glasses, holds them up to the light, and huffs and buffs them until I swear she's going to polish right through the lenses. Finally she pops them back on her nose and says, "Are you implying I might be sensitive about this because . . ."

Her voice just trails off, so I look her square in the eye and nod. "Because of Gramps." She looks down, so I touch her arm and say, "Grams, I know about the Biker Babe."

Her mouth scrunches up, down, then all around. Then she straightens her skirt and says, "This has nothing to do with that."

"But Grams—"

"Your grandfather was going through a midlife crisis. It's very typical for a man that age to . . . to . . . to develop a wandering eye. But Hudson Graham is well beyond midlife! Besides, Diane Reijden is not really a 'younger woman.' She's fifty if she's a day!"

"But still, you're sixty—"

"Don't remind me! It's not something I want to hear right now, okay?" And with that she got up and said, "You can fix your own supper, can't you? I need to go lie down," and shut herself in her room.

So after sitting by myself for a few minutes, I got up and yeah, I fixed myself supper—about ten bowls of cereal with buckets of sugar and milk.

But the more I shoveled, the more I couldn't stop thinking about Grams and the story I'd overheard about my grandfather leaving her for a bimbo at the Harley-

Davidson shop. All Mom or Grams had ever actually *told* me was that he'd died in a motorcycle accident shortly before I was born, but after I caught whiff of the Biker Babe—or the "Harley Hussy," as Grams once called her—well, things like why Grams didn't have any pictures of my grandfather around and why she never really had much to *say* about him started making sense.

So I sat there, stuffing myself full of oats and corn and other nutritious grains, thinking. And when I was finally full, I cleaned everything up and headed for the couch. And even though I did read a little and watch some TV with my cat Dorito, after a while I just shut out the light.

And as I lay there on the couch, wrapped in my afghan and the sweet smell of fresh cut flowers, I couldn't help wondering. About my grandfather. About my father. About my mother and my grandmother and what they had been like at my age. What had junior high been like for them? When and where had they fallen in love? At school? At work?

At a Renaissance Faire?

And it's funny—I had always thought of them as being old. Or, at least, *adults*. But they'd been kids once, too. And I could tell from the hurt in Grams' eyes that she'd felt all this before.

Maybe many times.

And that seemed so strange.

So . . . impossible.

But as I drifted off to sleep, the one thought that kept cycling through my head wasn't actually about my grandparents or parents. It was about Hudson. And the more I thought about it, the more I could just see him—his boots kicked up, the wind in his hair.

Hudson Graham, right at home on a Harley.

I had dreams about ants. Little red ones with yellow antennae, tiptoeing up my finger. Up my hand. Up my arm. Tickling, tickling, tickling. Then they'd rear back and duke it out with those wild antennae, jump off my arm, and start all over again.

Up my finger.

Up my hand.

Up my arm.

Tickle, tickle, tickle.

"Who are you shouting at?" It was Grams, shaking me awake.

"What? What?" I sat up and whipped around, looking for ants.

Grams was holding her heart. "You scared the daylights out of me!"

"I'm sorry," I told her, still looking for ants.

"It didn't even sound like you! You had an English accent!"

"I *did*?"

"Distinctly English."

"Well . . . what was I saying?"

"Something like, Unhand me! and, Thou shalst pay!" She holds her temples with her hands and says, "And there was something about 'Sir Hiss-a-lot'?"

I rubbed my arm, hoping she wouldn't notice how red my cheeks must have been turning.

"What were you dreaming about? Was it something about the Faire?"

I shook my head, happy to be able to tell her the truth. "I was dreaming about ants."

"Ants?"

"Angry little red ones with yellow antennae."

"Oh." She studied me a minute. "Were they *talking* ants?"

"I don't think so."

"Were they wearing British uniforms or something?"

"Grams! They were just little red ants."

"But with yellow antennae."

"Yeah."

She sighed and said, "Well, I can make hide nor hair of that one." She stroked my head. "Did you want to try to get some more sleep?"

I looked at the clock. "It's eight already?"

"But it's Sunday. I can read a little longer if you want to rest."

"Nah," I said, swinging my legs off the couch. I eyed the flowers, then looked at her. "How are you, anyway?"

"Fine," she said real primly.

"Well, I have some information that I didn't get the chance to tell you yesterday."

"Oh?"

"Yeah. I ran into Jojo at the Faire yesterday."

"And . . . ?"

"And I found out that Diane Reijden isn't going to have the police investigate who tried to steal her paintings."

All of a sudden Grams is sitting right beside me, grabbing my forearms. "She *said* that?"

"Jojo said she wants to put it all behind her."

Grams let go and raised an eyebrow. "Is she an artist or a politician?"

"Huh?"

"Never mind," she says, rubbing her hands together. "Just tell me this—why *wouldn't* she have them investigate?"

"I know. It does seem kinda strange."

"So . . . ?" she says, turning to look at me.

"So . . . what?" I ask, staring right back at her.

Her face zooms closer. Her eyes burn brighter. And out of her mouth come words I never in a million years thought I'd hear.

"I think you and I should prove it."

EIGHT

"*Prove* it? Grams, I've been trying to stay *out* of it! I thought you'd be all proud of me for that. And now you want to go and *prove* it?" I shake my head. "Besides, I don't even think it was her."

She just looks at me. Level stare. Pursed lips. Hands folded calmly in her lap. "Well, I do."

I take a deep breath and try again. "Look. Even if she did hire some guy to make it look like her art was worth stealing, so what? She's just got, you know, creative publicity strategies."

"What she's *got* is a coy, deceptive, cunning mind."

"Oh, come on! You barely even met her. Besides, she seemed like a perfectly nice lady to me."

"A perfectly nice lady wouldn't scare a room full of people out of their wits just to pull off a publicity stunt."

"Exactly!"

We stared at each other for a minute, then she said, "Well, obviously what we need is some more information."

"Grams, I don't see why—" I stopped short. Her eyes were twinkling. Her lips were curving up.

My grams had come up with a plan.

"What are you thinking?" I asked her.

She took a deep breath, squared her shoulders, and said, "I'm coming with you."

"Coming . . . with me?" I followed her into the kitchen. "Where am I going?"

"You've forgotten already? To interview Ms. Reijden, of course!"

"Oh." I watched her move around the kitchen. Bending for a pan, twirling around to click on the stove with one hand as she flicked the water on with the other. Then she practically did a pirouette as she pulled the milk out of the refrigerator, snagged a wooden spoon from the utensil jar, and tapped the refrigerator door closed with her foot. It was like a tightly choreographed dance. And for the first time in my life, I realized that my grams—my sixty-something guardian with the gray hair and over-sized glasses—wasn't stodgy or stiff.

She was agile.

Smooth.

Graceful.

"What are you staring at, child?"

"I . . . Nothing. I just never saw you do that before."

"Make oatmeal?" She laughed. "You've seen me do this nearly every day for over a year!"

I got down the bowls. The sugar. The walnuts. I set the table and poured us some juice. And the whole time I tried to act normal, but I had my eye on Grams, and the truth is, I was feeling very, very strange.

By one o'clock, Hudson had called three times. The first time it was, "Make a list of questions, Sammy. If you're going to interview someone, you can't shoot from the hip. It's disrespectful."

The second time it was, "Would you like to borrow my tape recorder? You don't want to misquote her, you know."

"Hudson!" I told him. "It's for a junior-high art class. Not *The Washington Post*!"

The *third* time it was, "How's it coming with those questions?"

"Fine, Hudson. I've got plenty."

"Let's hear them."

I tried to protest, but he made me read the whole ten questions to him.

"That's it? That's all you've got?"

"Hudson," I said, trying to sound as polite as possible. "The report only has to be a page or two."

"Hmm," he said. "Well listen, I have a couple of questions I think you should add to your list. Ready?"

I rolled my eyes but jotted them down, just to make him happy. And the whole time I'm writing, Grams is pirouetting and sashaying around the house, dusting her little knickknacks. I swear I even saw her moonwalk out of the corner of my eye, but it was over by the time I actually looked.

When Hudson was finally done, my list of questions had doubled. "I hope you left plenty of room for answers."

"I did," I lied.

"Good. I'll be out front in about half an hour."

"Half an hour? I thought you said it was right off Morrison."

"It is, but we don't want to be late."

"We sure don't want to be *early*."

"Hmm. Okay. I'll meet you out front in forty-five minutes."

"Fine. And oh, Hudson?"

"Yes?"

"Grams is coming along."

Silence.

"You don't have a problem with that, do you?" I was eyeing Grams, frozen with one foot kicked up behind her, the feather duster in midair.

"No, no! But I'd hate for Ms. Reijden to feel . . . invaded."

"So . . . maybe I should go in by myself, then."

"Well—"

"Or why don't you just drop us off? *Or* if you give me the address, we could just walk there ourselves. I mean, we managed to walk home from the Vault the other night. This can't be farther than that. . . ."

Sometimes I can be so bad.

But it worked, because all of a sudden he's rushing to say, "No, no, no. I'll be out front in forty-five minutes. We'll just play it by ear."

"Great," I said. Then I hung up the phone and grinned at Grams. Already I could tell—this was going to be fun.

We couldn't see Diane's house from the street. All we could really see was a narrow gravel driveway with an arch of out-of-control creeping roses and lots of plants everywhere. But we knew we were in the right place because of the two mailboxes that were T-ed to a post. One was labeled 580—MOSS, the other 584—REIJDEN.

"Do you mind walking?" Hudson asked as he pulled off the road. "I'm afraid Jester'll get scraped up if I drive through there."

It was true. Hudson's car is pretty big. And pretty old. And, according to him, pretty valuable. Not that *I'd* ever want to own a 1960 sienna-rose Cadillac, but Hudson loves it, and I've got to admit—it glistens.

Anyway, we got out and started hiking down the gravel driveway, me in dirty white high-tops, Hudson in Panamanian iguana boots, and Grams in her best leather pumps.

Thirty feet past the archway the wind seemed to vanish and we found ourselves in the middle of a jungle. Seriously. There were plants everywhere, growing wild, tangling into each other, and twisting up into tall pine trees. We could hear birds twittering and bees buzzing and water trickling somewhere off in the distance.

So we're crunching along the gravel, passing by 580—a weathered wooden house with a rickety fence and a splintery-looking rocker on the porch—when I hear, *"Ch-ch-ch-ch-chee!"*

Hudson puts his arm out like a crossing bar at a railroad track. "What was that?"

"Ch-ch-ch-ch-chee!"

Grams catches up and says, "Sounds like a squirrel."

"Ch-ch-ch-ch-chee!"

"That's no squirrel," Hudson whispers, one ear strained forward like a hound dog. "Maybe a bird?"

"It's a *squirrel*," Grams says, pushing down his arm and walking past.

Then from high in a pine tree we hear a different voice cry, *"Chee-te-te-te-te-te-te!"* and all of a sudden a big, bushy gray tail flashes from behind the trunk and a squirrel spirals down the tree.

Grams gives Hudson a little I-told-you-so grin over her shoulder and says, "Pretty bird."

Hudson and I look in the yard, and what we see is a man on his knees in the dirt. He's wearing a red-and-black flannel hunter hat with the big earmuffs sticking straight out, and about three layers of flannel shirts. In one hand he's got a planting trowel, and in the other he's holding out something sort of round and dirty-looking for the squirrel.

Grams backtracks to join us, and when she sees the squirrel taking the dirt ball out of the man's hand, she says, "Will you look at that!"

The squirrel scurries off a few yards, then starts pulling and prying at the dirt ball with its front paws. And while it's busy doing that, the man digs in the ground, pops up another dirt ball, and calls, *"Ch-ch-ch-ch-chee!"*

Hudson eyes Grams and whispers, "That was not a squirrel, that was a man."

"Hrmph."

"Ch-ch-ch-ch-chee! Come down, Guiditta! Supper's ready!"

Another squirrel comes twisting down the trunk of the pine tree. The tail of this one's not nearly as bushy as the other's, and she doesn't go over to Flannel Man like the first one had. Instead, she sneaks up to the first squirrel and snatches his dirt ball from him. And even though the bushy one is bigger than the second one and even though Flannel Man scolds, "No, Guiditta! Naughty girl!" in the end she's running off with the Bushy One's dirt ball.

So Flannel Man holds it out to Bushy, saying, "Thar ye go, Luciano." And when Luciano scurries over to snag the dirt ball, Flannel Man says, "Isn't it time ye stood up to 'er, boy?"

Now, I have a big urge to shake out an ear, because Flannel Man sounds English. Distinctly English.

Hudson calls, "What are you feeding them?"

"Huh?" Flannel Man says, then stands up like he could use a good oiling at the joints. "Why, hallo. Didn't see ye there." He hobbles our way, saying, "They're walnuts is wot they are. I bury 'em 'cause that's how they like 'em. Good and rotten. Turn their noses up at the fresh ones, they do. Especially Guiditta. She's a picky one, that."

By now he's over at the fence, dusting off his hands. "Come ta visit Lizzy, have ye? Or might ye be lost?"

"Lizzy?" Hudson asks. "No, we're here to see Ms. Reijden."

"One and the same." He motions down the driveway. "The Reijden place is there, at the end of the lane. She knows you're comin'?"

Hudson nods. "We have an appointment."

"All right, then," he says. Like he's the gatekeeper, letting us through. "Tell Lizzy hallo for me, will ya? Haven't see her about much these days."

"Will do," Hudson says.

As we got closer we could see the house through the vines and trees. It was only one story, but it had lots of wood and spindles and shutters, a tall stone chimney, and a vine-covered porch. We followed a cobblestone path under another, smaller arch of roses and passed by a pond with water from a clay pipe trickling into it and lily pads growing all over it.

"Wow," I said. "What a cool place!"

Hudson agreed.

Grams didn't say a word.

A minute after Hudson rang the bell, Diane opened the door and sang out, "Hudson! Welcome," like he was a long-lost friend. She had a small paintbrush in one hand and was rubbing the bristles clean with a cloth in the other. She turned to Grams. "It's . . . Rita, right? How nice you could come." And before Grams could say anything, she turned to me and positively beamed. "Sammy. My gutsy little heroine."

I blushed and shrugged. "I took down a guy with a squirt gun. No big deal."

"I beg to differ!" she said as she let us into the house.

The house smelled wonderful. Like cinnamon and oranges and . . . honey. And while I'm sniffing the air, Hudson's saying, "Your neighbor told us to tell you hello."

"Pete? Oh, he is such a dear. I really must stop in and see how he's doing."

I said, "He was digging up nuts for squirrels when we saw him."

She nods. Like she knows all about it. "Luciano and Guiditta have him wrapped around their little paws," she says with a laugh. Then she notices my notepad and says, "Why, look at that! You have questions all written out. Very professional."

All of a sudden I was grateful for Hudson's advice. "Yeah. I hope I don't have, you know, too many."

She chuckled. "We have plenty of time, don't worry. Now come. I've prepared cookies and tea." She smiled at me. "Or cookies and milk, if you prefer."

"Thanks," I said. "But tea's fine. Hudson's kind of got me in the habit of drinking it."

She taps Hudson on the hand with her paintbrush and says, "Shame on you!" but her eyes are twinkling.

Now, I can tell that steam's beginning to billow from around Grams' collar, but she's doing a beautiful job of smiling, anyway. And as we follow Diane and Hudson down the hall, I notice that she's not just following along. Her head's jerking around, her eyes are darting back and forth, and as we move from the hall through a living room with a big stone fireplace, it hits me what Grams is doing.

She's *casing* the joint.

I nudge her and mouth, "Grams!" but she keeps right on scanning the room and mouths back, "Keep your eyes open!"

So, okay. To do Grams a favor I check the room over, too. Lots of lace. Old books. A rocking horse, an old trunk with big brass hinges. A telescope. Dolls. A spinning wheel. Old, no, *ancient,* ice skates. And here and there among all this old stuff are statues. Three big rough-looking plaster statues of human bodies.

Now let me tell you, these are no Michelangelos. No tucked torsos. No jutting jaws or chiseled cheeks. These statues have parts sagging everywhere, wrinkles galore, and hands with long spindly fingers. And even though two of them don't have heads, the one that does has a face that would make its body run for the hills if it could.

"What do you think of those?" Grams whispers in my ear.

"They look like they were cast off of nursing home patients," I whisper back.

Grams doesn't scold me like she normally would. Instead she eyes me and nods. And from the look on her face, I know just what she's thinking.

There's something strange about this woman.

Something very strange.

NINE

Diane leads us into a sunny sitting room that has a piano, red velvet armchairs, and a window that takes up nearly one whole wall, ceiling to floor. The view through it is amazing, too. There's tall grass blowing in the breeze, an enormous tree, and dark green vines with little blue flowers weaving around a little picket fence. And birds. Birds fluttering everywhere! It's like her very own little wildlife park.

Trouble is, there's also one of those headless statues standing right outside the window like some sort of ghastly guard. And even though it's off to one side, once you notice it, you don't really see the yard anymore. It's like a nasty scar on someone's face keeping you from noticing how pretty the rest of them is.

Anyway, Diane puts aside her brush and rag and says, "Here we are," as she motions for us to sit in the chairs around a tea table. And as she takes a seat next to Hudson, he points to a guitar that's on a stand beside the piano. "That's a beautiful Gibson."

"Pardon me?" she asks.

"The guitar?"

"Oh, that. It was my father's."

"He was a musician?"

"A doctor, actually, but he was also musically gifted. As was my mother. She bought him the guitar, he bought her the piano." She sighed. "They were serious collectors, and everything you see here was theirs. At first it was very haunting, but now I find being surrounded by their things comforting."

"How long ago did they pass on?" Grams asked her.

"Dad's been gone nearly three years. I cared for Mother until the end—about a year and a half ago."

"I'm sorry," Grams told her, and I could tell she meant it.

"So!" Diane said, taking a deep breath and turning to me. "Before we begin with your questions, I want to thank you again for saving the day on Friday. What an absolute nightmare that was!"

Now, I'm about to say, No biggie, but Grams has already downshifted into snoop mode and jumps in with, "Do you have any idea who that fellow was?"

I look at Grams, sitting primly in her chair, looking oh-so-innocent.

Innocent like a hawk.

"Some desperate individual, to be sure. And," she adds as smoothly as she's pouring tea, "I suspect a drunk to boot." She smiles at Grams as she hands her a dainty cup and saucer. "Milk or sugar?"

"Oh, no thanks. But a drunk? He seemed very sober to me!"

"I'm sure I detected alcohol." She hands a cup to me, saying, "Did you notice any strange odor on him, Sammy? You were certainly close enough."

"Uh, nuh-uh. He did seem kind of dirty, though, and kinda *wiry.*"

Hudson says, "Are you sure you don't want Sammy to tell these details to the police?"

She twinkles at him. "That he was dirty and wiry?" She laughs, then pats his hand. "Sweet man!"

I checked Grams—steam was billowing.

"Well, then," Diane says, holding the pinky of her right hand out as she takes a dainty sip of tea. "What questions do you have for me?"

I put aside my cup and saucer and pick up my pad and pencil. "How about, Where were you born?"

She gives me a very regal smile. "That's better than *when* were you born. Let's hope you're not planning to work up to that."

I shook my head. "No, ma'am."

"Well then, I was born in Boston, I studied in New York and Paris, and spent many years refining my style in the quaint town of Orlean."

The word Orlean seemed to come through her nose, and since I wasn't real sure, I asked her, "New Orleans? In Louisiana?"

She laughs, "Oh, how precious! No, dear. Orlean as in Orlean, France. Have you ever studied Joan of Arc? Well, she came from Orlean. A charming city, and the one *New* Orleans is named after. Like New York is named after York? In England? And New Jersey after Jersey?"

My face must've looked pretty blank, because she said, "You didn't know that, dear?"

I shook my head.

"Well, nonetheless, I spent many years in France."

A phone began ringing in a different room as I was jotting down notes, but Diane waved it off, saying, "I'll just let the machine get it."

Now, this was not one of the questions on my list, but it popped out of my mouth anyway. "So how in the world did you wind up in Santa Martina?"

She laughs. "Good question. One I used to ask my parents all the time. They moved here when I was quite young, and believe me, I spent a great deal of energy trying to escape this town." She looks out the window and says, "Seems quite ironic how content I am to be here now."

I didn't really know how to go about jotting *that* down, so I just went on to my next question. "Can you tell me a little about your process? Like, how often do you paint, how do you decide what to paint, where do you paint . . . that sort of thing."

"Well, let's see . . . I'm very disciplined about my art. I paint every day. Sometimes the result is inspired, often it's not. What I paint can range from real-life images, to recollections, to dreams. I get a lot of inspiration from dreams."

I scribbled like crazy, then asked, "Do you have a studio?"

She laughs. "Yes, but it's really just a back bedroom that I use as such. I'll show you later, if you'd like, but it's nothing glamorous, believe me. I also do plein-air painting. I'll see a scene I love and then gather my easel and palette and go to it."

She smiles at me and waits, so I ask, "What kind of paint do you use?"

"Oils. Strictly oils. Cut with linseed and turpentine, of course. And since I'm going for an Old World depth, I treat my work with an antiquing spray to put in the teeny tiniest of cracks."

"So that's it!" Hudson says. "That's fascinating!"

Diane laughs, "Perhaps I shouldn't be giving away my trade secrets like this." She warms Hudson's tea, but as she starts to top off Grams', Grams stops her and says, "Might I use your bathroom?" She smiles. "Tea, you know."

Diane smiles back and motions behind her. "Through this doorway, take a left, second door on your right."

When Grams takes off, Diane asks me, "What's next?" So I ask her questions about who her influences were and how long a painting takes her to make and stuff like that. And Diane's being patient and very nice, giving a lot of thought to what she's saying.

Her answers are making *me* think, too. Like when I ask her how she decides what to paint, and she says, "I like art to represent life as it should be or could be . . . an ideal to which you should strive," it makes me think about what that *means,* and how it isn't just the images in her paintings that I like, it's the mood. The way they make me feel like I *want* to feel.

And I'm kind of disappointed that Grams isn't hearing Diane's answers, because if she was she would almost *have* to start to like her, too. But Grams obviously has some serious business to attend to, because she hasn't come back. And pretty soon I'm down to my last two questions. So I just go ahead and ask, "Can you tell me why you paint?"

"*Why* I paint?" She studies me a minute, then takes a deep breath, looks up at the ceiling, and holds her breath.

Now, sitting there in her high-collared white blouse with the dainty ruffled cuffs, she looks so . . . regal. Her posture's perfect. Her ankles and knees are pressed together and angled to the side. Even the way she's holding the teacup with her fingertips seems regal. Her nails aren't long, but they're perfectly manicured and painted a soft pink that blends in with the flowers on her cup. Like little rose petals, set against porcelain.

When she finally lets her breath go and looks at me, what she says is, "I paint because I have to. It's something I'm called to do. Moved to do. It is who I am." And the way she says it is so intense—so sincere—it gives me goose bumps up and down my arms.

It also gives me the nerve to ask her the one question I really wanted an answer to. "Where did *Whispers* come from?"

"Where did it *come* from?" She smiles at me softly and says, "From my heart, dear."

"But I mean . . . who *are* those people?"

"They're not models, if that's what you're asking. And I don't use photographs."

"But . . . then who were you imagining?"

"Ah." She smiles again, but this time it's twinged with sadness. "Generalities are fine, but it's my policy not to discuss the specifics of my subject matter."

All of a sudden I wanted to shake her and say, "You've got to tell me!" It felt like I *had* to know who those people in the painting were. What was the girl whispering? And most of all, who was it she was sharing her secret with.

And I know this sounds stupid, but in two seconds flat I went from wanting to shake an answer out of her to feeling like I'd swallowed a golf ball. I couldn't seem to say a thing.

What *was* it about that painting?

"Dear? Are you all right?"

My voice came out low and choked. "Can't you tell me *any*thing about it?"

She sighed. "The idea is that you see what *you* see, and if I tell you what *I* see, that will alter your perception of it." She put her hand on my knee. "I'm glad it moves you. You've given me the most precious of compliments."

I nodded and managed to say, "Where is it, anyway?"

"*Whispers?* Why, it's still at the Vault."

"Oh. I thought you might bring them home after what happened."

"I threatened to, but Joseph has hired a security guard, who, he assures me, will protect them to the death."

"Really?" Hudson says.

"Yes." She smiles at me. "So for the next three weeks, you can see *Whispers* at the Vault."

"What happens to it after three weeks?" I ask her.

She keeps her left hand neatly in her lap as she refreshes Hudson's tea. "We'll see. Maybe someone will buy it, hmmm?"

100

I almost said, "No!" but just then Grams walks in the room. Her cheeks are rosy, and she's trying to act nonchalant, but I can tell—she hasn't been using the bathroom all this time. She's been nosing around.

The naughty little snooper.

Hudson doesn't even look at her as she takes her seat. He just tells Diane, "I have no doubt someone will buy *Whispers*."

Now if Hudson had stopped right there, he would have been okay. But no. He has to go and tell Diane about a summer he spent camped outside the Louvre in France, visiting the museum nearly every day, discovering new and breathtaking works of art. And then he goes and puts the cherry on top. He says, "Your paintings could hang in the Louvre, Diane. They're that good."

Diane blushes and looks down. "Oh, Hudson. You do know how to flatter, don't you?"

Grams turns red, too, but let me tell you, it's a whole different *temperature* red.

So I figure it's time to wrap this party up. "That was my last question, Ms. Reijden. Do you think we could see your studio before we go?"

"There's really not much to see, dear, but we can take a quick peek if you'd like."

"Great," I say, getting up.

Hudson says, "Now?" like he can't believe what I'm doing. But Grams stands up, too, and says, "I do think we have taken up enough of Ms. Reijden's time, don't you?"

Hudson sputters a minute like, Well, *no*, but then the phone starts ringing again. And since it's easy to see that

Diane's distracted by that and also not exactly begging us to stay, Hudson stands up, too.

So she takes us down the back hallway, then pushes open the door to a fairly small room. "See?" she says, holding open the door. "Not even remotely glamorous."

I peek in and can see an easel with a partly painted canvas on it. And on a stool right beside it is an oval wooden palette—the kind with a thumb hole and a cutaway for the hand.

"Cool palette!" I tell her, because I love those things. "My art teacher, Miss Kuzkowski? She has one just like it—it's so cool to watch her use it. She puts on a little beret and just gets *into* it."

She laughs. "Well, I don't wear a beret, but my palette certainly helps me get into the flow of painting."

"I wish they'd let us use them in class. We have to use *waxed* paper."

"Oh, really? Not even disposable palettes?"

"Nuh-uh. We use waxed paper and Popsicle sticks."

"To paint?"

"No! To mix."

"Oh," she laughs. "No palette knives?"

"Even the *word* knife isn't allowed on campus."

She laughs again and says to Grams, "Quite a character you've got here."

Grams smiles, but Hudson's hand comes down on my shoulder, and he says, "I think Sammy's just a little excited to see a real studio."

Diane laughs again. "Well, as you can see, there's really

not much to it. And I'm afraid it's a bit of a mess. I get so involved, and then I forget to tidy up."

"It's your work environment," Hudson says, then points to the canvas on the easel. "Is that the latest masterpiece?"

She shakes her head and sighs. "Let's hope. I've actually been struggling with it. Maybe tomorrow will be more productive than today has been."

Now, I was pretty interested in looking around a little. I mean, I could see scrolls of canvas and tools and brushes that were really different from the supplies in Miss Kuzkowski's classroom. But we weren't actually even inside, and then the phone starts ringing again.

"Oh *dear*," Diane says. "Someone is being annoyingly persistent."

"You probably should see who it is," Grams says.

"Please don't think me rude . . . ," she says as she pulls the door closed.

So I say, "Ms. Reijden? It was really nice of you to let me interview you."

She ushers us along, saying, "It was my pleasure, Sammy. And I do hope we'll all see each other again sometime soon. You're certainly delightful company."

"Thank you for your hospitality," Grams says when Diane lets us out the front door, but inside she's stewing. Stewing big time.

So as we're walking along the pathway I whisper to Grams, "And what did you discover, snooping around?"

She frowns. "Nothing."

"You looked pretty hard, too, didn't you."

She shrugs and frowns some more.

"I really can't believe you went snooping around her house. Do you know how mad you would have been at me if I—"

"Shhh!"

Hudson looks at us over his shoulder. "What are you two conspiring about?"

"Nothing!" we say together.

He stops in his tracks. "What on earth are you up to?"

"Absolutely nothing," Grams says, her nose hoisted primly in the air. But then the strangest thing happens. All at once, Grams' nose drops, her eyes bug, and her face turns white as winter.

"Grams? Grams, what's wrong? You look like you've seen a ghost."

"Listen," she whispers.

Then I hear it—*brum-bum-bum-bum-bum, brum-bum-bum-bum-bum*. And it's getting louder.

And *louder*.

And when it comes into view, I realize I'm right.

Grams *is* seeing a ghost.

A ghost that's riding a Harley.

TEN

Hudson looks from Grams to the Harley-Davidson thumping up the driveway, then back to Grams again. "Good lord, Rita, what's come over you?"

The motorcycle rider's wearing brown chaps, a leather jacket with long fringed sleeves, black boots, and one of those Hitler helmets. It's not Gramps. It *can't* be Gramps. But Grams is still frozen stiff, so I whisper, "Take a deep breath. It's not him."

Her head bobs like a dashboard toy and she says, "I know," but she's still not breathing right. So I whisper in her ear, "Maybe now would be a good time to try fainting . . . ?"

That gets her heart pumping again, let me tell you. Her head whips my way and her arms cross in front of her as she snaps, "Never!"

I shrug. "You looked like you were about to."

"Hrmph."

"What is going *on* with the two of you?" Hudson asks over the sound of the Harley.

"Nothing!" Grams tells him, then throws her head back and marches down the driveway, passing by the motorcyclist without even glancing at him. And when I

105

catch up to her, she keeps right on trucking, her arms pumping, her chin leading the way.

"Grams?"

"I'm fine, Samantha, and I'm sorry. I'm afraid the sound of a Harley can still get to me."

"But Grams, there are motorcycles everywhere, and you've never freaked out like *that* before."

"Not all motorcycles are Harleys, Samantha. And *that* Harley in particular . . . well, don't ask me. Maybe it's tricked out the same or something. It just got to me."

Tricked out? What kind of expression was "tricked out" for a *grandmother* to use?

Then all of a sudden she stumbles. I don't even know on what. One minute she's trucking along, chin jutting out, arms pumping high, and the next minute she's a heap of twisted grandma, sprawled on the gravel.

"Grams! Are you all right?"

"Owww," she says, grabbing her ankle.

"Did you sprain it?" And I really am worried about her until it hits me what's going on. I eye Hudson, who's talking to the motorcycle guy, and whisper, "Is this like fainting only not as stupid?"

I thought she was going to blow a gasket. "No!" She slaps the grit off her palms. "How can you even *think* such a thing?"

Out of nowhere, Flannel Man appears, kneeling right beside her, saying, "Are you all right, miss?"

Miss?

Grams looks at him. At his flannel ears sticking straight out. At his layers of shirts and the mud-caked knees of his jeans. "I'm fine," she tells him. "I must have slipped on the gravel."

He nods at her feet. "Lovely shoes, miss, but not much for walking, wot?" He helps her up. "Does yer husband know the rider?" he asks, looking over his shoulder at Hudson talking to Motorcycle Man.

"He is *not* my husband," Grams huffs as she dusts herself off.

Flannel Man looks from side to side. Like he's holding a stick of dynamite and not real sure how to get rid of it. So I give him a little don't-worry-about-it shake of the head and tell him, "They're probably just talking bikes."

It's like I snuffed the wick. He smiles at me, then says, "Never fancied motorbikes myself. And that one makes quite a racket."

I point up at the branch of a tree. "Your squirrels don't seem to like it much, either."

He spots Guiditta and Luciano scurrying back and forth along the branch. And I think he was about ready to march over and tell ol' Thumper to shut his contraption down, when the guy finally reaches over and turns off the key himself.

Now the bike doesn't just shut off. First it rumbles and sputters, then it blasts a huge flame out the tailpipe like a burning hot fart. *Then* it dies.

Motorcycle Man swings off the bike like the fire show was no big deal, and after talking with Hudson for another minute, he pushes the Harley up toward Diane's house.

Hudson hustles to join us, saying, "Sorry to make you

wait. I thought it might be a good idea to find out who that fellow was."

Now I'm just shaking my head, 'cause boy, is Hudson digging himself in deeper, or what? I mean, first he's got to go and gush about Diane's paintings belonging in the Louvre, then a mud-caked squirrel-feeding gnome with helicopter ears has to help Grams up 'cause Hudson's too busy protecting his purple-eyed princess from a gas-passin' Harley to notice the tumble.

And while I'm shaking my head and Grams is looking about as happy as a singed moth, Flannel Man asks, "And who exactly *is* he?"

"Oh, just her brother."

Flannel Man's eyes shoot open. "Lance? That's *Lance*? Crimy!"

"Why?" I ask him. "What's wrong with Lance?"

"We all thought he was dead, we did! Couldn't find him for Dr. Duane's funeral. Courtney tried, God rest her soul. And if you can't be found for your own father's burial . . ." His voice trails off and he frowns. "All these years. Imagine that."

All of a sudden Grams is back on the case. "Who's Dr. Duane?"

"Why, Dr. Reijden, miss. But he always insisted I call him Duane, so I called him Dr. Duane." He gives her a shy grin. "A compromise, wot?"

"And Courtney's the mother?" Grams asks.

He nods. "Yes, miss. Lovely lady. So full of grace and kindness. Lizzy, bless her heart, stayed with her to the end."

"You were neighbors a long time?"

"Have been, yes. Very private people, the doctor and the missus, but they treated me like family, they did."

"So what made the brother disappear?"

He shrugs. "He was always a bit of the black sheep. And being Dr. Duane's son, why, those were big footsteps to follow. That's always been my take on it, anyway."

We said our good-byes, and on the way back to the car Grams whispered, "He's the one. She got him to do it for her."

"Who? Flannel Man?"

"No! The brother!"

"But Grams, why? That doesn't make any sense!"

"Yes it does. Perfect sense. It explains everything."

"No, it doesn't! You've got the facts all mixed up. Whoever it was, was trying to get *away* with the paintings. They were *stealing* them. If I hadn't tackled them, they'd be out the door and down the street. Why would Diane get her brother to do that? I mean, she couldn't just pop them back on the wall after that, right?"

"But—"

"And excuse me, but a motorcycle does not make a very good getaway car. Besides, if this is the first time ol' Helicopter Ears has seen the brother, then they can't have been in cahoots. You can't exactly sneak around on that Harley!"

"You're just not seeing this right, Samantha. It's all for publicity! It's all for—"

"Grams, that doesn't make sense! Just admit it, would you? You *want* it to be her 'cause you're jealous."

Now Grams is about to say something back, but Hudson cuts in with, "What *are* the two of you whispering about?"

"Nothing," Grams snaps.

He looks at me, so I just shrug and sort of roll my eyes. But then I decide to toss him a bone. "You didn't notice Flannel Man coming to Grams' rescue when she fell?"

He gives me a really puzzled look. "You mean that Pete fellow?"

"Uh-huh."

He turns to Grams. "Rita, you fell?"

"Hrmph," she says, and picks up speed.

He looks at me, completely baffled, so I pat him on the shoulder and say, "Hudson, you're the smartest guy I know. I can't believe you're not getting this." He just stares at me, so I shake my head and say, "C'mon, let's go."

Grams made me sit up front on the way home. And it was weird—I wasn't mad at either of them, but they both seemed mad at each other *and* me. I tried breaking the ice by asking them stuff like, "Why do you think squirrels like rotten nuts?" and, "Where do you suppose *that* road goes?" and, "Is anyone else starving to death?" but all I got was a bunch of grumbling.

By the time I met Grams back at the apartment, she was in the strangest mood I'd ever seen. She raided the dregs of my Christmas candy, poured herself a big glass of my 2% milk instead of her fat-free stuff, and sat down at the kitchen table with a yellow pad of paper and a jar of colored pencils. Then she stuffed her face with chocolate, peanuts, and caramel and started scratching out a chart. "Why anyone else can't see this is beyond me," she muttered. "You want facts? I'll give you facts." And when I asked her, "You want me to make dinner?" she just ripped into a Three Musketeers and said, "Sure. Fine. Whatever you want."

Whatever I want? Well, this was a first. So while she scrawled away, I cooked up something Grams would normally never eat—some blood-cloggin', vein-stoppin' Pasta of Ill Repute.

That's right, I made us some mac 'n' cheese.

And when I brought two bowls of it to the table, she blinked at it, then at me, and said, "I can't eat that!"

I picked up her Three Musketeers wrapper and read, "Calories: 260. Calories from fat: 70." I grabbed the Snickers wrapper. "Calories: 280. Calories from fat: 130." And I was reaching for the PayDay wrapper when she said, "All right, all right! You've made your point. But could we at least have some kind of vegetable to go with it?"

"I am not mixing in peas or tuna or anything else, Grams. I—" and then I remembered something. "Salsa!"

"Salsa?"

I flew back to the refrigerator. "You know, tomatoes, onions, peppers . . . ?" I grabbed the salsa jar, a spoon, and an extra bowl and sat back down.

"Salsa is not a vegetable!"

"That's right, it's vegeta*bles.* Full of all those wonderful antioxidants you're always pushing me to eat."

"You're putting that *in* your macaroni?"

"I've heard it's really good. Actually, I've heard it's god-like."

"God-like?" She watched me mix up a little batch in the extra bowl, her face crinkled in disgust. "From whom?"

Actually, that was exactly what I was trying *not* to think about. I mean, I'd picked up this little tip clear back in January, so at this point I could easily have forgotten where I'd heard about mac 'n' salsa, right?

"Samantha?"

A lie flashed through my mind. A *meteor* shower of lies flashed through my mind. But since I'd recently made a pact with Grams that I wouldn't lie to her if she would try to trust me again, well, I didn't lie. I just shrugged like it didn't matter and said, "Just someone at school."

"And that someone's name is . . . ?"

"Casey," I said, then took a bite.

At first my mouth went into shock. Nothing moved. Then all of a sudden my tongue and teeth and palate and gums went crazy. Like they were jumping up and down for joy.

Casey was right.

It was god-like.

"Samantha?" Grams was looking worried. "Go on—spit it out!"

"Oh!" I started chewing like crazy. "Oh, Grams! This is so good, you won't believe it!" I spooned a bunch of salsa into my bowl and mixed, then grabbed her fork and gave her a bite.

"Say!" she said after chewing a minute. "That's wonderful!"

"Here." I passed her the salsa. "Have some veggies."

She laughed and mixed her own, then said, "So, who's Casey?"

Uh-oh. I stuffed my face. "Just somebody at school."

Now I could tell Grams was getting ready to sniff down a whole new trail of clues, so I reached over, snagged the pad, and said, "Let's see your 'facts.' "

Across the top she'd written SUSPECTS, but she'd only listed one—Diane "Lizzy" Reijden. And beneath her name she had:

1) Fainted during heist to cause diversion

2) Recognized bandit

3) Wanted to create reasons for the *L.A. Times* to write about her paintings

4) Was in no hurry to meet the reporter—knew he would be over to see her soon enough!

5) Dislikes Tess Winters

6) Does not want the police to investigate

7) Has a mysterious, black-sheep brother (who rides a Harley)

"Who rides a Harley? I guess that makes him guilty right there, huh?"

"Take it from me, Samantha, you can't trust a man on a tricked-out Harley."

"Well, the guy who kicked me in the jaw was wearing tennis shoes, not biker boots. Thank God."

She scowled at me. "Most people have more than one pair of shoes. And I don't know . . . maybe a Harley doesn't make for a quiet getaway, but who says he wasn't planning to just strap them to the sissy bar and blast out of there?"

To the sissy bar? The *sissy* bar? Who *was* this woman?

I shook my head. "Wouldn't that be really, really conspicuous?"

"Perhaps, but you did notice he only took four of them, right?"

"He couldn't *carry* all eight of them! Not under one arm!"

"Ah-ah-ah," she said, looking at me like she had the key to the universe. "He couldn't carry them all on the back of a Harley."

"But he could carry four? Gra-ams!"

"Okay, okay!" she grumbled, but then brightened. "So maybe he's also got a car."

"Not if he just came into town. Admit it, Grams. Your theory just doesn't hold up."

She crossed her arms. "I stand by my clues."

"Your clues." I shook my head and snagged her pad and a pencil. And while she ate zippy mac 'n' cheese, I made columns of my own. One for Tess Winters, one for Austin Zuni, and one for Jojo Lorenzo.

"Jojo Lorenzo?" Grams said, reading upside down. "Why on earth did you list *him*?"

So I told her all about seeing him at the Renaissance Faire and how he gets fifty percent of anything that's sold while it's at the Vault. "Diane's only showing her paintings there for three weeks, so he's got to move fast."

"Pshaw."

I blinked at her. "'Pshaw,' Grams?"

"You know—nonsense. Ridiculous. Absurd. Preposterous—"

"I know what pshaw *means,* Grams. I just didn't think it was something people actually *said.*"

"Well, I just did, and that's my exact assessment."

"Okay, well, what about the fact that Jojo 'forgot' to call the police the night of the robbery? Don't you find *that* a little odd? Maybe he was trying to give the squirt gun guy extra time to get away? Ever think about that?"

She waves it off. "That's perfectly in keeping with the way that man is." Then, just like that, she drops the only decent clue I've got and points to the paper, saying, "I know you've got things against that Winters woman, and heaven knows anyone would relish seeing her tried and convicted, but I place my money on Miz Liz." She wags her fork at me. "Intuition, child. You've got to trust it."

"Well, my intuition tells me Tess could very well have done it."

Grams shrugs. "List me some facts, then."

So I did.

1) Kept watching the front door.

"He came in the side door."

"Well, she was expecting *some*one."

"The reporter, most likely."

I scowled at her and wrote, 2) Needs publicity

"Any more than Diane?"

"Yes! Jojo says she hiked up her prices to be in the same ballpark as Diane's."

"Oh, pshaw."

I blinked at her, and then I couldn't help it—I cracked up. And when I quit laughing, I said, "You'd better not start using that all the time, all right?"

She grinned and scraped out her bowl, then eyed me. "It would be interesting to know whose paintings actually sell. Do you suppose that Winters woman has *ever* sold a painting?"

"Jojo said she sells a lot of them."

Grams quit licking her fork. "You can't be serious."

I nodded. "But that was at a price way lower than what she's charging now. He's not sure they'll move at the new price."

"Well, what about Austin Zuni? Why do you suspect him?"

"Jojo started to say something about him at the Faire."

"Like . . . ?"

"I don't know. There seemed to be something about him he didn't like. Didn't trust."

"Oh, that's concrete evidence." She smiled and shook her head. "Nope, the only real suspect is lovely Lizzy."

"Boy, Grams. She really bugs you, doesn't she?"

Grams scowled. "She's probably played off those eyes her entire life."

"What do you mean?"

"Why do you suppose her nickname's Lizzy? You can't very well get that out of Diane, now, can you?"

"So . . . ?"

She shakes her head at me like I'm dense as dirt. "Lizzy is short for Elizabeth? As in Elizabeth Taylor?"

"Oh come on, Grams. Who would do that?"

"Diane Reijden, apparently." She snags back the paper. "Now tell me about Casey."

"Casey?"

"You don't think I missed how your cheeks rosied up when I asked about the macaroni and salsa, do you?"

"I didn't blush!"

She took her glasses off, then huffed and buffed them. "The name Casey could be a boy's or a girl's." She popped her glasses back on her nose. "From your reaction, I'd say this Casey is a boy."

"So?"

"So who is he? How do you know him? Does he have a last name?"

I hesitated, then leaned forward and said, "Yeah, he has a last name: A-cos-ta."

She blinked. Once hard, then about ten times rapid fire. Then *she* leaned forward and whispered, "No . . . !"

"Yup. Casey is Heather's brother."

"They're not evil twins, are they?"

I laughed. "More like complete opposites. And he's in eighth grade."

"But still! You can't be—"

I shoved back and cleared our bowls. "Don't worry, I'm not about to get tangled up in a mess like that."

She just sat there, watching me rinse the dishes. And when I came back for the salsa and napkins, she gave me the same look she'd given me when I'd told her Diane hadn't set up the robbery. So I said, "Don't start thinking stupid thoughts, okay?"

"Then tell me why you blush every time you talk about him."

"I don't blush!"

She gave me a little grin. "Pshaw."

"Stop that!"

She grabbed my hand and said, "You can talk to me about this, you know."

"I know, Grams. But there's really not much to talk about. He's Heather's *brother*."

She kept her eyes locked on mine. "One's heart is not always as smart as one's head."

I laughed. "In your case, I think it's kind of the opposite."

"Samantha!"

"Seriously, Grams. You're completely deluded if you think Diane Reijden's an evil, scheming witch. Why can't you just admit you're jealous?" She looked really hurt, so I sat down across from her and said, "I'm sorry, okay? But I think it's true."

She sighed, then held her notes out in front of her and sighed again. "I wish I could prove it."

"So you can show Hudson what a blockhead he's being?"

She was quiet a long time, then said, "I guess it all just hits a little too close to home. I will never understand how your grandfather could have abandoned us for that Harley hussy."

"I'm sorry, Grams," I told her softly.

She got up and sighed again. "I think I'll go rest for a bit. Suddenly I'm very tired." She gave me a halfhearted smile. "But thanks for dinner. Tell Casey it was really quite good."

I shrugged. "If I see him." She eyed me skeptically, so I added, "I swear, Grams, I hardly ever run into him."

So she went off to her room and I cleaned up the kitchen. And while I scrubbed out the macaroni pan, I hoped really hard that I *wouldn't* run into Casey. Heather had probably told him everything Marissa had said at the Faire, and it wasn't something you could exactly explain away in the middle of a bunch of junior high kids. No, I'd just avoid Casey. Act like it was no big deal to me, 'cause it *was* no big deal to me. There was no way I was going to let a stupid little kiss on the hand make a fool out of me!

I should have known Heather Acosta would have other plans.

ELEVEN

I'd been on campus all of two minutes when I heard it.

A symphony of lip sucking behind me.

Don't turn around, I told myself. Don't turn around!

Smooch-smooch-smooch! Squeak-squeak-smack! "Oh, Romeo! Romeo! Wherefore art thou Romeo?" *Squeeeeeeak-smack!*

I kept lugging Marissa's tote bags along, my eyes glued straight ahead. But then all of a sudden Heather and her wanna-bes zoom around and block my path, their lips sticking out like a school of smoochy fish.

I roll my eyes and say, "Excuse me, Heather, but I think this is a violation of your, uh, *parole*. Twenty-five feet, remember? Unless you're *trying* to get expelled . . . ?"

It's kind of a long story, but after six months of Heather's lies and tricks and—as Grams says—shenanigans, this is Vice Principal Caan's latest brainchild: a "safety zone."

I guess he thinks you can fence out chiggers with chicken wire.

Anyway, Monet and Tenille are still making kissing noises, but their lips aren't sticking out quite so far, and they're starting to check over their shoulders for Mr. Caan.

Heather doesn't budge. "My brother says you're a liar, loser. Says he'd rather kiss a codfish!"

"He'd rather kiss *you*?" I wiggled my nose at her. "Didn't you take a shower after the Faire? Or is that your putrid personality passing gas again?"

She was about to shove me, but Monet grabbed her in the nick of time, saying, "It's the Caan Man!" And sure enough, Vice Principal Caan was making a beeline toward us.

Heather and her friends cut across the grass acting like everything was cool, but Mr. Caan wasn't fooled. "What was going on here?" he asked me.

"Just the usual," I said.

"I want to know what she said."

"Look, Mr. Caan. It's all right. I can take care of myself."

"I know that, Sammy. But I've promised you we'd be on top of her, so I want to know—did she threaten you? Because if she did, she's out of here."

Boy. Was this tempting, or what? But the fact was, she hadn't threatened me. And I suppose I could've told him all about her teasing me, but then I'd have had to explain about the kiss and really, I didn't want to get into it. Talk about embarrassing! So I just said, "She didn't threaten me. She was just being, you know, Heather. Don't worry about it, okay? It'll just get worse if you try and talk to her about it."

"You're sure?"

"Yeah. But thanks, Mr. Caan."

So I ran off to class, only the minute I walked into

homeroom and saw Marissa's face, I knew something was wrong. I put her tote bags by her seat and said, "Hey, what's up?"

She eyed my desk.

And that's when I saw it. Lying under my desk, wheels up, purple patch showing. "My board!" I yipped, and charged across the room.

Marissa followed me, whispering, "You're *happy* about this?"

I was all over my skateboard, flipping it around, checking it out, whipping the wheels, *zoom, zoom, zoom.* "Of course I'm happy! God, I want to go *ride.*" I tossed it on the floor and hopped on.

From behind the rulers and feathers and magnifying glass in her pencil jug, Mrs. Ambler barked, "Samantha! You can't ride that anywhere on campus, and certainly not in my classroom!"

I popped it up and called, "Sorry, Mrs. Ambler," then said, "Wa-hoo!" to Marissa.

Marissa leaned against a desk next to mine and said, "Don't you understand the significance of this?"

"Yeah! This means I don't have to *walk* everywhere I go. I can ride!"

The bell rang as she grabbed me by the shoulders and shook. "Sammy! The significance of this is that Casey isn't holding it hostage anymore."

"He should never have been holding it hostage!"

She threw her hands in the air. "You're hopeless."

"No, I'm not. You just read too much into everything. Danny says *maybe* he'll see you at the Faire and *you*—"

"Shhhhh!" she hisses, looking over her shoulder at the kids filing in.

I whisper, "—think it's a hot date. Casey's all caught up in being a thespian—"

"A what?"

"An actor! And *you* think he's kissed me for real."

Just then Heather struts through the door. And the instant she sees me she makes that stupid kissing sound. *Squeeeeeeak-smack.*

I give Marissa a dirty look. "And thanks to *you,* I now have to put up with *that.*"

Squeeeeeeak-smack!

Marissa cringes and whispers, "I'm sorry . . . !"

"Plus the embarrassment of hearing that he'd rather kiss a codfish."

"What?"

"That's what she told me this morning."

"Who? Heather?"

"Yes, Heather."

"Well, she's lying."

"How do you know?"

Marissa laughs, "She always lies!"

"So why's my skateboard here? I mean, according to you, this means he doesn't care anymore.

"Oh," she says, and her face falls. "Oh, yeah."

The tardy bell rings, so Marissa hurries to her seat. And even though I tried to act like everything was fine—even though most of me was ecstatic about having my skateboard back—the truth is, I was embarrassed. Embarrassed that Casey thought I'd made a big deal out of him kissing my stupid hand. Embarrassed that Heather was going around telling people I was in love with her brother—'cause knowing Heather, that's exactly how she was spinning this. And embarrassed that after all this time, Casey'd finally given my skateboard back without a word.

So for the rest of the day I did the only thing I could think to do about it—I hid. Not behind trash cans or in bushes or anything like that. More just in classrooms. And when I thought the coast was clear, I'd jet over to where I was supposed to be. Even at lunch. It was so windy that Holly, Marissa, and Dot all wanted to move from the patio tables to the cafeteria, but I wasn't about to go in there.

Heather and her friends eat there.

So does Casey.

So I dragged them into an open classroom, and that's where we ate lunch instead. And I *did* do a pretty good job of forgetting about Heather and Casey and that whole mess by catching Holly and Dot up on everything that had happened at the Vault and about getting to interview Diane. I didn't tell them too much about Grams and Hudson and the Harley, 'cause I didn't think Grams would appreciate it, but I did tell them about Grams being a snoop.

"Your *grandmother*?" Holly asks. "I can't quite picture that. She seems so, you know, normal."

I just shook my head and said, "I know. It's bizarre. And Hudson's been acting weird, too."

"How's that?" Dot asks.

"He's just been kind of *out* of it. Doesn't really tune in to what's going on."

Dot shrugs. "Well, he is kind of old."

"Hudson? No he's not."

They all stop chewing and stare at me.

"Well, he never *acts* old. He's really, really sharp."

"Yeah, that's true," they all say, and start chewing again.

So I was back to thinking more about Hudson and Grams and what was going on at the Vault than I was about Casey. And since Mr. Pence actually posted Heather in the back corner for "disruptive behavior" when she tried her smoochy-coochie sounds in science, I had the luxury of not having to dodge rubber bands or flying tacks or cutting remarks. I could just listen.

So I was in a pretty good mood when I blew into art. And then Miss Kuzkowski greets me with a great big, "Sammy!" like I'm a long-lost friend.

"Uh, hi, Miss Kuzkowski."

She comes right over to me, switching to a whisper. "Wow, did you ever put on a show Friday night! I'm sorry I didn't get the chance to say hello or congratulate you. The evening disintegrated awfully quickly, as you know."

"You can say that again."

She leans in even closer. "Was that the wildest reception you've ever been to, or what?"

Now until that moment, all the teachers I have ever had have been, well, *teachers*. Adults who tell you to be quiet; who give you homework and send you to the office. And not only have they always been adults, they've always been, you know, *old*. Maybe it's the way they act or the clothes they wear. Maybe it's the way they talk to you like you're a child—which makes them automatically old. Even the ones who try to talk like they're cool—you know, use all the slang that the kids use—well, they seem even geekier than the regular teachers. I mean, you do *not* want to hear your teacher say, "Sw-eet!" or, "Chill!" It's like seeing a guy with a big gut wearing a Speedo. You just want to look the other way.

But there was Miss Kuzkowski, perched on the stool next to me, and all of a sudden it hit me—she's kinda young. Maybe barely an adult. So instead of answering her question about the artist reception, I ask, "How . . . um . . . How many years have you been a teacher?"

She pulls herself up straighter. "Why do you ask?"

"I don't know. Just wondering."

"Well," she says, dropping her voice, "this happens to be my first year, but I had a full year of student teaching, so I'm definitely qualified."

"I didn't mean *that*. . . ."

"That's okay," she says. "Anyway, I just wanted to tell you I was so proud of you on Friday! I bragged to everyone that you were my student."

She was sort of gushing, and since other students were all around I was starting to feel pretty uncomfortable. So I said, "I hope you didn't brag to that Tess Winters lady—she hates me."

"Tess? Oh, she can be very temperamental, but don't take that personally. It's just part of her creative process."

"You *know* her?"

"Absolutely! She was one of my college professors, and now I'm one of her Disciples."

"Her . . . disciples?"

She laughs. "I'd forgotten how funny that sounds. What I'm saying is, I'm in her artists' group."

"What's that?"

"Just a group selected by Tess to meet and discuss art. We critique each other's projects, discuss art, encourage one another. . . . It's sort of a cross between an artist workshop and philosophers' forum." She stands up to let Emma sit down next to me. "Didn't you think her work was brilliant?"

"Are you serious?"

"Absolutely!"

I jumped off my stool and followed her back to her desk. "Miss Kuzkowski, I don't get her stuff at *all*. It looks like something a two-year-old could do!"

"Aaaah," she says, looking at me with a sort of sappy sympathy. "You just don't see it. Believe me, Sammy. It's deep."

"I tried to get her to explain it, but she wouldn't. She was really mean about it, too."

Miss Kuzkowski shakes her head and says, "She can be that way. Thank heaven I didn't tell the whole class to show up like I was going to. She was *not* in the mood."

"Well, maybe she wouldn't talk to me, but I did get an interview for your assignment. With Diane Reijden."

"Oh . . . ?" she says, and both her eyebrows go up. "I'm sure Ms. Reijden didn't have much nice to say about Tess, am I right?"

"I didn't really ask her about Tess. But why do you say that?"

"Because a couple of years ago, Tess was the head of a committee that approved art for a big showing in Santa Luisa. Apparently Miss Reijden was one of the artists whose work was refused."

"Refused? Like, rejected?"

"Uh-huh."

"You're kidding."

"Well, she wasn't the only one. There was a whole slew of artists who didn't make the cut—that's just how these things work." She shrugs. "But this time, the refused artists made a big stink and had a show of their own. It was all over the papers."

"I don't get it. How could they not have liked Diane's paintings? Don't you think they're amazing?"

"Truthfully?" She eyes me and settles onto her stool. "I find them to be rather clichéd."

"Clichéd? I've never seen anything like them!"

She smiles at me. Like I'm a little bird, perched on her windowsill. "You've just started looking, Samantha."

At this point my cute little feathers are plenty ruffled, let me tell you. So I blurt out, "Well, what's so great about *Tess's* paintings? Can you tell me that? And why does she get to be head of some committee that rejects other people's art?"

"Oh, Sammy, Sammy," she says with a sigh. "It's not something I can explain in two minutes." The bell rings and she checks the door for tardies, then flips open her grade book to take roll. "You would learn so much if you could sit in on a Disciple meeting, but I'm afraid that's a no-no." She scans the classroom, counting heads. "Hopefully I'll be able to enlighten you in class before the end of the term."

I took my seat, and for the rest of school my thoughts were like a pinball pinging around all over the place. Art. Casey. Heather.

Art.

My skateboard. Tess. Diane.

Art.

Grams. Hudson. Grams.

Art.

And I don't really know why the art thing bothered me so much. Why should I care if Tess told Diane her paintings weren't good enough for some art show? Why should I care if people thought a giant orange splot was brilliant, when what I saw was a mess? Wasn't it like food? I mean, some people like Chinese, some people like Mexican.

Some people like salsa in their macaroni and cheese.

But still, it bugged me. I didn't like that I didn't *get* it. How could any committee have rejected a painting like *Whispers*?

So I told myself, okay. Maybe I'd just imagined it. Maybe Diane's paintings had just looked great in comparison to orange splots and wild-eyed Indians. Maybe I'd seen something that wasn't really there.

Maybe.

After school, I threw on my backpack, grabbed my board, broke a few no-skating-on-campus rules, and met up with Marissa, who was strapping the tote bags to her bike. "You are not going to be able to keep up with me," I told her. "Man, I feel like I can *fly*."

She laughed and chased after me. "Sammy, wait up!"

"*Catch* up!"

I hit the sidewalk running, then threw down my board and jumped on. My hair flew up behind me. The wind was everywhere, whooshing in my sweatshirt, pushing back my face. I pressed along, faster, faster, faster, ducking down driveways, zigzagging past kids walking, hopping curbs at intersections, doing ollies. . . . I felt like I haven't felt in ages. Charged. Electric. Like I could do anything. *Be* anything.

Marissa caught up on the street beside me and shouted, "Awesome!" and that's when it clicked that what I was feeling was something every kid in junior high wants to feel.

Free.

When we got to the intersection of Cook and Broadway, Marissa said, "Wow! I'd forgotten how good you were!" Then she checked her watch and said, "We've got tons of time before we're supposed to be home. Want to go to the arcade?"

"You know what? I don't. I want to go to the Vault, and I want you to come with me."

"The Vault? Why?"

"Because there's something I want to see. And show you."

She looked over at the mall and I could practically hear the arcade, calling her name. "I've got all this stuff on my bike, Sammy."

"It's not that far . . . come on. I really want your opinion."

"You just want to ride some more, huh?"

I pushed off. "That too!"

The wind was behind us now, gusting us along. Faster, faster, faster! I was a sidewalk serpent! A barrelin' boarder! Or, as one old guy walking a mangy terrier put it, a bleepin' "MANIAC."

We got to the Vault in no time. And I was still all out of breath and buzzing at the knees as we headed for the Bean Goddess door, but as we start to cross a paved alleyway that runs between the Vault and the neighboring building, I pull back fast.

"What?" Marissa asks as I yank her down.

I put up a finger and whisper, "Hold on a minute," then peek around the corner and down the alley.

It's Tess, all right.

Talking to someone in the alley.

Someone she sure doesn't want this "ragamuffin" girl to see.

TWELVE

"Sammy, what are you doing? What's going on?" Marissa peeks around the corner, too. "Who are they?"

"That's Tess Winters—"

"The Splotter?"

"Yeah. And she just gave that guy an envelope."

"So?"

"So that's the same door the Squirt Gun Bandit used. And look at the way she's acting. Look at *him*."

He was sort of greasy looking. About 5'10''. Kind of wiry, with a ball cap and tennis shoes. And the more I watched the intense way Tess was talking to him while she kept checking over her shoulder inside the Vault, the more sure I became that something shady was going down.

When the man started off down the alley, Tess stepped back inside, closing the door tight. "You thinking what I'm thinking?" I whispered to Marissa.

She frowned at me. "I am not following anybody." She pointed to her bike. "Even if I wanted to, I couldn't."

It was true—with her bike saddled down the way it was, she'd be invisible as an elephant. So I parked my board and stripped off my backpack. "I'll be right back."

"Sammy, don't abandon me!"

"I'll be *right* back. Promise."

"Yeah, yeah, yeah," she grumbled as she slid down the building to sit. "I've heard *that* one before."

I sprinted down the alley, and when I got to a small parking area behind the Vault, I saw that there was *another* alley running behind all the buildings on the block. It was dirt and gravel and narrow, with a busted wooden fence running along the other side—the kind of alley I try to stay away from.

I spotted the guy unlocking a jacked-up purple Camaro. The car had gray Bondo patches on the door, but the chrome bumpers and mirrors were buffed to blinding. And when he fired that big boy up, it had a deep, ornery growl—like, Hey, you puny four-bangin' import, don't even *think* about messing with me.

I crouched low and zigzagged around cars until I was laying low behind the back fender of a silver Honda. And I would have had a great shot at the Camaro's license as it backed out, only there was no front plate. So I scrambled up to the intersection of the two alleys, but before I could make out the back license, he threw the car in first and tore out of there, kicking gravel and dust up behind him.

I raced back to Marissa, who did a double take when she saw me. Then she stood up, made a real exaggerated pinch on her arm, and said, "Wow. That *was* quick."

"Told you."

"So?"

I shrugged. "Drives a purple Camaro, couldn't get the plates." I picked up my stuff and started over to the Bean Goddess entrance, but all of a sudden I had an idea.

Marissa looks at me, looking at her. "Oh, no. *Now* what?"

"Why don't *you* go in and eavesdrop on Tess? You know her, but she doesn't know you!"

"But . . . why?"

"Maybe you'll hear something. Or see something."

"Sammy . . ."

I grab her bike and pull off her pack. "Just go snoop, would you? I'll be inside in a minute."

She rolls her eyes and gives a little *tsk*, but before you know it, she's shuffling into the Bean Goddess.

Now at first I'm just sitting against the building, surrounded by things with wheels and bags of stuff, looking like a junior bum-in-training. But after a while that gets old, so I decide to peek in the front window to see what I can see.

There are quite a few people inside. Some in line at the counter, being waited on by a couple of faux-bohemians with gelled hair and silver jewelry. There's another faux-bo collecting cups and wiping down tables, and then about fifteen customers, sitting at tables, reading and eating, and basically just worshiping the bean goddess.

But near the Vault archway, I spot Tess, wearing all black, and Jojo, wearing bright yellow boots and orange leather pants. They're rearranging furniture, making one long table out of a group of smaller ones. And sitting nearby, looking very self-conscious as she sort of hunches behind a plant, is Marissa.

I've got a real urge to pass her a magazine or a newspaper or shades, but all I can do is stand there, peeking in.

Then Jojo notices her. And even though he'd only ever seen her in that Renaissance dress, he recognizes her. He smiles real big, then goes over and sits with her, while Tess finishes arranging chairs around the long table she's made.

The minute Tess disappears through the Vault's archway, I lock up Marissa's bike, grab the tote bags, the backpacks, and my board, and go inside. And after I park all our junk in a corner, I go up to Marissa and Jojo and say, "Hi."

Jojo stands and gives me the brightest smile. "There you are, Sweet Pea. There you *are*."

I say, "Sorry I'm late," to Marissa, then ask Jojo, "How's it going?"

"Ducky! Everything is just ducky! I've got a security guard . . . ," he motions over to the rent-a-cop visible through the Vault doorway, ". . . and we've had lots of traffic." He claps his hands together and asks, "Can I buy you lattes? Iced mochas? Java swirls?" but before I can answer, his eyes get all big and he says, "Just tell the gals . . . tell them to put it on my account, would you?" Then he scurries off under the arch, disappearing into the Vault.

"That was weird," Marissa says, looking over for what had spooked him. And it *was* weird, because the only person coming into the Bean Goddess was a scraggly-haired woman with round wire glasses. And with her wrinkly corduroy pants, faded sweatshirt, and dirty Velcro-strap Nikes, she sure didn't *seem* like anyone to be afraid of— she just looked like a harmless bag lady coming in out of the wind for a cup of coffee.

So I shook my head and said, "I wonder what that was all about."

Marissa shrugs. "Maybe he just had to get back to work."

Tess had planted a RESERVED sign on her table and was now positioning a display easel at the far end of it. I asked Marissa, "Did you happen to overhear what that's about?"

"Some kind of religious meeting, maybe? She kept saying something about disciples."

"Disciples? Really? Miss Kuzkowski told me she was part of Tess's artist group called the Disciples."

Marissa's face crinkled. "That's kinda weird, don't you think? Sounds like a cult or something."

"You're right," I told her, and down my spine ran the tingle of a shiver. Not because a bunch of artsy-fartsy people were going to get together and talk about paintings. Big deal. No, my spine was tingling because my teacher—someone I'd known all year, saw almost every day, listened to, even *liked*—was one of Tess's "disciples." It just seemed . . . creepy. Like Tess had cast some sort of spell on her—a spell that made her think a big orange splot was brilliant.

I shook off the vision of Miss Kuzkowski with psycho eyes and zombie arms and said, "Did you hear anything else?"

"Not really. Jojo seemed kind of upset, but he was keeping his voice way down, so I couldn't really tell. And then he recognized me, which sorta surprised me."

"Me too. He's only ever seen you at the Faire, right?"

"Right. But anyway, he did, and it kind of blew everything."

I kept one eye on the bag lady as she moseyed through the Bean Goddess toward the Vault. "So what were you and Jojo talking about?"

"You, mostly."

"Me?"

"Uh-huh. He wanted to know if you were coming, too, and if you're always so brash."

"Brash?"

"He said it in a nice way." She grinned and pinched my cheek. "You plucky little tiger!"

"Oh, shut up."

"So what are we doing here, anyway? I thought you wanted to show me something, not involve me in some spying mission."

"I know. I do. Sorry about the sidetrack. Blame Grams, okay? She's the one obsessed with bringing down bad guys, not me."

"Oh, right."

"Seriously. This is all on account of her. I'm trying to stay out of it."

"Obviously."

I grab her by the arm. "Come on."

When we're inside the Vault, I whisper, "There's Tess," and nod over to where she's straightening one of her paintings.

"Ohmygod," Marissa gasps. "They *are* just splots!"

"Told you."

"She's charging eight *thousand* for those?"

"Yup."

Marissa moves a little closer, muttering, "Unbelievable," and that's when Tess notices her.

And me.

"You!" she says with a whole gust of air. "What are *you* doing back here?"

I almost said, "Just showing my friend what a splot'll cost ya," but I bit my tongue.

She swoops down on us. "I asked you a *question*."

I shrugged. "Just trying to figure things out."

Her eyes squint into little slits, then kind of dart from side to side. "Figure what out?"

Now the way she said it was plenty scary, but it was weird because under all that vampire posturing was something unsure.

Something worried.

So right then and there I decide to play a little longer. "Look, this is a public place; there's no law saying I can't look around."

She just glares at me, her pouty lips pulled tight like little pink worms. And she's trying to stare me down. To *intimidate* me. But I've had some intense intimidation training at William Rose Junior High, so I just stand my ground and stare back. And the whole time I'm thinking, You're a splotter, nothing but a snotty splotter. . . . You're a splotter, nothing but a snotty splotter. . . .

Finally, *whoosh,* she turns her back on me. But before she can walk away I say, "Yup, there's no law saying I can't look around. In here, or say . . . down the alley?"

She slows down, then stops and turns to face me.

"It's amazing what you can witness, looking down alleys. Drug deals, knifings, briberies, *payoffs* . . ."

She gives me a seriously scary look. And I can see the wheels spinning in her head, but I can't really tell what *direction* they're spinning, if you know what I mean. Then, without a word, she turns on her heel and marches her scary face right over to the scary table.

Marissa whispers, "Why'd you do *that*?"

"Just trying to make her give something away."

"God, Sammy. You're going to get yourself killed someday, you know that?"

"Nah. She's weak."

Marissa scowls at me. "Ever heard of poison? Dynamite? *Guns*? You don't have to be *strong* to kill someone."

I laugh. "I'm not worried."

"So is that why we came here? To meet the Splotter and see her splots?"

I laugh again. "Nu-uh. We're here because I want to show you these." I lead her over to Diane's wall and whisper, "What do you think?"

"Wow," she says after a minute. Then she leans in and looks at the signature. "Diane Reijden? So these are the paintings that guy tried to steal?"

"Uh-huh." I was staring at *Whispers*. At the girl's eyes, twinkling with excitement. At the way her hand was cupped near her mouth. At the moonlight across the room and the way it seemed to dust the background with light. The bookshelves. A birdcage. A rocking horse. All just barely there.

"Is that the one you like so much?"

Marissa's voice shook me out of the scene on the wall. "Huh? Oh. Oh, yeah." She had her head cocked at it, so I asked, "What do you think?"

She nodded. "It's great. They're all great."

Now, there are lots of ways of saying great. And depending on the way you say it, it can mean a lot of different things. And since the way she said it was sort of ho-hum, I was about to ask her, That's it? Just great? but then *she* says, "Wow, check *these* out!" and moves over to Austin Zuni's wall.

I follow her over, not quite believing what I'm hearing. "These are so cool! Look at those eyes! Whoa!" She moves from side to side, saying, "How do they do that? Wow." She grabs me by the arm and says, "You've got to try this. Stand right here. Now move like this . . ." She takes me by the shoulders and moves me to one side, then the other. "Intense, isn't it?"

I shake her off and turn to face her. "Are you telling me you like *these* better than *those*?"

She blinks, then shrugs. "I didn't say that. I just think these are, you know, cool."

So I was feeling a little confused. I mean, I didn't like the Indian eye paintings at *all*, but Marissa thought they were way better than Diane's—I could tell. And there across the room were big splots of paint that Miss Kuzkowski thought were amazing. How could anybody think they were amazing? How could anybody want Indian eyes staring at them from their wall? How could anyone not think *Whispers* was great? I mean *really* great.

So while Marissa danced around Austin Zuni's paintings, I wandered back to Diane's side of the room. And before I knew it, I was in front of *Whispers* again, staring at the girl, lost in the scene.

And I was just feeling like I was there, *in* the painting, when behind me I hear, "It is lovely, isn't it?"

I jumped. And it wasn't just because I'd been startled. It was also because I felt like I'd just been yanked from inside the painting, back to the Vault. I felt disoriented. Out of sorts. Like I'd just been woken from a dream. And when I whip around, who's there smiling at me?

The bag lady.

"Oh, hi," I tell her, and then nod. "It is. I like it a lot."

We look at it together a minute, and then she says, "The security guard tells me you were talking with Mr. Lorenzo earlier. Do you happen to know where he might have gone?"

"Uh . . . ," I look over my shoulder, "no." Then I see Tess behind the scary table and say, "But that woman over there probably knows."

"Hrmph!" she says, just like my grams might have.

I grin at her. "I take it she's been friendly to you, too?"

She eyes Tess across the room. "She's like that to anyone who dares call her a fraud."

Now this bag lady may have whiskers growing on her lip and a few poking out of her chin besides, but the more we talk, the more I like her. So before I can stop myself I whisper, "I call her the Splotter."

Her eyes light up. "*Hee-hee-hee.* Oh, that's rich!" And when we're done sharing a laugh, she sighs and says,

"Well, he can't avoid me forever. And you can tell him so, if you see him."

"But . . . who are you?"

"Mrs. Weiss. I'm the landlady."

"The . . ." I blink at her. "You mean you own the Vault?"

"Oh no, honey. The Vault is Joseph's business. I own the building."

"You mean this *part* of the building, or . . . ," I wave toward the Bean Goddess, "out there, too?"

The hairs on her lip move up. The ones on her chin poke forward, and some of her wrinkles compress on her cheeks as she shows me her crooked teeth. And as she's smiling at me, she waves out toward the Bean Goddess like I just had and says, "Out there," she waves past Tess's wall, "and down there, too."

"What do you mean?"

She levels a look at me. "Honey, I own this whole *block* of buildings."

"The whole . . ." I just stood there with my jaw dangling. And maybe it was rude, but you have to understand—this was my first millionaire bag lady.

Finally, I manage a real intelligent, "Oh." Then I ask her, "Does Jojo owe you rent or something?"

She nods. "And I can't wait any longer for his big break. With my property taxes coming due, I'm afraid I can't continue to float him."

"But I'm sure he'll pay it. . . ."

"Well, I'm not," she says, then asks, "What about his brother? Has he been around today?"

"His . . . brother?" I rack my brains for who that could possibly be, but just can't picture Jojo with a brother.

"That Zuni character?" She points at the wild-eyed Indian wall. "He's co-leasing."

Now I know I should've just nodded or shrugged or done something, you know, nonchalant. I mean, she probably would've kept on talking. Or at least asking questions. But shell-shocked me had to go bug out my eyes, and say, "Austin Zuni is Jojo's *brother*?"

"Never mind," she says with a frown. "I'm not here to spread gossip. I just want my rent."

So I'm feeling really stupid, really *lame,* but then as she turns to leave, she throws me a wink over her shoulder. "Splotter," she says. "*Hee-hee-hee,* that's rich."

And as I watch her walk away, it hits me that inside this world of art are shades of gray that I'm just beginning to see. Shades where people hide. And scheme.

And try hard to deceive.

THIRTEEN

Marissa had had enough of art. She was tired of doing the eyeball boogie with Indian chiefs and sure didn't want to spend any more time looking at anything else. But on our way out, I noticed that there were already three people sitting at the Disciples table and more were moving toward it. And there was Tess, at the head of the table, nodding and smiling and acting, well, like the biggest ant on the hill.

So I really wanted to hang around and catch a little of the meeting, just to see what it was like, but Marissa said, "Sammy, no!"

So I tried, "But I think Miss Kuzkowski's going to be here."

"And that makes you *want* to stay?"

I shrugged. "Don't you think it would be kinda interesting? Seeing a teacher as a student?"

"No! I like to forget about teachers when I'm away from school. Besides, she'll know you're here, so she'll either be embarrassed or show off." Then she adds, "Or worse, be an embarrassing show-off."

"But—"

"Why am I even having this argument with you? You can hang around if you want to, but I'm out of here."

Well, I didn't want to stay by myself. That would've felt awkward. So I was about to say, "Nah. Come on, let's go," but then the strangest thing happened. A man walked through the Bean Goddess door. A tall man. With white hair. And cowboy boots.

Green cowboy boots.

And my brain should've just said, Hey, wow. There's Hudson. But sometimes when you see somebody you know really well in a place you don't expect them, the part of your brain that's in charge of putting pieces together doesn't seem to work right. It holds the pieces right near each other, but takes forever to move them in for the big *click*.

So I didn't call out to him. I just stared. And as he's moving through the Bean Goddess straight for the Vault, Marissa's the one who finally says, "Hey, isn't that Hudson?"

Hudson didn't hear us. Didn't see us. He just beelined through the arch and disappeared into the Vault.

No one had to tell me where he was going. I could tell from the look on his face. And all of a sudden, more than anything, I wanted to talk to him about it, wanted to understand what it was that was making us come back. I mean, seeing *Whispers* a second time had only made me like it more, and already I wanted to go back and look at it again.

What *was* it about that painting?

I knew that if anyone could explain it to me, it'd be Hudson Graham. So I turned to Marissa and said, "Do you mind if I stick around and talk to Hudson for a bit?"

"No . . . unless you're gonna make me stay, too."

"No, that's okay. Sorry for dragging you all the way out here."

"Hey, it's fine. Those Indians were cool."

So she took off, and I slipped back into the Vault.

It wasn't *Whispers* Hudson was standing in front of. It was *Resurrection*—the one with autumn leaves swirling through the air. And I stood beside him for the longest time, but he didn't seem to know I was there. Finally I said, "So why do you like this one so much?"

His body jolted a little. Like he'd just stepped off a curb in a dream. Then he looked at me and asked, "Sammy?" like *his* brain was having trouble clicking pieces together.

"In the flesh," I said, then laughed. "I did the same thing when I saw you walk in." He was still sort of staring, so I asked, "Are you okay?"

"Yes, yes. I'm fine." He looked around a little. "Is your grandmother with you?"

"No. I came here straight from school."

"Oh. Oh, I see."

He was back to looking at the painting, so I said, "Hudson, I hope I'm not, you know, disturbing you because . . . well, I'm really glad you're here."

"You are?" He smiled at me, and this time he was all there.

"Yeah. Because everyone else I talk to confuses me."

"Everyone else you talk to about what?"

"Art!"

"Oh." He chuckles a little, then says, "Subjective topics usually render subjective comments."

146

"But you like these," I said, pointing to Diane's paintings. "You like them the way I do, I can tell."

He eyes me, but doesn't say a thing.

"Okay. Well tell me this—do they make you feel all jumbled up? You know—happy and peaceful one minute, then sort of tortured the next? Like any minute you're going to cry?"

Hudson just stands there studying me like *I'm* some odd painting. First his head cocks to one side, then to the other. But slowly a smile grows on his face. Not a ha-ha-ha smile or a patronizing smile. It's a gentle smile.

A grateful smile.

So I say, "And it's not just *Whispers* that does that to me. They're all a little that way. And I don't get how they can *do* that. I mean, they're just paintings."

Hudson nods, then turns back to the wall. "After reading the scathing review in yesterday's paper, I just had to come here and see again for myself."

"Wait a minute. What scathing review?"

"In our illustrious local rag. That's why the phone was ringing off the hook at Ms. Reijden's house. It's . . . it's libelous."

"But—"

"And it made me start doubting myself. So I came here to see whether what I was remembering was something I had simply projected onto the canvas. But here I am, completely mesmerized by these paintings again. Even more so than before." He starts walking along the Reijden wall, saying, "The reviewer called them 'conspicuously out of touch,' but I find them to be very much *in* touch. Compelling. They're serious, but uplifting. They each have a sense of hope—deep, steady hope. They touch upon fragility without apologizing for strength."

As stupid as this sounds, at that moment I wanted to crush Hudson in a hug, wanted to tell him how glad I was that he could put things into words in a way I couldn't and how relieved I was that someone else felt the way I did. Instead, what came out of my mouth was, "I can't believe she'd *sell* them."

He nods. "But she's an artist, and this is how she makes a living."

"Well if *I'd* made them, I wouldn't sell them." I point to the one with the gusting leaves. "Okay, maybe I'd sell that one to you, but only to you, and only because you like it so much. No way I'd sell *Whispers*."

"But if you'd painted them, you could make others." He looks at *Whispers* and says, "I hadn't noticed the bookcase before. Or the rocking horse."

"Neither had I. And the more I look at it, the more there seems to be to it."

He nods and murmurs, "The deeper it goes."

"I think that's the same rocking horse we saw in Diane's house, don't you?"

"I didn't notice it," he says absently.

"It was by the fireplace. See the star on the forehead? It had one, too." We both look at it a minute, and finally I ask, "So who do you think that girl is? At first I thought it might be Diane, remembering her own childhood, but the girl in the picture has brown eyes. Do you know if Diane has children? Grandchildren?"

He shakes his head. "I have no idea. But I do think she's right that not knowing the specifics is better. Project your own story into the painting. It'll have its own meaning for you that way. It'll become more personal to *you*."

We looked at the paintings a little while longer and finally I whispered, "Thanks, Hudson."

He grinned down at me. "Thank you, Sammy."

So I was feeling pretty good, but then as we were heading out of the Vault Hudson sighed and said, "I'm afraid I'm in rather a bad spot with your grandmother."

Now the way he said it was sort of heavy. Like just the thought of Grams was making his feet slow down, even stop. And that's when it hit me—he needed to talk. For the first time since I'd met him, Hudson was asking *me* to help *him*.

So I jingled around in my pocket, asking, "Can I get you an iced tea? Some cocoa?"

He laughed. "Only if you let me buy."

Good thing, too, with the seventy-four cents I managed to scare up.

So while he got us iced teas, I settled in at a table behind a big, plastic palmy plant and checked out the Disciple table. Miss Kuzkowski was there, all right, and even though she looked my way once, she didn't seem to recognize me. She just turned and smiled at a guy with a short curly ponytail who brought her coffee and a muffin.

There were twelve Disciples total, plus Tess. And when Hudson came back with the teas, he scowled in Tess's direction and said, "Looks like she's holding court, doesn't it?"

"She is." I leaned over the table and whispered, "Those are Tess's 'disciples.'"

His face scrunched up. "Surely you jest."

"Not I, sire," I said in my best English accent.

He laughed. "Say, that was good." Then we overheard Tess say, "Who's volunteering first today?"

At first none of the Disciples said a thing. Then they all seemed to talk at once. Finally Tess laughed and said, "Frank, you're elected."

So Frank lifts a covered canvas onto the easel, and when he whips the sheet off, the whole Disciple table gasps at the painting. It's a big red face, with black holes for eyes and a screaming mouth. And glued all around the face and sticking out of the mouth are blue and red tubes of some kind.

"What *are* those things?" I whisper to Hudson.

"Shotgun shells," he whispers back.

"Comments?" we hear Tess ask the group.

There's a moment of silence and then one Disciple says, "It's powerful."

"Arresting," Miss Kuzkowski chimes in, then adds, "No pun intended."

There's a little laughter, then someone calls out, "It's electrifying!"

"Stunning!"

"Nice depth to the acrylic, Frank."

Then after a few moments of silence, Tess says, "Very powerful, Frank. Leaps ahead of your last presentation."

Frank was nodding away, beaming like a little kid.

I whisper to Hudson, "Comments?"

He shakes his head. "It strives to evoke a sense of hatred. I find it emotionally contrived and aesthetically distasteful."

"Hey, I think you ought to join the Disciples."

He scowls. "I'm afraid I'd be more of a Dissonant."

The next Disciple's painting was already on the easel. It was waves of color overlapping from top to bottom with some long drips running through like stretchy faucet drips. Tess stands there, nodding. "I feel the rhythm."

"Yes, yes!" the artist cries. He's actually bouncing up and down on his toes, his thick glasses bobbing on his nose. "It represents rhythms of civilization. Paths crossing, lives intersecting. . . . I've tried to be submissive to the materials, allowing them to take me, rather than trying to dominate them!"

Tess nods. "Just as we discussed, Koto. Good progress." She looks around the Disciple table. "Comments?"

"It's mesmerizing!" some Disciple gushes.

"Very Zen, Koto."

"It projects heat as it moves from cool to warm and then back to cool again."

"And I feel a . . . a fluidity of cooperation."

"Nicely stated," Tess says. Then after Koto sits down she smiles around the table. "Those were the only presentations this week, am I right?"

Personally, I'd had enough of Tess and her dopey Disciples. But when I try and get Hudson to tell me about what's bothering him, he holds up a finger and says, "She's brought something, I'd bet my boots."

And sure enough, the Supreme Splotter lifts a large sheet-covered painting onto the easel, then waits. And when she's sure she's got the attention of everyone at the table, plus all the people in the Bean Goddess who've been listening in, she says, "I present to you . . . ," then throws back the sheet, *"Looking Glass."*

The Disciples all *oooh* and *aaaah*. Everyone in the Bean Goddess stares. And what we're all gaping at is the world's biggest . . .

Oval.

That's right. All it is, is a big white oval on a jet-black background. Well, jet-black except for her signature slashing across the bottom right corner in turquoise.

"Fabulous!" one of the Disciples cries.

"It's so . . . so deep!" another one gasps.

"Why, just *look* at it!" someone else chimes in.

Tess stands beside it like she's wearing a crown. "Gaze into my *Looking Glass.* See inside your soul!"

Then that Koto guy with the bouncy glasses stands up and moves around the table, shifting from side to side as he looks at her painting. And seriously, he's acting like he's about to bust at the seams, he's that excited.

"What is it, Koto?" Tess asks him.

"This is so brilliant! *So* brilliant." And Tess is looking oh-so-pleased with herself but then, *then* Koto says, "Did you consider using silver paint? Or some reflective medium? So you could actually have *seen* yourself. Or some contorted version of yourself?"

Tess's face changes like clay on a potter's wheel. From top to bottom it comes squeezing down into a frightful frown. All the Disciples hold their breath. Koto freezes with a big OOPS on his face, then dives back into his seat. And Tess just stands there, nostrils flaring, lightning bolts shooting from her eyes.

"It was just a suggestion," Koto squeaks, but Tess doesn't let him off the hook. She takes a deep breath and says through her teeth, "It reflects your *soul*, not your face!" Then she sits down with a pout while all the Disciples swoon around her, telling her how brilliant *Looking Glass* is.

Hudson shakes his head and mutters, "The Empress is wearing no clothes."

I bust up. "Exactly!"

So after we sip and laugh for a minute, he holds his tea high. "Here's to not exposing ourselves in public."

I clink my glass to his, then kick my high-tops up on the empty chair next to me and ask, "So, Hudson. Tell me about Grams."

He frowns, then shakes his head.

I sit back up. "Hudson, look. I always feel better when I talk to you . . . give it a try, will you?"

He just shakes his head some more.

"Okay. Well tell me this: Are you *mad* at Grams?"

"No. I'm more mad at myself."

"Because . . . ?"

"Because I'm afraid your grandmother's right."

My hands were suddenly clammy. My heart seemed to forget how to beat. And I tried to make it sound funny, but it came out real quiet when I asked, "About you being all blather-brained about Ms. Reijden?"

He gave me half a grin, then did something that about ripped my heart in two.

He shrugged. Like, yeah, okay. So I'm blather-brained.

I sat up. "But Hudson—"

"I know! And I swore it was just her paintings, but the more I look at them, the more depth I see in them, the more they stir my soul . . ." His voice trailed off and he gave a helpless shrug. Like it was too late for him to stop it. Too strong for him to fight it.

"But Hudson," I whispered. "I love her paintings, but I'm not in love with *her*."

His eyes looked pained. "Don't you see? They are who she is. Her hopes and her fears, her joys and despairs. You know who she is by knowing her paintings."

"But Hudson, come on. That doesn't mean—"

He shook his head, cutting me off. "She's committed to attending an Art Society dinner in Santa Luisa Wednesday evening, but after that horrific review, she just can't face going alone. She's asked me to escort her, and I've agreed." He looked at me, his eyes pleading. "Sammy, she was just devastated by that review."

"But . . . couldn't she have asked somebody else?"

"I'm sure she could have asked any number of people."

"So why you? I mean, you just met, and you're so much . . . you know, *older* than she is."

His eyes flashed. "No one likes to be called old, Sammy."

"I didn't say . . . I mean, I didn't *mean* . . ." But he was already standing up. "Hudson, wait!"

He shook his head and said, "I'm not some old fool. I'm sorry that's how you see me."

And with that, the one person I can always turn to— the one person I can always talk to, the one person who knows me better than I know myself—turned his back on me and walked away.

"Hudson!" I cried, but he kept on walking, straight out the Bean Goddess door. And I did chase after him, but it didn't do any good. I'd hurt his feelings, and besides, ol' Purple Eyes had him under a spell.

Now if it hadn't been for Grams, I would have been happy for him. But I knew that Grams really liked Hudson, even though she wouldn't admit it. So I wasn't happy. Not for anybody.

I went back inside the Bean Goddess to where I'd stashed my stuff, and as I was strapping on my backpack, I noticed part of an abandoned Sunday paper on a table nearby. So I paged through it, looking for the review Hudson had talked about. I mean, Hudson had called it horrific, but how bad could it be? Was this just some damsel-in-distress game Diane was playing? And why Hudson? Don't get me wrong—I love the guy. And yeah, for seventy-two, he's kinda handsome. But he's seventy-two! Why couldn't Diane find someone, you know, fifty-two? Or *sixty*-two?

I spotted the review. And halfway through, I had to sit down. The reviewer said that Tess's paintings "demonstrate unbridled courage" and "allow us to liberate our imagination from our mechanical mind" and that Austin Zuni's work "haunts the continuum of dominance"— whatever that means. Then came the part about Diane's paintings.

Ms. Reijden's installment is a throwback to an era gone by. It wallows in subtle shades and clichéd lighting. The feel of her work is conspicuously out of touch with modern times. In this competitive age, where we are all but suffocating beneath the weight of industrialization and technology, Ms. Reijden arrogantly portrays man with an aura suggesting he is larger than life, that he holds a power beyond mortality. Her work is neither suitable nor appropriate, either stylistically or thematically, to the conditions of today.

At first I couldn't even breathe. Then my heart started pounding and my hands started sweating and I wanted to punch something. Some*body*. How could they say that about *Whispers*? About *any* of her paintings? Sure, I could hear catty ol' *Tess* saying something like this, but a reviewer?

I looked at the top of the column. At the reviewer's name. Ned Bristol. At his chumpy little picture, smiling from the page. "You're a jerk!" I yelled at the paper. "And a moron, too!" And I had lots more to say, believe me, but all of a sudden I stopped and looked at the picture again.

Closer.

In my mind, I took off the faddish glasses.

Erased the smile.

And slowly a wave of heat spread from my head, down my back and out my arms.

It was him!

It *had* to be.

I looked over at Tess and her Disciples, laughing and yapping and drinking brewed bean juice. And I knew right then that Hudson was right.

The Splotter was wearing no clothes.

FOURTEEN

I tore out of the Vault and rode my skateboard hard and fast. I don't remember the turns or the lights or the traffic—I was too busy *thinking* to pay much attention to what I was *doing*.

Inside, my head was a jangly, jumbly mess. On the one hand, Tess Winters was mean and I *wanted* her to be guilty. She was snobby. She was cold and hateful and phony. I wanted to throw a bucket of paint on her and her broomstick and make her dissolve.

But on the *other* hand, I was confused about Diane. I mean, I liked her, but she had come between Hudson and Grams, and I was sort of panicked about it. I didn't want Grams to be sad or hurt or any of that, plus I didn't want to lose Hudson as a friend—something that was already happening, thanks to my big mouth.

But even though I knew Grams thought that Diane was a sneaky manipulative purple-eyed dragon—even though it might hurt Grams' feelings for me to help Diane—if I was right about Tess, someone had to expose her.

When I reached the arch of roses, I popped up my board and carried it down the gravel driveway to Diane's house. And as I got close, I noticed that Diane already had company. Near her walkway was one of those European motor scooters. You know, bigger than a bike, but not quite a motorcycle?

Anyway, this thing was bright white and had about fifty rearview mirrors on it. Seriously, they were different shapes and different sizes, sticking out all around the front end like a wall of glass.

I checked it out long enough to learn that it was called a "Vespa," then went up and stood at the front door. And when I finally reached up to ring the bell, my arm seemed heavy. Weak. Like it just didn't want to do it.

But I knew I had to tell her. So I pushed the doorbell, took a step back, and waited.

The door didn't open, but a curtain to my right moved slightly. I waved like, Hey, I know you're there, even though I couldn't see who it was.

Forever later, the front door swings open and Diane peeks out at me saying, "I'm sorry, Sammy, but it's not a good time."

Her eyes are all puffy and her cheeks are flushed, and she's got a mangled hankie in her hand.

She starts to close the door on me, so I cry, "Wait! I have something I have to tell you!"

She cocks her head a little like, Oh?

"It's about Tess. She . . ." I pull the newspaper review out of my back pocket and hand it to her.

"She what?"

"First, do you know this Ned Bristol guy?"

She nods. "He's interviewed me several times."

"Does he always wear glasses?"

She shakes her head. "No . . ."

"Do you know what he drives?""

She focuses on me a little closer. "Why?"

"Just tell me—does he drive a purple Camaro?"

"Yes . . . he does."

"That's him!" I said, slapping the paper in her hands.

"That's who?"

"The guy who took an envelope from Tess! Out the side door of the Vault! A couple of hours ago! I'm sure she was paying him off." I tapped on the paper. "For this!"

Her face morphs from soft-puffy-smile to eye-popping surprise. Then she grabs me by the wrist and hauls me through the house and into the living room. And who's sitting on the fireplace hearth?

Jojo.

Big surprise, huh? I mean, who else would drive a motor scooter with fifty funky mirrors?

Anyway, he jumps up when he sees me, looking sort of guilty and very confused. "Sammy?"

"Tell him," Diane says to me. "Tell him everything you just told me."

So I do, and when I'm done, Jojo says, "Wait a minute, wait a minute. Are you sure it was Ned?"

"I followed him down the alley. I watched him zoom off in a jacked-up purple Camaro with chrome bumpers and Bondoed doors. You know anyone else who has one of those?"

"No, but come on. Tess could have been handing him tickets to the movies. You can't just accuse people of paying people off."

"You should have seen the way she did it, Jojo. She kept looking over her shoulder."

"But that doesn't mean he's the guy! It could have been—"

"Joseph, clearly this review is the result of a bribe. Ned Bristol has never written anything even remotely scathing in his life! It's always been gushy small-town puff pieces. And now this? It's Tess's style, Tess's thoughts, Tess's words. He just took the bribe to place it."

"Yeah!" I said. "And I'll bet he's also the Squirt Gun Bandit! She was probably desperate to get your paintings out of there because of that *L.A. Times* guy!"

"Why . . . I'll bet you're right!" Diane says, then adds, "First she tries to steal my paintings, then she tries to destroy them this way."

Jojo shakes his head and tisks. "But Ned wouldn't risk his *job*—"

"He'll never *admit* it, Joseph. Although he's certainly made no secret of the pittance he gets paid at the paper, so maybe he doesn't even care. The point is, this all makes sense now. Tess is just trying to push me out of the limelight, and frankly, I'm more than happy to leave." She puts her hands on her hips. "I want my paintings back, Joseph. Today."

"No, no! You don't! Don't you see? All she's done is push you *into* the limelight! That ridiculous review will make people curious! They'll be coming in in droves."

"To see my 'conspicuously out of touch' paintings? No thank you."

"But Di, be *reasonable*. None of this is my fault! And

I'm heavily invested in you! I've taken out ads, I've done promo three counties wide. I got the *Los Angeles Times* to cover you! When that hits stands around the globe, none of this will matter!"

"It does to me."

Jojo takes a deep breath and puts both hands up. "Okay, okay. I'll investigate. I'll get to the bottom of this and—"

"*You'll* investigate?" She shakes her head like, Oh yeah—fat lotta good that'll do.

"Wait and see! And if Tess is behind this, we'll expose her and *she'll* be the one to suffer. Not you, not me. Tess."

Diane crosses her arms. "But none of this will happen before your contract with her is up, am I right? After all, you're invested in her as well, no?"

He gives her a helpless shrug. "What can I do? I'm legally bound to her."

"Not if she's broken the law!" She shakes her head again, then sort of crumbles into the folds of a worn-looking armchair. "Oh, let's stop bickering. I don't want this. You don't want this." She sighs. "Perhaps I *am* ready to pursue other avenues." She looks at Jojo. "Like you encouraged me earlier?"

Jojo's eyes get bigger. And bigger. And *bigger*. "Do you mean . . . ?"

She nods. "I think lithographs might be a good idea after all." She lets out a big sigh and says, "The art world has been run over by people like Tess—I just can't stomach it any longer." She gives him a tired smile.

"Would you release me from my contract if I agreed to prints?"

Jojo dashes over and slides down on one knee, holding one of her hands with both of his. "Yes! Yes, yes, yes! I'm so glad you've finally seen the light! Do you remember how reluctant you were to show them at all? How you priced them so high, hoping maybe they *wouldn't* sell?"

"Did I say that?"

"You didn't have to! It was obvious to me! Obvious from the day you unveiled the first one. You wouldn't even show me the others, remember? They're *personal* to you." He pats her hand. "This way, we'll sell the prints, you'll keep the originals—it'll be the best of both worlds!"

She smiles at him, then lets out a choppy sigh. "Okay, then. Let's do it."

Jojo jumps up. "Darling, I am on it. I'll get Michael to shoot the negs right away and—" He stops short and says, "I *am* your agent and distributor on this, then, right? We *do* have an exclusive agreement, right? One you won't renege on, right?"

She laughs and waves a hand. "Write it up. I'll sign anything that's fair. I just want my paintings back."

He sort of spins around like he's not sure which direction to run, then says, "I'll put it together right now! Right away. No, no, I'll get Michael going first. Oh! You won't regret this, Di. This is the smartest career move you've made!" He kisses her hand, then whispers, "And expect Tess to be catty and condescending when she hears. She'll call it crass commercialization, but only because she'll be green—just green! And don't you think I'm going to let this review thing drop. I have friends at the paper, too." He winks at her. "Let's see what trouble I can cause Neddy boy!"

So he dashes for the door, but I intercept him and whisper, "Uh, Jojo? Your landlady was looking for you at the Vault. . . ."

His face squinches up. "You didn't tell her where I was, did you?"

"No! I didn't *know* where you were. But Jojo, I think you'd better pay her. Real soon."

"I will, dumplin', I will."

"No, Jojo, I mean like, today." I hesitate, then say, "Why don't you ask Austin to help you? She said he's co-leasing." And before my mouth knows when to shut up, out comes, "I can't believe he's your *brother.*"

Jojo's eyes get all big, then they come down to half-mast. "He's my *half* brother, and a pitiful one at that."

"But—"

"Thinks he's such a star." His face comes in real close and he says, "Do you know what his real name is? It's Harold *Flunk.*"

"But—"

"And blood's only important to him when he *wants* something."

"But—"

"The opportunist! He won't do lithographs with me! He's holding out for 'better distribution.' But now, *now* I'll show him!" Then with a huff, he spins around and darts for the door.

I just kind of stand there blinking after him, and when I turn around, there's Diane on the sofa with her head cocked like, And what was all that about?

It probably would have been polite for me to tell her, or at least *leave,* but instead I went over and said, "Um, Ms. Reijden?"

"Yeeeees . . . ?"

"There's something I have to know."

"Oh?" she says, but it comes out more a sigh. Like she'd rather I'd just go away.

"It's about Hudson."

"Ah," she says, then smiles softly. "My silver knight."

My heart was sinking. Sinking fast. "Well, I was wondering . . ."

"Yes, dear?"

"Well, I know it's none of my business . . ." I look down at my high-tops and sort of toe the rug, saying, "He told me that you asked him to escort you to some Art Society dinner or something?"

She nods. "Yes, that's right."

"And I was wondering, you know, why him?"

She laughs, then smiles at me very sweetly. "Why, because he's a real gentleman. And intelligent and charming and . . ."

Inside I wanted to die. So it was true—she was sweet on Hudson.

What in the world was I going to tell Grams?

But then Diane leans back, lets out a little sigh, and says, "And he reminds me quite a lot of my father."

"Your . . . your *father*?"

"Mmm-hmm. They even look a bit alike." She motions to her left. "There's a picture of him on the desk. Have a look."

It was the coolest desk I'd ever seen. It looked like something Ben Franklin might have had. Or Thomas Jefferson. It had a leather top with a gold design all around the edge. And the whole desk was kidney-shaped. Even the drawers curved around.

I picked up the picture of her father and studied his face. To me, he looked nothing like Hudson. Oh sure, his hair was white, but Hudson has way more hair. And Dr. Reijden had little round glasses. I could not picture Hudson wearing little round glasses. There were tons of books in the background, just like Hudson has in his library, and the picture was friendly enough, but something about it made me feel a little strange. I mean, in the picture he's sitting *at* the kidney desk, looking up from a letter he's writing. But now that he's dead, he sits *on* the kidney desk. It made me feel sort of sad. Like he was never going to get to finish the letter.

"See what I mean?" Diane asked.

I put the picture back where I'd found it and said, "Yeah."

"Well," she says, coming over to me, "I hope it hasn't caused any trouble with your grandmother. Is that what this is all about?"

I gave a little shrug and looked down.

"Ah," she says. "Well, I hadn't intended to give off any romantic signals." She eyes me. "Would you like me to cancel my invitation?"

I wanted to say, Yes! But I knew that would be a very bad idea. So I shook my head and said, "Hudson's one of my best friends in the whole wide world. He's smart and he's wise and he's really good company." I looked her in the eye and added, "Today I found out he can also be kind of . . . tender. Just kind of keep that in mind, okay?"

She smiled at me real sweetly, then put her arm around my shoulders and said, "I promise."

I left there feeling better. A lot better. And I was just kind of strolling along gravel, lost in feeling sorry for Hudson, when all of a sudden Flannel Man pops out from behind a hedge and says, "Hallo there, missy."

I jumped back a little, then couldn't help laughing. With one of his cap muffs sticking straight out and the other one sticking straight down, he looked like an old hound dog who was having trouble perking up his ears. "Oh, hi," I told him. "Out feeding your squirrels?"

"Just buryin' them treasures for later. How's Lizzy today?"

"Oh, she's okay."

"Been a little concerned since the row last night."

"The . . . the row? Like, there was a fight?"

His mouth scrunches closed, then moves to one side as he studies me. Finally he leans closer. "Mmm-hmm," he says, his flannel ear bobbing up and down. Then he points to the big tree on Diane's property and says, "I was over picking up walnuts from under their tree—" He stops himself and says, "Mind you, that's just fine with Lizzy. Anytime, she told me. Anytime a'tall. And that's when I heard the yellin'. I got myself home right quick.

Never been a meddler, but I can't say it didn't shake these old bones. Dr. Duane and the missus would be crushed, they would, to hear their kids carryin' on so."

"She was fighting with her brother?"

He nods. "I sense he's layin' claim on some of the estate." He shakes his head. "Lotta nerve after all these years." Then he adds, "Ah, well. S'long as Lizzy's all right. S'pose it'll work itself out."

He turns to go back to burying walnuts, but I stop him, saying, "Uh, Mr. Moss?"

"Yes, missy?"

"Why do you call her Lizzy?"

"Why, because it's her name."

"Like when she was born, her mom named her *Lizzy*?"

He shrugs, "Well, Elizabeth, wot? But they all called her Lizzy."

"So why's she go by Diane?"

He shrugs again. "Didn't know she did."

He turns to go, but I can't help wondering just how isolated his world of squirrels really is. So I stop him with, "Mr. Moss?"

"Yes, miss?"

"Do you get the paper?"

"The newspaper?" He shakes his head and gives a little snort. "No time for that." Then he disappears behind the hedge.

So I left him to his squirrels and hit the street, telling myself that everything *would* work itself out. Jojo'd take care of Ned Bristol, Tess would be exposed for the lying cheating phony that she was, and Hudson would get over being blather-brained about Diane. Like he had told me about Marissa—I just had to be patient.

But as I clicked along on my skateboard, the back of my mind didn't feel like being patient. It was busy churning away. First slowly, then faster and faster, stirring up questions. Stirring up doubt.

And, as it turns out, a whole new batch of trouble.

FIFTEEN

I snuck up the fire escape and through the fifth-floor door without a sound. And I had my whole story lined out about why I was so late—which for once wasn't hard to do. No tracks to cover, no lies to construct—I was just going to tell Grams the truth.

Trouble is, when I let myself into the apartment and looked around, well, she wasn't there to tell the truth *to*. I said hi to Dorito, fed Dorito, then started checking around for signs of how long Grams had been gone.

No mail on the table, no mail in the trash. No lunch dishes in the sink or dishwasher. Just breakfast bowls. But I did find a knife with a little mustard on it.

So I checked the fridge. Half a turkey sandwich wrapped in cellophane and stashed in the meat drawer. I unwrapped it and looked inside. Mustard.

I checked the trash again and found a rumpled paper towel with crumbs and a smudge of mustard inside.

Okay, so she'd been home for lunch, but probably not as late as one or two—which is when she usually goes down to the lobby for mail. She hadn't just taken a quick trip to Maynard's Market, either. She'd been gone a long time. I could feel it.

I thought about starting on dinner, but I started on my homework instead. Who knew when she'd come home? A month ago I could have told you *exactly*, but now, well, things felt sort of out of control. Like Grams was all wound up one minute and completely wound *out* the next. I felt kind of sorry for her. I mean, it had taken her a long time to be comfortable around Hudson. To let her guard down. Slowly she'd started trusting him. Liking him.

Counting on him.

And from what I could tell, he really liked her, too. But then ol' Purple Eyes had come into the picture and now Hudson seemed out of control, too.

So where was Grams? And how in the world was she going to react to the things I'd found out.

Maybe I wouldn't tell her.

Maybe that would be for the best.

But then I remembered our pact—I tell her the truth, she trusts me.

But would it be lying to just *not* tell her?

Now, before I can totally talk myself into or out of anything, Grams blasts through the door. She's all out of breath and windblown, and when she sees me, she whooshes into the chair across from me, saying, "You will never believe what I found out!"

"What?"

Her eyes are all wide and shining, and she's just dying to tell me, but she takes a deep breath, trying to calm herself down. "First, I'm sorry I'm so late. I would have called you but . . . but the reference desk was closing and I had to pay for my copies, and then there was this pokey old grouch using the phone, so . . . so I decided to just hurry home."

I laughed, "Grams, you're sounding a lot like me, you know that?"

She holds completely still for a moment, then laughs, "So I am!" Then she leans forward and her eyes are huge as she says, "Anyway, you will never guess what I dug up today."

"So tell me!" I go to snag the papers she's holding, but she pulls them to her chest. "Ah-ah-ah! First," she says, sitting up straight, "has Hudson told you his excuse for why he's fallen for Lovely Lizzy?"

"Uh . . ."

I was looking for a way to phrase it when she says, "Oh, come on. I know the two of you talk. Surely he's told you about her work being a window into her soul? How you know her by knowing her paintings?"

I cringed. "He *told* you that?"

"He most certainly did."

"Well, you know how philosophical Hudson can get."

"Delusional is more like it! It's the violet eyes, and I told him so."

"You did?"

"I most certainly did! And I asked him, If those paintings had been done by a fat old hag with warts and bad teeth, would he be in love with *her*?"

I laughed. "What did he say?"

She huffs. "He said a fat old hag with warts and bad teeth wouldn't create such masterpieces."

"Hmm." I reached for her papers again. "So what are those?"

"A *real* window into Elizabeth Diane Reijden's soul," she says, handing them over. "One with a completely different view."

"So her name really is Elizabeth?"

"According to these articles."

The papers were thin and sort of shiny and looked like bad copies of old newspapers. "Is her *middle* name Diane?"

"I suppose so."

"But why—" The feel of the paper interrupted my train of thought. "These are weird," I said, rubbing one between my fingers. "Where'd you get them?"

"At the library. Off the microfiche machine."

"The micro-*fish*? What kind of—"

"Just look at them, would you!"

So I did. The first one was an article with the title JURIED ART SHOW PROTESTED. It was long and looked pretty dense with no pictures, so I went to the next paper, which had the headline REVENGE OF THE REFUSED. There were some pictures of people I'd never seen before, posing with their artwork. But there was also a picture of someone I did know. Too well. "That's Tess!" I said. "These are about that art show where Diane got rejected?"

Grams nodded. "That's right. The refused artists made a big fuss and put together their *own* show." She pointed to the bottom right of the paper. "Right there Tess justifies why the panel rejected some of the art."

I snorted. "I'll bet she does. Like she's really going to say Diane's art makes hers look bad . . ."

Now, I was expecting Grams to nod or maybe just shrug, but instead, she raises one eyebrow and smirks. Like, Girl, you have no idea what you're about to see.

So I turn over to the next page where there are more pictures of rejected artists. And there's Diane, smiling up at me from fishy paper. She's not alone, either. She's surrounded. Not by other artists. Not by paintings or painting supplies. No, she's surrounded by statues.

Big, white, ugly statues.

Ones that look like they've been cast off of nursing home patients.

"No!" I whispered. "*She* made those?"

"That's right," she says with a really smug smile. "What do you suppose he'll say about her inner soul now?"

"But—"

"Samantha, it's all right there," she says, slapping the paper with the back of her hand. "She studied here, there, and everywhere, she was mentored by some famous French sculptor in New York, some famous German in France . . . she drops names like you won't believe, but they don't help the end result. Those statues are hideous!"

I skimmed the article. Everything Grams said was true, and if I didn't know Diane in person, I sure would not like her from what I was reading. The article made her sound really . . . snobby.

"But Grams, her paintings are so good. Maybe we just don't get something about these statues—"

"Oh nonsense. What neither you nor Hudson seem to understand is that her paintings are just a new contrivance."

"A new con*triv*ance?"

"They don't mean anything to her. They're just product. Fabricated emotions. They move you by *design*, not consequence."

I stared at her. "Wow, Grams. You've given this a lot of thought, haven't you?"

"Yes, I have," she said. "How else do you explain this?"

I looked back at the fishy picture and shook my head. "Maybe I just don't get art."

She smiled at me, then kissed my temple. "What you don't get, child, is men."

At school the next day, I realized that Grams was right—I didn't get men.

Or, at least, junior high boys.

I was charging up the school steps *shwap-bap-bap-bap-bap-bap-bap*, when all of a sudden *shwap-bap-bap-bap-bap-bap-bap*, there's Billy Pratt charging up the steps right beside me. "Hey-ya, Sammy!"

Hey-ya, Sammy? I didn't even think Billy Pratt knew who I was. I mean, everyone knows who *he* is—he's Billy Pratt, Class Clown.

Strike that. He's *school* clown. No one else even compares. You can't *not* know the guy. He's everywhere, just being funny.

Anyway, I didn't slow down out of shock or anything, I just said, "Hey," back and kept on bapping up the steps.

"Cool board."

Cool board? This was turning into a real conversation. "Thanks," I told him, eyeing the one under his arm. "Yours, too."

Now what was weird was that he didn't pass me by. I mean, if some guy's going to come bapping up behind you on the front steps, usually they'll just bap on past you. And if they do say hey to you, that'll take all of two steps and *schwap-bap-bap,* off they go. But Billy kept running along beside me—kinda *close* beside me—and at the top of the steps he *stays* beside me as I head to homeroom. And I'm starting to feel kind of uncomfortable. Like, go be Billy Pratt somewhere else, why don't you?

But he hangs with me all the way to homeroom, jabbering away about some mouse that's living in the walls of his house, and how it does laps up and down the two-by-fours and makes a big old racket all night long, chomping and scratching and whipping its tail around.

"Its tail?" I ask him. "How do you know it's whipping its tail around?"

"You can just tell. It's got this thwacky sound. *Thwack! Thwack! Thwack!* All night long. Maybe it's whipping on ants or something, you never know."

"Ants? You've got ants, too?"

"Or roaches, maybe."

"Oh, gross!"

"But that would make him whip his tail around, wouldn't it? He's probably going . . . ," he makes like he's grabbing his tail, then whips it through the air, shouting, "Take that, you dog! Outta here, vermin! Out of my wall! Out-out-out! Ooowwwww!" He shakes his hand like he's hurt himself, then grins at me. "Busy mouse."

Now, I'm sorry, but I just couldn't help it. I cracked

up. And even after he took off, I kept on laughing. I mean, Billy is just so . . . *hyper.*

But then after homeroom, there he was again. "Hey-ya, Sammy!" he says, walking right beside me.

I looked around like, Where'd you come from, because I'd never seen Billy Pratt outside of homeroom before in my life. And Marissa looks at me like, What's this? And Holly raises her eyebrows, too, but then they fall back and let Billy jabber away next to me, all the way to my next class.

Then at lunch, Billy comes and sits beside me at the patio tables, and that's when I start to smell a rat. "Hey-ya, Sammy," he says. "What's for lunch?"

I look at him, then at Marissa, Holly, and Dot. None of them says a word, but they're all looking at me with their eyebrows up. "All right, Billy," I say to him. "What's going on."

"Waddaya mean?"

I dig out my peanut butter sandwich and shoot him a look. "I'm gonna start whacking my tail around pretty soon here."

He makes an exaggerated hurt look. "Are you sayin' I'm *bugging* you?"

I squint at him and whisper, "I'm saying I'm not stupid, okay?"

He nods, and his eyes get a little shifty. Like he wants to check around but he's making himself not. "I know that."

"So? You going to be straight with me?"

He shrugs and grins. "Just thought it might be fun to hang with you."

But looking into his eyes, I can tell—he's lying. "You're talking turds, Billy."

He laughs, then gets up, saying, "And here I thought you were cool."

Then he blindsided me. I swear, I didn't see it coming, didn't in a million years *expect* it. I mean, one minute he's leaving, the next he's leaning over, smooching my cheek. I'm talking a mushy, gushy, air-sucking, high-decibel kiss. And then he's waving, laughing, "See-ya, Sammy!" over his shoulder.

I just sat there like a statue with bird poop on its cheek. And while I'm trying to come to grips with what's just happened, Holly's going, "What in the . . . ," and Dot's going, "When did you and Billy . . . ?"

But then Marissa says, "Wait a minute . . . ," and dashes to the end of the tables. And then Marissa—Little Miss Gross-out Germaphobe—starts digging through a trash can.

"What is she *doing*?" Dot asks.

Holly shakes her head. "It's got to be important."

We watch as Marissa flies through crumpled scraps, opening them up one by one until she finds what she's looking for. In a flash she's back at our table, smoothing out a paper in front of me.

And with one look I know—Heather Acosta is at it again.

SIXTEEN

"What *is* that?" Holly asked.

I took the paper from Marissa. "How'd you find this?"

Marissa asked, "Did you *write* it?"

"No!" I scanned the patio area and spotted Heather's wicked red head jetting away. "There she goes! That sneaky, creepy, mentally deranged . . . tarantula!"

"Oh, boy," Marissa says, sitting down. "Oh, *boy.*"

"What is going on?" Dot asks.

"Here," Marissa says, shoving the note her way. "I just saw Casey chuck this in the trash."

"*Dear Casey . . . Meet me at our lunch table on the patio. There's something I have to tell you. Hang ten, Sammy.*" Dot looks at me all wide-eyed. "You didn't write this?"

"Me? Sign off 'hang ten'? That chowderhead probably thinks that's something you do on a skateboard."

"You think Heather wrote it?"

"Yes!"

"Whirling windmills!" Dot cries. "You've got to *do* something!"

Marissa nods. "Casey looked pretty upset, Sammy."

"He saw Billy here?" I asked. "He saw the whole thing?"

"I think so."

I slammed my fist on the table. "How does she *do* that? How does a person manage to pull something like that off?"

"But I don't get it," Holly says. "*Why'd* she do it?"

I sighed, then looked at Marissa, then at Holly and Dot. And since Marissa's giving me the You've-Got-to-Tell-Them nod and Holly and Dot are just sitting there with big question marks on their faces, I break down and tell them. About Casey and the kiss, Heather and the fish, my skateboard coming back, and Billy Pratt. And when I'm all done, Dot jumps out of her seat and says, "You've got to find Casey and tell him!"

"I know," I tell her, staying put.

"No! You've got to go *now*."

"But if I track him down, he'll think I *like* him."

All three of them lean in like a flock of buzzards. "Well, *don't* you?"

"You guys are crazy, you know that? What kind of *mess* would that be? How can you like someone and not give them your phone number? How can you like someone and not tell them where you live? How can you like someone if you can't trust them with really basic stuff?"

They were all quiet a minute, kind of shrugging and looking down. And finally Holly says, "So what you're saying is, you can't like *any*one, right?"

I snap, "Yeah, so it's a good thing I don't like him, okay?" But to tell you the truth, what she said sank in heavy. Sank in hard. *No*, my living situation wasn't temporary. Grams wasn't going to marry Hudson and move into his big house, like I'd started daydreaming might happen. His porch would always be *his* porch, not *our* porch. And I knew my mother wasn't going to sashay home anytime soon. To her, life on a soap opera was way more meaningful than life in Santa Martina. No, things were the way they were, and they were going to stay that way for as long as I could see.

"You okay?" Marissa asked.

"Yeah. Yeah, I'm fine."

"You've got to talk to him."

"I will." I folded the note and put it in my back pocket. "Later."

Heather was her usual smug and hateful self in science. And I really wanted to let on that I was wise to her, but I made myself keep quiet. The less she knew about what I knew, the better. But believe me, by the time I got to art, I was in a really bad mood. And one look at Miss Kuzkowski just made it worse. She was standing in front of her "Art Teaches Nothing, Except the Significance of Life" poster, wearing her beret and holding her precious wooden palette in her left hand while she poked paint onto a canvas with her right. *Jab-jab-jab. Whoosh-whoosh-whoosh. Jab-jab-jab. Whoosh-whoosh-whoosh.* The class was piling in, but she didn't stop. She was *into* it, shuffling all around her easel. *Jab-jab-jab. Whoosh-whoosh-whoosh.* And her punches and slashes of brown and yellow and purple made me understand that it was true—she was definitely the Splotter's disciple.

When the tardy bell rang, she took a break from her jabbing and whooshing and said, "Hey, gang! Your reports are still due on Friday, but as of today, we're back to projects."

Who cared? Right then I wanted nothing to do with art or paint. I just wanted to go home.

But as she explained what the new project was, well, I began to get an idea. A very *bratty* idea.

See, our assignment was to paint joy.

That's right, joy.

She didn't care what medium we used—watercolors, oil paints, acrylics, colored pencils—she didn't care. She just wanted joy. "Get to it!" she cried, then went back to punching on purple splotches.

So while everyone else is thinking and talking out their ideas, I get up, get a recycled canvas, splot out some red and white oil paint on a sheet of waxed paper, mix them into pink, and thin it out with turpentine. Then I get to work.

Tony Rozwell's in the back, singing, "La-la-la-laaaa! La-la-la-laaaa!" and someone shouts, "Knock it off, Rozwell, you're annoying!"

"La-la-la-laaaaa! La-la-la-laaaaaaaaa!"

Miss Kuzkowski calls, "Tony!"

"Just trying to feel joy, Miss K! Looking for my inspiration! La-la-la-la-laaaaaa!"

"Tonyyyyyy," she warns.

"Turn on the radio, Miss K! That'll shut him up!"

Emma watches me and says, "How do you know what to do? How can you be painting already?"

I just smile at her and keep on going.

"I have no idea what to paint. How come everyone else always knows what to paint but me? I am so lame at this." She looks at my canvas. "What *are* you making?"

"Joy," I tell her. "Don't you feel it?"

She looks at the ridiculous circles I'm painting, one around the other, around the other, all in pink. "Nu-uh," she says. "They're just circles."

I smile at her again and say, "Oh, no, Emma. This is joy."

"Miss Kuzkowski!" she calls, her hand shooting in the air. "I don't know what to paint!"

"La-la-la-laaaaaa! La-la-la-laaaaaaaaaaaaaa!"

"Somebody turn on the radio!" Brandy calls from the back of the class. "Or I'm gonna have to burp!"

Miss Kuzkowski lets out an impatient sigh and cranks on some music. Then she comes over to Emma, whose hand is flagging around like crazy, and says, "Okay, Emma, how can I help you?"

"Sammy says that's joy. Can we do that? Just paint anything and call it joy?"

"Hmmmm," Miss Kuzkowski says, watching as I paint the next, bigger circle. "What's your plan here, Sammy?"

"Plan? How do you plan joy?"

She blinks at me.

I blink at her.

Then I move on to the next, bigger circle.

"But . . ." Her eyes narrow down on me. Her beret seems to grip on tighter. "You're not being facetious, are you, Sammy?"

"Facetious? Miss Kuz*kow*ski!" I hold out my painting, which now looks like the ugliest psycho pink eye you'd ever want to see. "Don't you feel *joy* from this?"

She cocks her head, then very slowly starts to shake it.

"Miss Kuzkowski!" I point to the center dot. "This is how joy begins. As a little warm spot in your heart. That's why I chose pink. Then it radiates outward, filling the world, the galaxy, the *universe* with jubilance, warmth, delight! It's like a pebble tossed into a pool, where the ripples go out, out, out, changing the . . . the landscape, the mood, the perspective on existence!" I look at her with wide eyes. "Don't you *see* it?"

"Wow," she says, taking the psycho pink eye from me. "Sa*man*tha!"

Emma is squinting away, shaking her head. "So that right there is joy? We can turn that in and get credit?"

"No," Miss Kuzkowski says, turning to face her. "*Sammy* can turn this is. This is *her* joy. You come up with your own joy." Then she smiles at me and hands back my psycho pink eye. "*Very* nice."

When she's gone, Emma shakes her head and says, "I hate art."

"Me too," I tell her. "Me too."

I did look for Casey after school. Sort of. When I headed for the bike racks to meet up with Marissa, I kept one eye on the buses waiting at the front of the school, but didn't see him.

Not that it would have done any good anyway, but I

was feeling pretty bad about what had happened. Bad and sort of responsible. I mean, maybe I wasn't the one who had made things such a mess, but still, I was the one who could fix them.

Or, with the way things had been going, make them worse.

The whole situation just made me frustrated and mad and confused and . . . *irritated*. And it didn't help matters any that I was being whipped around in the wind, waiting for Marissa, who was just not showing up.

Finally I couldn't take it anymore. So I crammed a "Gotta get out of here—catch up" note under her bike's brake grip, then tore off campus.

I had a tailwind, so I flew down the sidewalk even faster than I had the day before. I hopped curbs. I blasted down one driveway and blasted up the next. I didn't slow down for anyone or anything. And when I heard the buses growling in the distance behind me, I pumped even harder. I wanted to get *away* from school, but the buses gaining on me made me feel like I was being chased by it. Chased by wicked diesel-spewing schoolhouse demons in ugly yellow trench coats.

They roared past me anyway, and when they did, I finally let up. And at the corner of Broadway and Cook, I waited a few minutes for Marissa, but then decided it would be better for her if I just headed home. Even after a hard ride, I was still too dangerous to be around.

Boy, was I crabby!

So, it turns out, was Grams. I swear, she made *me* seem sweet as Snow White. I found her sitting on the kitchen floor, ripping pots and pans out of a cupboard, thumping and bumping, muttering and *hrmph*ing, steaming like a pressure cooker.

"Hi, Grams."

Grumble-grumble.

"I take it you saw Hudson today?"

Grumble-grumble-grumble.

"Showed him the fishy papers?"

She looked at me from around the cupboard door. "Micro-*fiche*, Samantha! It's a type of film, not something from a seafood market."

I couldn't help grinning. "But he didn't find anything, uh, *fishy* about them?"

She burrowed back into the cupboard. "Very funny. And no, he didn't."

"Are you looking for something or just cleaning?"

"Organizing," she says as she yanks out more pots and pans. "Making sense out of years of accumulated clutter and debris."

I dropped my backpack and sat down on the floor, too. "So what did he say?"

Bang, clank, thwonk. "He told me it's who you evolve into that matters, not the missteps you've taken along the way." She eyes me over her shoulder. "I don't know why I bothered."

So there she is, surrounded by pots and pans, baking dishes and muffin tins, about to say something more, when all of a sudden her eyes get real big and she freezes. Then I swear her *ears* perk up. Like a bunny that senses a fox near the meadow.

186

"What, Grams?"

"Shhh!"

Before I can hear a thing, Grams is up and out of the kitchen, on her way to her bedroom.

I chase along behind her, and that's when I hear it, too. *Brum-bum-bum-bum-bum*.

Grams already has her binoculars out from under her bed and is heading for the window.

"Grams, it's probably just a—"

"No, it's not," she snaps, then points. "There he is." She puts her binoculars up to her glasses, but I don't need them to know she's right. I watch as the bike growls up Broadway, and even from five floors up, I recognize the rider.

Plus, Grams was right—nothing sounds quite like that Harley.

"What's his name again?" Grams asks from behind her binoculars.

"Lance, I think."

"That's right, Lance."

We watch as he flips a U-ie. Across four lanes of traffic, right there in front of the highrise, he does a U-ie and pulls up to the curb of the Heavenly Hotel across the street. Then he snaps down his kickstand, peels off his helmet, and saunters inside.

Grams lowers the binoculars. "He's staying at the *Heavenly*?"

Now, the Heavenly is the seediest hotel in town. I know—I've been inside. So whether he's staying there or just visiting someone there doesn't really matter. As Grams says, it's a safe house for unsavory characters.

'Course there are also nice people at the Heavenly. Like my friend Madame Nashira. And André—the guy who runs the front desk—he's okay, too. So it's not like I'm afraid of the place. I just don't hang out there much, is all.

Anyway, Grams is practically rubbing her chin, going, "I wonder what he's doing there. . . . Mizz Lizz has got plenty of room, so why isn't he staying with her?"

I almost told her what Mr. Moss had said about him and Diane having a "row," but I didn't really want to get into *why* I'd been over there again. Not just then, anyway. So instead I said, "You want me to cruise over and check it out?"

"No!"

"Why not? I'll just go in, ask André if the guy's staying or visiting, and come back."

"No. You know how I feel about the Heavenly."

"I also know how you feel about Diane Reijden."

"Hrmph."

"Okaaaaay, Grams, then you go."

"Me?"

"Yes, you."

"But—"

"*Or*, we could go together . . . ?"

She looks at me. Then the Heavenly. Then me again.

Then my grams does something I've never known her to do.

She *giggles*.

And with that, we're off to the Heavenly Hotel.

SEVENTEEN

Not only did Grams decide to go to the Heavenly Hotel with me, she decided to take the fire escape. "It's certainly more direct," she said.

"But not exactly made for *pumps*," I told her.

"Look, Samantha. Quit it about my shoes, would you? I've worn pumps my whole life, and I'm not ready to give them up yet." She clanked along behind me. "Would you rather I wore shoes like Rose's?"

"Oh yuck, Grams!" I said, 'cause Mrs. Wedgewood next door wears the world's most revolting shoes. They're rubbery and black, and her ankles balloon out over the tops.

"Well then quit making fun of my pumps."

I started saying something about some happy middle ground, but she caught my eye from half a flight up. "I said, quit!"

"Okay, okay! I'm just worried about you tripping on nothing again and having to haul your broken bones to the hospital—"

"I did not trip on nothing!"

"Well then—"

"Stop it!"

I rolled my eyes. "Whatever."

When she joined me on the ground, she snorted and said, "See? I managed just fine," but then she wouldn't jaywalk across Broadway. Not because she was afraid of getting a ticket—no, she was afraid she couldn't cross fast enough to make it without getting hit by a car. So we had to go clear up to Main, cross at the light, and then walk back down to the Heavenly.

She might as well have taken the elevator.

The minute we stepped inside the Heavenly, Grams' nose started twitching. And I knew she was thinking that the place reeked, because it does. Like giant moldy potatoes have been hanging around the lobby smoking cigarettes.

I put a hand on her shoulder and whispered, "I know it stinks, but check out the furniture and stuff. It's really pretty cool." I pointed to the fuzzy green high-back chairs. "Don't you love those?"

She wrinkled her nose. "They look like the pope's hat."

I laughed, "Exactly!"

André was in his usual spot—sitting behind the check-in counter, chomping on a cigar and leafing through the paper. He does a double take when he sees me, then pulls the cigar out of his mouth and says, "Saaaaaay, Sammy! How ya doin'?"

"Doing all right." I motion to Grams, saying, "This is my grandmother."

He leans over the counter and shakes her hand. "Nice to meet you. You after a room?"

"Heavens no!" Grams says, then clears her throat and

takes it down a notch. "I live right across the way. In the highrise."

"Ah . . . ," he says, then turns to me. "She's the one with the binoculars?"

I grin at him, 'cause it was thanks to Grams' binoculars that I spotted a thief in his hotel once. "That's right."

He nods. "I remember now. So, what can I do for ya?"

I look at Grams like, Well? So she clears her throat again and says, "The fellow that just came in? Is he visiting someone or staying?"

André studies her a minute, then me. And the whole time he's looking at us, thinking, his cigar's rolling from one side of his mouth to the other and back again. Finally he clamps it between his front teeth and says, "Stayin'." He eyes me. "Should I be concerned?"

I shrug, then ask, "How long?"

There goes his cigar again, rolling back and forth. Finally he nods and says, "We're going day by day."

"You think maybe we could talk to him?"

He shrugs, then picks up the phone and dials 2-2-7, and after a few seconds he says, "Mr. Ryder? You've got visitors down here . . . a gal and her grandma . . . let me ask." He covers the receiver. "What's it about?"

"Uh . . . his Harley," I tell him.

André's eyebrows go up a bit as he uncovers the phone. "They say it's about your Harley . . . no, I can assure you it's a gal and her grandma . . . All right, then."

"So?" Grams asks him after he hangs up.

"He'll be right down."

I ask, "Is that how he registered? As Mr. Ryder?"

He holds my gaze, then checks the book. "Uh-huh."

"*Lance* Ryder?"

He leans forward, "You know privacy's a big deal to my guests. Don't push too hard, Sammy."

"I know, but—"

"I only told you so much 'cause I owe ya. But let's leave it at this, okay?" He motions to the pope-hat chairs and says, "Why don't you take a seat. Save your questions for him."

So Grams and I sit down, and I whisper, "What are you going to ask him?"

"What am *I* going to ask him? Samantha, this was your idea!"

"Yeah, but—" Then there he is, coming out of the stairway, still in chaps and his fringed leather jacket. I wave and call, "Hey! Over here!"

He walks toward us. Cautiously. Suspiciously. Like the granny and the girl might be packing heat or something. Finally he asks, "Do I know you?"

"Sort of." I stand up and stick out my hand. "I'm Sammy, this is my grams, Rita." I plop back down in my pope-hat chair and wave at a third chair, but he keeps right on standing. "We saw you outside your sister's house a couple of days ago."

He just squints at me.

"We were leaving when you were driving up?"

"You sure it was me?"

"Uh-huh. Unless you just bought that Harley."

"There's lots of Harleys in the world."

"Apparently not like yours. My gramps had one that Grams says was tricked out the same."

His eyebrow goes up in Grams' direction, but since *she* doesn't say anything and *he* doesn't say anything, I lower my voice and say, "Gramps ran off with a bimbo from the Harley shop, so it's sort of a sore subject."

He kind of nods at me, then looks at Grams. "Well, that Harley ain't your old man's, if that's what you're wondering. It's been mine for nearly thirty years."

Grams still doesn't say anything, so I say, "Actually, Mr. Reijden, we didn't really want to talk about your Harley. We want to talk to you about your sister."

He just levels a look at me. Real calm. Real even.

"Why are you staying here and not with her?"

He shakes his head and says, "I'm afraid I don't have much to say about that or Lizzy."

Now the way he said it was like he was pushing through the doors of a saloon, kinda surveying the joint, sauntering up to the bar for a shot of whiskey. And all of a sudden I could just see him, all jacked up, shouting "FREEZE" across the room, holding the place up. And I tried to look at his eyes and see if they were the same eyes I'd seen behind the Squirt Gun Bandit's mask, but shoot, I couldn't tell. They were just your average medium-brown eyes.

Kind of *shifty* medium-brown eyes, but still, medium brown.

But Grams laughs and says, "If it's any consolation, I don't have much good to say about Lizzy, either."

His head tilts to one side, and half a smile creeps up his face. "Is that so?"

She nods, then starts plucking imaginary fuzz off her

skirt. "I find her to be deceptive and coy." She rolls her eyes my way and adds, "Not that I can convince anyone *else* of that . . ."

His smile creeps across, invading the other side of his face. Then he sits down, stretching his legs out in front of him. "So what's she done to you, Rita?"

Grams looks right at him, then looks back at her skirt.

So *I* say, "Her friend's sort of . . . you know . . . *mesmerized* by her."

"Boyfriend?" he asks.

Now that term seemed like a really stupid way to describe Hudson. I mean, he's seventy-two, for crying out loud. But still, I couldn't come up with a better word to explain it. "Kinda."

He nods. "He's not the first."

That got Grams' attention. "Oh?"

"Won't be the last."

"You're saying this is a . . . a *pattern* for her, then?"

He shrugs. "My sister's always been a dabbler."

"In men?" Grams asks.

"In everything."

"Well, wait a minute," my mouth shoots off. "I don't know about men, but she sure doesn't dabble in *art*. She's really talented and—"

Grams shuts me down with, "And what do you call those *statues*?"

Lance throws his head back and laughs. "Lady, you just hit the nail on the head." He stands up, saying, "And that's really all I have to say about Elizabeth. People do wise up eventually. She's got a string of exes to prove it."

He sticks his hand out to Grams and covers hers with his other hand when they shake. "It was nice to make your acquaintance. And don't worry about the Harley. Once I settle things with my sister, I'll be off."

Now, before I can say, "Settle *what* things?" he winks at Grams and says, "Between your ex and your boyfriend, it sounds like you could use a good man in your life."

Grams blushes. Heck, I do, too. But before either of us can say a thing, he's heading for the stairs.

I whisper, "He did just hit on you, right?"

"It's been a long time," she says, still blinking at the stairway.

The phone was ringing when we got back to the apartment. Grams snatched it up, saying, "Yes?" then, "Hold on." She gives me the phone. "It's Marissa."

"Sammy!" Marissa says when I get on the line. "I've got his number!"

"Danny's?"

"No, Casey's!"

"Mar-is-sa . . . !"

"You'd better not be mad at me. I went through a lot of trouble and embarrassment to get it."

"Embarrassment? What do you mean?"

"Well, he's not in the phone book, but he *is* in that Drama Club play on Thursday."

"So?"

"So I found out they were having a rehearsal and—"

"Good grief! Why'd you do all this?"

"Because I'm your friend, that's why."

"But—"

"Anyway, I had to, you know, interrupt the rehearsal, so I couldn't exactly explain things to him. Besides," she adds really fast, "I figured it would make you mad at me if I did."

"Got that right," I grumbled.

"So I made it quick, but Ms. Pilson was still plenty annoyed." I could practically see Marissa rolling her eyes. "You know how she gets."

It was true. Ms. Pilson's nose seemed to get really sharp and pointy when you interrupted her. Warts popped up everywhere. But all that was beside the point. I didn't *want* Casey's number. I didn't know what I *did* want, but having his number was certainly not it. That would just make me nervous. Like if I had it, I *could* call when I didn't really think I *should* call. Or *should* call when I didn't really *want* to call.

It made everything way too complicated.

"Well?"

"Well what?" I ask her.

"Aren't you going to at least say thank you?"

"Marissa I . . . I . . ."

"I cannot believe what an absolute coward you're being about this. Why are you so fearless about everything but Casey?"

I just stood there, gripping the phone.

"Huh? Why?" she asked.

"I'm . . . I'm not *afraid* of him, I just—"

"You just what? Don't want to get involved? Well, I've got news for you, Sammy, you already are. And if you don't straighten this mess out, Heather wins."

"She can't win if I don't play."

"Fine. So I'll play for you. I'll call him and tell him what happened."

"No!"

"Why not?"

"Because it's . . . it's *my* mess."

She was quiet for a minute, then grumbled, "You are so stubborn. . . ." Then all of a sudden she switches gears. "Oh! Billy Pratt is in Drama Club, too! And you're never going to believe this—he was dressed up as a girl."

"No way."

"Seriously! He plays a barmaid."

"A *barmaid*? At William Rose Junior High?"

"Yup. At least he was wearing a wig and a barmaid costume. They even had him stuffed."

"No way."

"Yeah! And while Ms. Pilson was going over lines, he was pulling out Kleenexes and blowing his nose. 'Course when Ms. Pilson saw what everyone was laughing about, she had a meltdown.

"I'll bet."

"Anyway, look. I told Casey you would call tonight, so you'd better."

"Tonight?"

"Yes, tonight."

"Okay, then you can go ahead and call him. And you can tell him that I can't call tonight. Tell him I'll call him . . . later."

She was quiet for a minute. So quiet, I wasn't even sure she was still there. "Marissa?"

"Nine-two-two three-three-four-four. I'm not talking to you until you talk to him."

Click.

She'd said it before I could plug my ears. Before *I* could hang up in the middle of it. It was such an easy number, too. One I wouldn't be able to block out of my mind.

No matter how hard I tried.

EIGHTEEN

I chickened out. I even went down to a phone booth to call, just in case Casey had caller ID or something. And I did dial, but after one ring I hung up. And then after standing around the phone booth fighting with myself for twenty minutes, I went home.

The next day in homeroom, Marissa asked, "Well?"

I cringed. "I started to, but . . ."

She scowled at me, then made like she was buttoning her lips and sat down.

"I *will*," I told her. "I just have to figure out how."

She just looked down her nose at me, then turned away. And that's how she acted the whole day. After school I waited forever for her in the stupid wind, but when she finally showed up, she just slipped me a note that said, "I hate not talking to you. Call him!" and took off without me.

So I felt really lonesome, okay? I know it's pathetic and all my own fault, but that's how I felt. And since Dot takes the bus or gets picked up by her dad and I hardly ever see Holly after school anymore because she volunteers at the Humane Society, I headed home on my own. I didn't even ride my board at first, that's how bad I felt. I just tucked it under my arm and shuffled through the wind, thinking. Thinking about how everything was all mixed up and turned around. Hudson and Grams were acting like a couple of moody teenagers, my best friend wasn't talking to me, and who knows what Casey Acosta really wanted from me. Maybe he did like me, maybe he didn't. And who knows how I felt about him. He *was* cute. He *was* funny. And nice, and smart, and even, you know, *courageous*. But I was scared to find out more. Scared that he might be just another version of Billy Pratt, taking a dare at my expense.

So I was all caught up in thinking dark, stormy thoughts, when suddenly I realized I was riding my board. And I wasn't exactly rolling toward home—I was headed for the Vault.

The minute I was in the gallery, standing in front of Diane's paintings, I started feeling better.

Like I had company.

I looked at *Whispers* first, but then I found myself in front of *Resurrection*—Hudson's favorite. And the more I looked at it, the more I liked it, too. That one leaf with its tips dipped in gold, swirling, *dancing* above the others. It felt happy. Light. Free.

Just like I wanted to feel inside.

Then I moved over to *Awakening*—the one with a young tree arching over a small meadow. The grass was a soft green, spotted with wildflowers. And all the flowers were still folded closed, except in one strip where the sun shone. There they were turning up, opening. Like they were sunning their faces, breathing in the joy of a brand-new day.

I hadn't even noticed the flowers the first time I'd looked

at the painting. I'd noticed the tree and the ray of sunshine and the tidy olive green fence in the background, but I'd missed the flowers. They were a subtle yellow. Quiet. But the more I looked at the painting, the more I understood that they were the focus. They were the picture.

I just stood there, wishing I could sit in that meadow and soak in the comfort of starting fresh. And I wondered where you could go to feel that way. Where *she* had gone to see this.

And then very slowly this odd sensation crept over me. Like I *had* been there before. Only . . . only not.

I stared at the painting for the longest time, trying to remember something. A dream, maybe.

But what dream?

I went over to *Whispers* and stared at it, too. Then back to *Awakening*. And my heart was starting to do really funny things. Really *weird* things. Like beating too fast, then not beating at all.

It was coming to me.

Yes, it was.

But . . . was I just imagining it?

I mean, it didn't really make sense.

I took one last look at *Awakening*, then decided—I had to go see for myself. See if it was real or just my runaway imagination again.

So I'm backing away from Diane's installation with a lot on my mind when I sort of stumble, right into someone. And when I whip around to say I'm sorry, who's standing there smiling at me?

One millionaire bag lady.

"Well, hello again!" she says.

"Hi, Mrs. Weiss," I tell her, but really, I don't want to stand around and chat with any millionaire bag ladies.

But she holds on to my arm and whispers, "Have you seen him around, dear?"

I knew she meant Jojo, so I shook my head.

"How about the Splotter?" she asks with a grin.

Now, okay. I couldn't be rude and just bail on her, so I stopped pulling away and said, "Sorry, Mrs. Weiss. I don't think anyone's been here—just the security guard."

She tisks and says, "Well, I can see that this business is going nowhere. And I think I've been patient long enough."

The way she said it sounded so . . . final. And all of a sudden I felt really bad for Jojo. I mean, obviously he was *trying* to make his art gallery successful—maybe he just needed a little more time. "Mrs. Weiss, I think Jojo's a really nice guy. I'm sure he'll come through with the rent. . . ."

She shook her head. "The man is trying to sell watercress sandwiches at a rodeo. He's made a gallant effort, but it's a hard sale to make, and it's time to face facts."

"But—"

"There, there. He's resourceful and charismatic. He'll be just fine." Then she turned around and hurried away.

I wanted to find Jojo and warn him. But I really didn't know where to find him, and besides, there was someplace else I needed to go.

So the minute I was outside, I tossed down my board and rode. But the closer I got, the more uneasy I felt, and by the time I'd reached the mailboxes, I'd decided that I really didn't want anyone to see me. So I stripped off my backpack and stashed it with my board behind a bush, then started tiptoeing up the driveway. Trouble is, no matter how you walk on it, gravel crunches.

It seemed to take me forever to get to the Reijden property, especially since I was on the lookout for Flannel Man and his tattletale squirrels. So by the time I reached the picket fence, I felt like a real sneak thief, which was stupid—I wasn't there to steal anything!

Still, my heart was bumping around like crazy, so I crouched low for a minute behind the fence. Then, when I'd calmed down a little, I moved to where I could see beyond the pine trees and vines, into the center of Diane's yard.

The grass was knee-high—much too tall for dainty yellow wildflowers. And there was no graceful little tree, just the big walnut tree, with rough, chunky bark.

But off in the distance, between bushes and weeds and vines, I could see sections of the white pickets that marked off the Reijden property. The same fence that wound its way around to where I was standing.

I crouched behind the fence again and just stayed there for a minute, thinking. Finally I picked up a rock and started scraping paint off the fence.

It wasn't hard to do. It was flaky and weathered. And underneath the white paint was . . . yellow.

Yellow?

I started scraping again. Harder. Faster. And when I'd dug through the yellow paint, there it was—olive green.

Just like the fence in the painting.

I looked out across the yard again, hearing Diane's words

in my head: . . . *I like art to represent life as it should be or could be . . . an ideal to which you should strive.*

So what about those hideous statues she had made?

I sure wasn't striving for *that* ideal, let me tell you.

"Hallo, missy. What'cha doing there?"

I fell over, right on my rear end. And when I turned around to face him, Flannel Man laughed and said, "Bit of a guilty heart?"

"No!"

"Then . . . ?"

I stayed sitting, hugging my knees as I faced him. "I was thinking, is all."

He nodded slowly with his lips puckered out. Like he was doing some thinking of his own. Finally he says, "About . . . ?"

"Art."

"Art, is it?"

"Yes! I just don't get it."

He laughs. "And you're going to discover its truths by hiding behind a fence, are you?"

"I'm not hiding. I'm . . . I'm thinking."

"Ah," he says, like, Uh-huh.

"Well, I am. I mean, for instance—have you ever seen Diane, uh, *Lizzy's* statues?"

His eyebrows pop up and his eyes drift around, and I can tell he doesn't know how to say what he's thinking.

"They're ugly—just say it, that's what they are."

"My mum always told me it was all in the eye of the beholder."

"Well, behold this—they're ugly. But her paintings! Have you seen those?"

He shakes his head.

"They're displayed at the Vault right now. You should go look. They are amazing."

"The Vault?"

"The art gallery. Next to the Bean Goddess?"

He shakes his head some more. "I don't fancy going out."

"Well, ask her to show them to you when she brings them home. Or ask her if you can see the one she's working on. Then you'll see why I'm all confused. It's like she went from being Elizabeth Reijden, Sculptress of Grotesque Bodies, to Diane Reijden, Awesome Painter. And her paintings have so much, you know, *feeling* in them. There's this one with these leaves just dancing in the air. And another of a little girl whispering something. It's just so . . . magical. You feel like you're there. Like any second you're going to get to know the secret. And there's one of a tree and a little meadow and a fence—it's this fence, I swear it is, 'cause in the painting it's olive green, just like this one used to be. Only it's *not* this fence. It's all tidy and . . . I just don't get what's going on in her head. Is she remembering her childhood? Is she—"

"Why, hello there."

I jerked. Just bounced on my bottom like a rubber ball. Then I turned and said, "Oh, Ms. Reijden, hello," and stood up.

She looks from me to Flannel Man and back again. "This is an odd place to be having a conversation. . . ."

"Well, I . . . I . . ."

She turns to Flannel Man. "How are you, Pete?"

"Fine, Lizzy," he says, but he's suddenly looking like

205

he's got a bit of a guilty heart. "I should be gettin' back to my critters." And before she can ask him anything more, he's scurrying away.

"What did you say to him?" she says with a smile. But her face is sort of twitching, and she's not looking too happy.

I dusted off my pants. "Nothing! Really, nothing. I was just telling him how awesome your paintings are."

Now, the way she was looking at me made me feel really small. Really pesky. And I just wanted to throw myself at her mercy and say, "I'm sorry! I'm just trying to *understand*," but for some reason I was sort of scared to. Like I'd already blown it and making excuses for snooping around her property would just make things worse.

"Hmmm," she says, still twitching around the mouth. Then after what seemed like forever, she says, "Samantha, this is my home. And I would really appreciate it if you would respect my need for privacy."

"Yes, ma'am," I said. "I was just—"

"Just *don't*," she says, then turns away.

I got out of there fast. And as I dug up my board and backpack, I tried telling myself to just let it go. To leave it alone.

But the back of my brain wouldn't let it go. It was fighting for a way to make all my scrambled thoughts make sense. And it was telling me that it couldn't be as hard as I was making it. That this whole thing was like doing a giant word-search puzzle. It was all right there.

I just had to look until I found where the answers were hidden.

NINETEEN

By the time I snuck through the apartment door, I was more confused than ever. And talking to Grams about it didn't help a whole lot, let me tell you. She was mad at Hudson, mad at "Lizzy," and especially mad at herself. "Why did I let myself get fooled by him? Why did I ever let my guard down?"

"Because he's a really nice guy and he's interesting and he's smart," I told her.

"He's an old fool, Samantha, and I won't abide it any longer."

"Meaning?"

"I'm through with him! I've had it! I don't even care anymore."

I grinned at her. "Oh, pshaw."

At first she looked pretty mad, staring at me through her owl glasses and sputtering a bit at the mouth, but in the end she chuckled and shook her head, saying, "At least let me pretend to have some pride, won't you?"

I kissed her on the forehead—just like she would have done for me—then went back to telling her what had happened at the Vault and at Diane's house. And I was trying really hard not to say anything that would hurt her feelings, but it was like walking through land mines, because *every*thing seemed to touch on something that would set her off—Hudson, Diane, even Diane's paintings. I mean, the more I saw the paintings, the more I loved them, only Grams didn't want to hear that, or see it, or understand it, because it reminded her that Hudson felt the same way about them. And, of course, he had taken everything one step further—right off the cliff, into that scary Abyss of Love.

So when I finally managed to navigate my way to the part about the olive green fence, I thought she'd actually find it interesting—maybe even suspicious—but she dismissed it right away. "For all we know she painted those scenes *before* she did those statues. It would certainly lend credence to my theory that the woman has a vagrant soul."

"A vagrant soul?"

"Sure. It wanders about, leaching on the emotions of others. Let Hudson think those hideous statues were the ugly caterpillar of her evolution into 'magnificent art.' My intuition tells me otherwise."

I shook my head and said, "Wow, Grams." And I was going to add that when it came to Diane Reijden, she was *cold*, but I decided to skip it. Instead I told her, "Well, she couldn't have done the paintings first."

"Why not?"

"Because in those fishy-paper articles about her statues, they called her Elizabeth, and her paintings are signed Diane Reijden, clear as day. I think she switched to Diane to start over, don't you? Like maybe she wanted to ditch the reputation of being a rejected artist?" I shook my head. "I just don't get how you can go from making something so ugly to something so amazing."

"Amazing, *pfttt!*" she says, making a little raspberry sound. "They're simply the by-product of a vagrant soul."

"Grams!"

"Well, your name-change theory just serves to make my point."

"It does?"

"Look. There are eight of her paintings at the Vault, right? Who knows how many more she has at home."

"So?"

"So she's just cranking them out. They don't mean a thing to her. They're a calculated attempt to tug at your heartstrings, nothing more."

"But when we were over at her house, she said—"

"I don't care what she said. The facts speak for themselves." She stood up and headed for the refrigerator. "She just gave you answers she knows work."

I helped Grams with dinner, but we didn't talk to each other much while we were making it. She was pretty broody, and I felt bad. I mean, for once I was doing my best not to keep secrets from Grams or hide things from her—for once I really wanted to talk it all out with her—but I couldn't. She was too defensive.

Too hurt.

And it wasn't just Hudson who'd hurt her. It was probably me, too. After all, I wasn't exactly jumping over to her side, saying, Yeah, that Diane—boy, is she an evil witch, or what? And it wasn't because I thought Diane was so wonderful—she was fine, but she wasn't Grams.

Not in a million years was she Grams. So I *wanted* to be on Grams' side, but those darned paintings kept getting in my way. They *were* wonderful. And the fact that Grams couldn't get past the creator and just admit that the paintings were amazing bothered me as much as Hudson deciding he was in love with the painter because the paintings were so brilliant.

They were both wrong.

So Grams and I made chicken salad and soup together. We ate chicken salad and soup together. We cleaned up the chicken salad and soup dishes together. And the whole time we barely said a word. And after dinner we *still* didn't really say anything to each other. Grams went to the couch to read, and I took out my schoolbooks and started on my homework.

Which is when everything about school came flooding back and I remembered—I couldn't even talk to Marissa.

How did my life get to be such a mess?

About halfway through my math, I couldn't stand it anymore. Yeah, things were a mess, but there were at least *parts* of it I could clean up.

So I checked the change in my pocket, then headed for the living room. "Grams? I'm going for a walk."

She looked up from her book and said, "A walk," like it was the most ridiculous lie I'd ever told. And since I'm usually sort of quarantined to the apartment after school, it did seem a little suspicious that I suddenly thought I'd just breeze out for an evening constitutional. But before I could even say, Grams, I need to get *out* of here, *she* says, "I suppose this means you're going over to Hudson's?"

I didn't have the heart to break it to her that Hudson wasn't even home. He was out with the Other Woman, probably wearing his fanciest boots.

I sighed and sat down next to her on the couch. "Look, Grams. You may be right about Diane, but I think you're wrong about her art. Hudson may be right about her art and wrong about her—I don't know. I feel confused about the whole thing, but what bothers me most is that I can't talk to either of you."

"*Hrmph,*" she says, all defensive-like. "Why can't you talk to Hudson? You two seem to be on the same page about . . . about . . . *her.*"

"No, Grams, we're not! And besides," I say, kind of looking down and at her at the same time, "I was talking to Hudson about Diane, and I made the mistake of calling him old."

Her eyebrows pop up. "You didn't."

"Well, you're right, I didn't, but that's how he took it. The last time I saw Hudson, he was making fast tracks away from me."

"Oh," Grams says. It's a really little oh, too.

A *guilty* oh.

And with that little "oh," the way she was looking at the whole picture seemed to change. She whispered, "I'm sorry. I know he's been a good friend to you. And I haven't forgotten how helpful he's been to us. I didn't mean to make trouble between the two of you." She took a deep breath, then let it out, saying, "If you want to go see him, that's fine."

"Seriously, Grams. I wasn't going over to see him."

She looked me right in the eye. "Then where were you going?"

I toed the carpet with my high-top. "There's another mess I have to try and straighten out."

"Oh? And what mess might that be?"

I shrugged. "A school mess."

She lifted my eyes with hers, and she didn't have to say it—I could tell what she was thinking: We had a pact.

"I know, I know, but really, it's nothing."

She sat back a little and said, "Let me guess. Heather?"

"Sort of."

"Casey?"

"Sort of."

"Marissa?"

"Sort of."

She was quiet a minute, then said, "My. That certainly does sound like a mess."

I nodded. "So I have to go make a phone call."

"Why don't you just call from here? I'll go in the bedroom if you need some privacy."

I shook my head. "I'm afraid he might have caller ID."

"He? So you're calling Casey, then."

Man, I can be so lame.

She just looked at me. Steady. Calm. Waiting.

"Okay, okay!" I told her, and then filled her in on what had happened at school. And when I'd finished explaining about Billy Pratt smooching my cheek and Marissa finding the note I'd supposedly written, Grams just shook her head and said, "That girl's an idiot."

"Marissa? Why? If it hadn't been for her—"

"No, Heather!" She shakes her head some more. "She's just driving the two of you together."

I blinked at her a minute, then said, "No, she's not."

"Sure she is! Look at you—you're going off in the middle of the night to call him and—"

"It's not the middle of the night! And I have to call. Marissa won't talk to me until I do, and I need *some*one to talk to."

Grams' bottom lip pouted a little. "What do you mean by that?"

"Oh, come on, Grams. Look—I'm just going to go down, call, and come right back, okay? I've got to try and straighten this out."

The minute she nodded, I bolted. Just tore down the fire escape like an avalanche of boulders was rolling behind me. And when I got to the pay phone, I took two seconds to catch my breath, then popped in the coins and punched in the number. And the minute I heard Casey's voice on the other end saying, "Hello?" *I* said, "Casey, this is Sammy. I just wanted to tell you that I didn't have anything to do with that note, and I didn't have anything to do with stupid Billy Pratt smooching my cheek. Your sister was hanging around the patio, and you know she's never there unless it's to jab me in the rear end with a sewing pin or something lame like that. So we're pretty sure Heather wrote the note and set the whole thing up. Actually, I'm positive, because Marissa told her how you kissed my hand at the Faire and she got all bent out of shape about it. *I* know it was all just part of the act you were doing, but Marissa gets all, you know, blather-brained sometimes when it comes to boys, so she went and made a big deal out of it to Heather, but I want you to know *I* didn't, okay? I know it was just part of, you know, that live theater thing you were doing."

Now the whole time I'm blurting all this out, he's saying, "But," and "Wait a minute," and "Hold on," and stuff like that, but I knew if I didn't get it all out right away that I'd probably chicken out. So I didn't let him say a *thing*. I just kept on going until my breath was completely run out. And when I finally come up for air, there's a second of silence, and then he says, "Uh, you said you were Sammy, right?"

Uh-oh.

"What I've been trying to tell you is that Casey's in the shower. This is Warren Acosta, Casey's dad?"

I wanted to slide down the phone booth and dissolve into a pathetic pool of moronic goo. "Oh."

He laughed. "Don't be embarrassed. I like to know what's going on in my son's life. And my daughter's, too, for that matter." Then he says, "Sammy . . . ," like he's trying to remember something. "You wouldn't be the girl that has a restraining order on my daughter, would you?"

Come on, sidewalk! Swallow me up. "Uh . . . ," I squeaked out. "That was Vice Principal Caan's idea, not mine."

"So it *is* you." He laughs some more. "Well, well. And believe me, I'm not criticizing. I sometimes wish I had one on her myself." Then he adds, "Just kidding, of course, but she is a handful." He chuckles. "But very resourceful, you've got to give her that."

What could I say? I wanted to die. Disappear. Erase my-self from this conversation. And he was in the middle of asking me if I'd like Casey to call me back, when he inter-rupts himself with, "Oh, here he is now. Hold on."

So there I am, gripping the phone like I'm trying to kill *it,* when I hear his voice. "Sammy?"

I said, "Yeah," but it sort of stayed trapped in my throat.

"Are you there?"

"Yeah," I said again, and this time it actually made it out of my mouth.

"What's up?"

I almost said, I'm an idiot, that's what's up, but instead I choked out, "Your dad sounds just like you."

He laughs. "So I've been told." Then after a minute of painful silence, he says, "Uh, Marissa said you had some-thing you wanted to tell me?"

"Yeah," I said again, feeling like a cement truck was parked on my chest. "Only I just told it all to your dad."

Silence.

"I thought he was you."

Another second of silence and then, "That's cool. So, what was it?"

By now my grip on the phone is starting to shake. And all of a sudden I can't think of what to say. Of how to start. "I . . . I don't know if I can do this twice."

"Are you telling me I should go ask him?"

God, was I lame, or what? So I took a deep breath and told him. The whole thing. From the beginning. And it didn't come out smooth and fast like it had the first time, but at least I got it out.

I could now hang up and die.

Then he asks me, "So . . . you *don't* like Billy?"

"No! Right now I kinda hate him."

He laughs. "He's just Billy."

"Yeah, I know." Then I add, "So I'm sorry, okay? I'm sorry for the misunderstanding and for Marissa telling Heather about how you kissed my hand. I know you were acting, and I want you to know that *I* sure didn't go around making a big deal out of it, okay?" Then before I can stop myself, out of my mouth pops, "It's a little cold to say that you'd rather kiss a codfish, but hey, I can understand why you said it."

"What?"

I hesitated, then said, "Never mind."

"No, seriously. I never said anything about a codfish."

"You didn't?"

"Nuh-uh. Where'd you hear that one?"

I shook my head. "Where do you think?"

"And you *believed* her? God, she is such a pain!"

All of a sudden I remembered. "Oh! I forgot to tell you—I am *so* glad to have my skateboard back. Thank you for bringing it to school."

"Man, you *smoke* on that thing. I had no idea."

I could feel my cheeks turning roasty. "When did you—"

"Everyone on the bus was going, Dude! That's a *girl?*"

"Yeah, well, I was just happy to have it back. So thanks."

"No problem. Sorry it took me so long."

I kind of muttered, "Sorry I never asked nice."

He laughed, then I heard some clinking and rustling on the other end. "Let me have your number, okay?"

"Uh . . . I can't do that."

"Why not?"

"My mom . . . um . . . I'm not allowed to talk to guys on the phone."

"You're not? So . . . what do you call what you're doing now?"

"I'm, uh . . . I'm calling you from a pay phone."

"You're kidding."

"No, so . . . I'll just see you around school, okay? And thanks for being so nice about all of this—"

"Wait a minute. You're calling me from a phone booth?"

"Right."

"You're risking parental wrath to talk to me?"

This was not good. Not good at all! I could feel him smiling clear from his house in Sisquane. "Well, I . . . you know . . . I felt bad that you thought I would . . . And Marissa, you know . . . she really thought I should call . . ."

"Uh-huh," he says, like, I know better.

"Seriously, Casey. I—"

"It's okay, Sammy. I'll look for you at school. And hey! Tell me to break a leg tomorrow. We're either gonna smash or bomb—I don't think there'll be much middle ground."

"What's the play about, anyway?"

"Laddies Gone Amok?"

"All Ms. Pilson'll say is, 'You'll see.' "

He laughs, "You'll see!" Then he adds, "But pretty much, it's just what it sounds like—we lads have gone amok! So have some of the lasses, but I don't want to give it away."

"I already heard about Billy's . . . uh . . . *costume*."

"He's a wild card, no doubt. Like that's something I need to tell you, huh?"

I laughed and said, "Right," then added, "Well, break a leg."

"Thanks," he says, then switches into an English accent. "'Tis better by far than a broken heart, I say! And now, fair lass, I must be off. I have serious matters to attend to before morrow's light. I bid thee adieu!"

I laughed again and told him, "Adieu." And when he hung up, I just stood there, listening.

Listening to the hum of the phone in my ear.

TWENTY

The next morning I didn't do any fancy curb hopping or maneuvering on my way to school. I just *click-click-clicked* along on my board. There was a pretty strong head wind, but the truth is, I was also feeling a little self-conscious. I didn't want to get pegged as a show-off, when all I was, was happy to ride. I mean, junior high is such the high wire. One wrong move and you're doomed. Unless you've got some good friends willing to catch you, that is.

So I'm in the middle of thinking about how nice it is that I *do* have friends—and specifically that Marissa-the-Mute would have to break her silence once I told her I'd called Casey—when who do I see on the sidewalk about fifty feet ahead of me?

Pratt-the-Brat.

I hung back for a few kicks, then decided to lay down some rubber.

Some high-top rubber.

When I caught up to him, I said, "Never really pictured you as one of Heather's stooges. I thought you were cooler than that."

He nearly fell off his board. "Oh, hey, Sammy, how's it goin'?"

"Pretty good, Stooge. Your germs washed right off."

I powered on past him, but he worked to keep up. "Hey, Sammy, wait! I was just doing a dare, you know how it is. . . . Sammy? Hey, come on!"

"Don't sweat it, Billy," I called over my shoulder. "I'm disappointed, is all. I used to think you were an original. Now I know better." Then I dusted him. Just left him behind calling, "Sammy! Sammy, wait!"

Like I've got time to waste on stooges.

Marissa was already in homeroom when I gusted through the door. "Talk to me, sister!" I called across the room.

"You did it?"

I parked my skateboard behind the coatrack. "Everything's fine."

"Fine? Or *fine*."

"Fine, okay? Misunderstanding cleared up."

"And?"

"And what? Don't make this into a big deal—it's not. And you were right—he never said anything about a codfish."

"Told you!"

Just then Heather walks in the door, and the minute she sees me she lets out a really big *smooooooooooch*.

Mrs. Ambler's oblivious. She's hunched over her desk pretending she doesn't need reading glasses, looking at someone's microscopic scrawl through her magnifying glass. So let me tell you, it's real tempting to say something back or *do* something back, but I'd just gotten everything straightened out, and the last thing I needed was to give Heather a reason to think she had to mess them up again. So I *don't* say, Hey, your daddy'd like a restraining order on you, too! or, Pratt-the-Brat confessed, Fishface, or any number of things that would have lit her fuse. I just roll my eyes and turn away.

But she keeps at it, making little kissy sounds and acting oh-so-superior as she struts to her desk. So believe me, it's not easy keeping my lips buttoned.

And then, real loud, Marissa asks, "Oooo. What *is* that smell? You smell that?" Then she says it across the room. "You guys *smell* that?"

"Smell what?" Mrs. Ambler asks, with one eye looking at us through the magnifying glass for a second before she lowers it.

Now really, I don't smell a thing. But I can't exactly *say* that. So I wrinkle up my nose and say, "Pweeeu! It smells like . . ." I look at Marissa and pull a face, like, What? What's it smell like?

"Like . . . rotten *fish*," she says, giving me a sly wink. "Like a stinky, slimy, rotten . . . *cod*fish!"

All of a sudden Heather's lips pooch out and her eyes get all big. And let me tell you, she's looking like a big old bass with a lure through its lip. And it's easy to see that any second she's going to start whining to Mrs. Ambler about how *we're* harassing *her*, only just then the strangest thing happens. Across the room Brandy Cavaletto says, "Oh, gross! I smell it, too," and Tawnee Francisco says, "God, who farted?"

Now, Rudy Folksmeir is standing near them looking like a dog that's been caught lifting his leg on the couch, but he chimes in with, "Yeah, what *is* that?"

"Kids, kids!" Mrs. Ambler says, tapping her magnifying glass on the stack of papers in front of her. "If it smells that bad, just go out—" The tardy bell rings right over her speech, so she stops and shakes her head. "Never mind," she says with a sigh. "Another glorious day has begun."

So all through my morning classes I was in a pretty good mood. What did I care about Heather and Billy and their stupid smoochy prank? Big deal. And since all of our classes were shortened a little to make time for the assembly, the day seemed to go by pretty quickly. And I have to admit, I was looking forward to seeing what *Laddies Gone Amok* was all about. Between what Marissa had told me about Billy's barmaid costume and what Casey had said, it sounded like it was at least going to be interesting.

So when it was showtime, Marissa and I hurried over to the cafeteria and got really good seats. Center section, up close and near an aisle. We planted our fannies on the floor, saving room for Holly and Dot, then checked out the stage.

"What's that supposed to be?" Marissa whispered, pointing to the painted cardboard backdrop on the right. "Looks like something out of *Alice in Wonderland*."

"Sure does." It had a big yellow spiral background, with dirty, overflowing pots and pans and foamy mugs painted over it. And on an angle in front of it was an arched sign in Old English script that said BEDLAM'S TAVERN.

On the opposite side of the stage, there was a tall wooden ladder leaning against the wall beside another cardboard backdrop—this one of a bunch of painted windows with WEARY WARRIOR'S INN stenciled across the top. And against the back of the stage were bales of hay and tables with bowls of vegetables, and an A-frame contraption with rubber chickens hanging from it.

Just then Holly and Dot slide in, saying, "Wow. This looks like it's going to be wild."

Ms. Pilson is up front with Mr. Caan, hugging a copy of the script. And she's smiling and nodding and talking away, but even from where I'm sitting I can tell—she's completely amped with nerves.

Finally Mr. Caan gives her one last nod, then clicks on the mike he's holding and says, "Boys and girls? Find a seat. We've got to get this show on the road if you don't want it to eat up your lunchtime!" He watches the crowd for about thirty seconds, then says, "Hey, guys—Rusty, Will, José? You can't sit there. We need both these aisles clear. That's it. Just scoot over for them, will you?"

Now of course everyone has to turn around to watch Rusty, Will, and José find their seats, including me. And while I'm doing that, I notice Heather's red head about halfway back on the left side. She's sitting with Tenille and Monet, and you can tell—they think having to be there is the lamest thing since kindergarten.

Holly whispers, "At least she's a safe distance back, huh?"

Dot says, "Why's she always got to go and look like that? Why can't she just be, you know, *nice*?"

I turn back around, saying, "She doesn't know how."

When everyone's finally sitting, Mr. Caan says, "Very good. Now, I don't have to remind you—eyes and ears up front, everyone, eyes and ears up front." He waits a few seconds, then says, "And I know I don't have to remind you that William Rose students are . . ." He holds the mike out to the student body, and on cue, one out of every fifty of us mumbles, "Attentive, respectful, and kind."

"I can't *hear* you. . . . Let's try it again. William Rose students *are* . . ."

"Attentive, respectful, and kind." Mumble, mumble, mumble.

"Well," he says, giving up, "please do be attentive, respectful, and kind. And remember—your classmates have worked hard to put this play together for you. Treat them as you would want to be treated. And now here's Ms. Pilson to explain a little about today's production."

Ms. Pilson takes the mike from him and says, "You guys are in for such a treat. This play was written, produced, and choreographed by the Drama Club. As you should know by now, it's called *Laddies Gone Amok*. 'Laddies' as in boys, and 'amok' as in . . . crazy, wild, out of control! There'll be a little adjustment period for your ears as they become attuned to Old English, but don't despair! You'll catch on. The club has spent hours and hours and *hours* preparing this for you, so let's give our own William Rose Players a rousing William Rose welcome!"

Everyone starts clapping and whistling and yipping while Ms. Pilson says, "Ladies and gentlemen, *Laddies Gone Amok*!"

It's like she let loose a family of mice. Heads start popping out of Weary Warrior windows, and kids scurry onstage from the wings.

The two heads sticking out of the Weary Warrior windows have on big wigs and plumed hats, and around their necks are dangling rows and rows of beads. One of the wigs is blond, the other black, and I don't recognize the faces. I also don't recognize the group of boys near the rubber-chicken contraption. But it's definitely Casey standing on the fourth rung of the ladder. And of course I recognize Billy Pratt, in a barmaid's apron and skirts, stuffed to a triple-D, in front of Bedlam's Tavern.

All the players are wearing blousy shirts and dresses— like they've just come in from the Renaissance Faire. And they're busy milling around, making like they're carrying on conversations with their neighbor, when all of a sudden a guy in big black *waders* bursts onto the stage, shouting, "O fate, O cursed fate! I shall find thee soon! And then thy fate shall be that of a fox before the hound!" He looks around madly, then says to Casey, "Have you seen him, m'lord? Have you? The scourge, the miscreant! The bane of my soul!"

" 'Tis Sir Calwell you seek again, m'lord?"

"Aye!"

"He's not been about today."

"Nor yesterday! Or so you say!" The guy in waders moves toward the ladder with his nose twitching in the air. "But there's an odor most foul, and *you*, sir," he says, producing a sword from inside his coat, "might well be on task to conceal it!"

"Not I, sir," Casey says, but he cuts a look at the blond hanging out of the Weary Warrior window and gives her a nod.

The guy with the sword and the waders looks up to the windows, too, but Casey isn't giving away anyone's hiding place. He's asking for a sword. The blond tosses him one while the black-haired girl in the lower window shouts, "Lords, lords! Let him rot and perish, but be calm to-night!" But then the blond calls, "Nay! The justice of a duel pleases! A duel, a duel!"

Now, Marissa, Holly, Dot, and I all look at each other and start whispering because we can tell from their voices—the girls in the windows aren't girls at all—they're boys. And then Holly says, "And look! Those boys back there by the chickens? Isn't that Sandra Wayze and Lisa . . . what's her name? Lisa . . ."

"Ronaldi! You're right," Marissa says. "That's Lisa Ronaldi!"

So while we're figuring out that all the girls are boys and the boys are girls—well, except for Waders and Casey anyway—Blondie is hanging out of the window waving her—well, *his*—arms at the audience, trying to get us to join in with his chanting, "A duel! A duel!"

So we do. And pretty soon the cafeteria's shaking from the whole school shouting, "A duel! A duel!"

So Casey and Waders give each other a little bow, then hold their swords up, tip to tip. Then Blondie makes a grand throat-cutting motion out at the audience, and all at once, we all hush up.

What Mr. Caan would give for the powers of a cross-dressing blond.

Anyway, Waders and Casey broaden their stances, raise their left arms for balance, and the duel begins.

Only, *thwap, flap,* these are not metal swords. They're *rubber* swords. Really soft rubber swords. They bend and U-turn and make for really ridiculous dueling, and pretty soon the whole audience is laughing its collective head off.

Now the rest of the cast gets in on the action, too, taking turns shouting or wailing or both. And everyone's busy, moving around. The two in the Inn are popping back and forth between windows, putting up little masquerade masks as they go from one window to the other, pretending to be more than one person, squealing stupid girlie stuff like, "Oh, m'*lord,*" and, "Such a dastardly duel!" and, "M'lord, be careful!" while the guys, well, *girls* from the back part of the stage move forward carrying rubber chickens. And after another exchange of words between Casey and Waders, Sandra and Lisa and the other "boys" start swinging their chickens. And then someone backstage lets a bag of feathers go, and pretty soon there are little downy feathers floating around everywhere.

Now, the amazing thing is, this is not a brawl. It's more like a dance. I mean, in a brawl it's just chaos and noise. But here, the players are ducking under and hopping over flying rubber chickens, steering clear of rubber swords, saying their lines one right after the other instead of all in one big roar. It's loud, and there's a lot of action, but it's not a free-for-all—it's *tight.*

And things seem to be building louder and louder, getting more and more intense—like a crescendo in a

227

symphony or something. But then Casey presses Waders back, back, back with his sword until he backs right into Billy Pratt.

Suddenly the whole stage freezes. Even the little feathers seem to hold still in midair.

Now all this time, Billy Triple-D Pratt has had his back to the action, making like he can't hear or see the ruckus all around him, whistling and wiping down a little round table at Bedlam's Tavern.

But when Waders backs into him, Billy turns to face him, then sort of hides behind his cleaning cloth. "Why, good evenin', m'lord," he says in the stupidest girlie voice I've ever heard. "Hast thou come to Bedlam's for a spot o' tea?"

Waders seems to forget all about the duel. He lowers his sword and says, "A spot o' tea? What sort of rubbish is this? Tea, indeed!"

"A beer then, perhaps? Brewed straight from the root!"

"A root beer you say?"

"Aye, 'tis most delicious, *teee-heee-heee.*"

"My, you're a saucy one, wot? All right then, a beer it 'tis." Then he looks to the audience—first at Mr. Caan, then at the rest of us—and calls, "Wot kind of beer?" and as he cups his ear, all of William Rose shouts, "Root beer!"

Well, except for a couple of idiots in the back who shout, "Coors!" and, "Bud!"

"Aye, that's it, then."

So while Billy pretends to pull him a root beer, Waders checks him over, saying, "Don't suppose you've seen a certain Lord Calwell about, eh?"

Billy's eyes get all big in the direction of the audience, then he hides his face a little and giggles, saying, "Nay, sir. I heard rumor he'd left for London."

"Have you now," Waders says, taking the mug from Billy.

Then Casey comes over and says to Billy, "I've worked up a wicked thirst, too, m'lady." He claps a hand on Waders' shoulder as he sits down next to him. "So let's toast! And then perhaps we'll duel to the death?"

"Nay," says Waders. "Your sword is fierce and your tongue sharp. Let's leave it be." Then he draws his sword again and stands up, moving in on Billy. "But *you*, m'lady . . ." He lifts Billy's chin with the tip of the sword, then suddenly snags his wig off and cries, "Or should I say, Lord Calwell!"

Billy squeals. Then after spinning in a circle, he jumps offstage and gets chased by Waders down one aisle, around the back of the audience, and up the other aisle. Then he jumps back onstage and hides behind Casey, shaking in his D cups.

"Hold!" cries Casey with his sword out to Waders. "Methinks I have a solution!"

The three of them huddle in the middle of the stage while all the other players cup their ears and lean toward them. And after a few seconds, Billy steps to the edge of the stage, puts one finger up, and says in a big boomy voice, "My penance, fair folk? I must kiss a codfish!"

"What?" Marissa and I gasp at each other. Then Ms. Pilson moves forward from her spot at the side of the stage, looking from her script to Billy and back to her script. And she's frantically mouthing something at Billy, but Billy's already on his way off the stage, charging down the first aisle.

Now, to tell you the truth, I was scared to death that he was coming right for me. But he just winks at me as he goes by and heads straight back.

Straight for Heather.

Heather screeches when she realizes what's happening, then makes everything even worse by trying to run away from him. She tears down the aisle, around back, and up the other aisle, crying, "Stop him! Somebody stop him!" But Billy's just hamming it up, reaching down his blouse while he's chasing after her, flinging Kleenex into the audience left and right, crying, "My codfish! My slippery, onion-eyed codfish! Don't let her get away!"

Everyone thinks this is all part of the play, so nobody's stepping in to stop Billy. And then Marissa starts chanting, "Catch the cod, catch the cod, catch the cod," and pretty soon the whole room is shouting, "Catch the cod! Catch the cod! Catch the cod!"

But when they make it around to the front, Ms. Pilson comes to Heather's rescue, putting her arms out to block the aisle.

That doesn't stop Billy, though. He grabs Heather's face and lays a big, loud smooch right on her cheek.

Heather screams, *"Aaarrrhhh!"* then charges for the side door, wiping off her face, screeching, "I am not a codfish!"

Billy just smiles and hops back onstage. Then he throws his arms in the air and shouts, "*This* laddie's gone amok!"

Everyone in the audience whistles and claps and yips, because even with Ms. Pilson blocking the path, it did seem like it was all just part of this crazy play.

I don't know what was *supposed* to have happened in the play, but I guess they decided that this was a good way to end, because after a few seconds the whole cast steps forward, links arms, and shouts, "The more we practice, the better we fake it!" then takes a grand bow.

What I do know is, nobody clapped harder than me.

They cleared us out of the cafeteria so they could pull the tables out and set up for lunch. And normally Dot, Holly, and I would have just parked at our patio table with our sack lunches while Marissa went back to the hot-lunch line, but we couldn't stop talking about the play, so we all waited in line with Marissa.

And we were just laughing away, when all of a sudden Marissa's eyes get all big and she gasps, "Ohmygod!"

"What?" I ask her, thinking something's wrong.

"They're serving . . ."

The rest of us look and cry, "Fish sticks!" then totally bust up.

"So that's where Heather ran off to," Holly says. "Around back to get caught . . ."

"Cut . . ."

"And fried!"

Marissa shakes her head, still laughing. "I think this is what Ms. Pilson calls 'poetic justice.'"

But then Dot reels us all in by whispering, "Nuh-uh. It's called wishful thinking . . . there she is, right there."

We watch as Heather walks up and takes cuts from Tenille and Monet and then just stands there, glowering at us from twenty feet back.

So. Heather wasn't fried filet after all. She was just hate bait, as usual.

It had been a fun fantasy while it lasted.

And even though I could tell she thought I'd masterminded what had happened to her—even though it was very tempting to start up a chorus of "Codfish! Codfish! Codfish!"—I just turned my back on her.

She'd started it, Billy'd finished it.

I was going to stay *out* of it.

So I'm just standing in line with my friends, feeling kind of proud of myself for swimming away from temptation, when all at once Holly's face pulls back, Marissa's eyes bug out, and Dot takes a nervous step backward. And from the looks on their faces, I can tell who's coming up behind me.

Heather.

So I whip around, ready to put up a karate block or something, only it's *not* Heather.

It's her brother.

He's not wearing his hat, and he doesn't have his sword, but he is still mostly in costume. He grins at me, saying, "Hey, take it easy! I was just hoping you'd let me have cuts."

I was so embarrassed! Then, like a moron, I popped off with, "You gotta ask nice," and before I know it, he's on one knee, grabbing my hand with both of his, saying in a loud, stage voice, "I beg thee, fair Samantha! This weary traveler's had but a morsel all day. 'Tis a small thing I ask—"

"Okay, okay!" I tell him, trying to pull free.

He doesn't let go, though. He just holds on and grins. And then, very slowly, he brings my hand closer, closer, closer.

Right up to his lips.

Then he jumps up and gets into line, saying, "So, what's for lunch?"

Now, personally, I can find no vocabulary. It's like my hard disk has been demagnetized by my hand.

But Marissa, Holly, and Dot are completely connected. "Fish sticks!" they say together.

"Fish sticks," he says with a grin and a glance back in line at Heather. "Perfect."

TWENTY-ONE

We wound up eating lunch in the cafeteria with Casey and a bunch of his eighth-grade actor friends. And the strange thing is, they were all really nice. They were goofy, but not too goofy. Friendly, but not too friendly. And just nice.

And when Casey made me put some Triscuits and peaches on my peanut butter sandwich—which, by the way, is really good—I told him how Grams agreed that mac 'n' salsa was god-like.

"Your *grand*mother tried it? Mine won't try anything. She thinks I'm nuts."

I laughed. "Mine's the greatest."

He kind of cocked his head and looked at me.

"Well, she is!"

"Okay! I believe you." He grinned at me, then added, "Does she ride a skateboard, too?"

I busted up. I mean, something about that seemed really funny to me. But then I thought about it a minute and said, "No . . . but I'm working on it."

Then Danny Urbanski came over to the table and said, "Hi, guys," as he scooted in next to Marissa. "Hey, Missy."

Now, I could tell that Marissa's heart was going all pitter-patter. But she looked right at him and said, "Uh, please don't call me that. *Heather* calls me that."

"Oooooh," he says. "Wouldn't want to be in the same camp as her. Y'all'd probably kill me."

Well, all of a sudden that's just what I wanted to do. Or at least make him back off a little. I mean, here he is, thinking he's all, you know, *suave,* and there's my best friend, getting swoonier by the minute. And *I* can tell that *he* can tell that she's all blather-brained about him, and to me, there's no doubt about what he's doing.

He's working her.

So I tell him, "You've got nothing to worry about, Danny. Not unless you plan on being a two-faced, back-stabbing, smooth-talking snake."

His eyebrows go way up, and he says to Casey, "You gonna let her talk about your sister that way?"

Casey shrugs. "I believe that was directed at you." Then he grins at him and adds, "And man, I wouldn't risk it."

Now, I thought Marissa might be kind of mad at me, but she wasn't. She actually gave me a little nod. Like she knew she'd been about to spin out of orbit and was glad I'd pulled her back. And then when Danny found out that Marissa hangs out at the mall arcade after school and said, "Well, maybe I'll see you there sometime," Marissa just shrugged and told him, "You'll need a lot of quarters if you're thinking you'll beat me."

After lunch, Casey walked with me clear over to science, which wasn't weird or anything. We just, you know, walked and talked. He told me about how he got into acting because his dad was into it and took him to auditions and stuff when he was younger because he didn't want to stick him with a sitter or his wacky mom and sister. And then he started trying out for parts, and pretty soon he and his dad were in plays together.

I almost told him about my mom being an actress, but I bit my tongue in time. Like I need him to know about her!

Anyway, Heather saw us outside of science, but she just sulked into class. Then sulked all through class. Not one word.

Now, that could be a good thing or a very bad thing. I guess time will tell. For now, I'm just enjoying the silence.

Anyway, with all of that going on, art was about the last thing on my mind. Even on my way over to Miss Kuzkowski's classroom, I still wasn't thinking about art. Especially since Billy Pratt ran up to me and whispered, "You still think I'm a stooge?"

I just laughed and said, "What you are, Billy, is a maniac!"

He blew me a kiss and charged off to class.

So my mind *still* wasn't on art when Miss Kuzkowski told us our reports were due the next day, or that she'd be gone to a conference for part of next week, or that we should come up and get the still-life sketches she'd made us do weeks ago and had finally graded. I just fished my still life from the stack she'd fanned out on the front table and went back to my stool.

But then Tammy Finnial says from up by the front

table, "Miss Kuzkowski, mine's not in here," which sort of brings my head into art class.

See, Tammy has the world's whiniest voice. Everything she says sounds like a complaint, even if what she's saying is that she *likes* something. She may say, I like your sweatshirt, but what she's really saying is, I like your sweatshirt, and I don't get why *my* mom didn't buy something like it for *me*. *My* mom never buys anything great for me. Why does everyone *else* have a mom who buys great sweatshirts for *them* and mine won't do that for *me*?

The girl's a whining wonder.

Anyway, there's Tammy, up front, whining about not finding her paper. And we're all kind of rolling our eyes while Miss Kuzkowski looks through the few still lifes that are left on the table, comparing who's absent to which papers are left, when she looks up, right at me. "Sammy? Whose sketch is that?"

"Mine," I call back. But then I look at the name on the sketch and it's *not* mine—it's Tammy's.

"Oh, wait!" I say, jumping up. "I took the wrong one. Here, Tammy. Sorry."

Tammy rolls her eyes and tisks and snatches her lopsided fruit out of my hand. "No biggie," she says, and huffs back to her seat.

So, fine. Now I've got my own ugly still life of the fruit bowl, not hers. And it really *was* no big deal. A simple mistake. Tammy's *T* had been covered up by the paper on top of it, so all I'd seen was *ammy*.

Still. Something about it felt strange to me. I mean, Tammy and I are so different. She wears fashion clogs and pink nail polish and velvet hip huggers. No kidding. They're sort of a maroon red and the velvet on the butt is all crushed or worn off from sitting, but she wears them all the time anyway. I guess she figures if *she* can't see the bald patches, neither can we.

Anyway, the point is, Tammy's nothing like me. And I'd never made the connection before that our names were exactly the same except for the first letter, because to me *Tammy* and *Sammy* are as different as worn jeans and balding velvet pants.

But knowing my mom, she could very easily have named me Tammy instead of Sammy. And then what? Would it have made any difference in how I turned out? Would I be into nail polish and velvet pants?

Could a single letter have such power?

Then I started thinking about Marissa's name and why *didn't* she like to be called Missy?

Well okay. It rhymes with sissy and prissy, so scratch that. It'd be like Henry Regulski going by Ichabod, which *is* his real first name. And maybe he actually went by Ichabod for the first five years of his life, but the minute he hit school, kids probably started calling him Icky.

How are you supposed to survive school with a name like that?

*Any*way, there I was, just sitting on my stool, obsessing over names, when this little thought sort of fluttered through my brain. It felt like a dandelion seed spinning up, up, up, into the sky. I'd lose sight of it for a second, then see it again. Drifting. Spinning. Disappearing. Reappearing . . .

And something about trying to follow this thought was making my heart beat faster. Sort of taking my breath away. Pretty soon it felt like I was spinning. Faster and faster. Higher and higher.

Emma shook me back to earth. "Sammy? Sammy, are you all right?"

"Huh?"

"You look like you're going to fall over. You're all pale."

"Huh?"

"Miss Kuzkowski?" Emma calls, flagging her hand through the air. "Sammy's all . . ." She kind of crinkles her face up at me and says, "Are you contagious?"

All of a sudden Miss Kuzkowski's right in front of me. "Sammy? Are you all right?"

I almost said, Yeah, yeah, I'm fine. But really, I wasn't. My heart was bouncing all over the place, I could barely breathe, and my head was spinning.

Then all of a sudden I broke through. Just sailed through the wall in my head, into the light.

I could *see*.

"Sammy?" Miss Kuzkowski asked.

"What?" I whispered.

"Are you going to be sick?"

"I . . . I need to go home, okay?"

"By all means, go!" She hands me my backpack and says, "Emma will help you to the office."

"No!" I tell her. "I'll . . . I'll be fine."

"Are you sure . . . ? I think I should send Emma with you."

"No, really. I'll be fine. I just need to get home."

"Okay, then. If you're sure."

Now maybe it would've been easier to wait for school to let out, but I felt like this thought—this *idea*—was going to burst inside me if I stayed at school. So I headed straight for Mrs. Ambler's classroom. Straight for my skateboard.

Trouble is, the room was locked up tight. So I raced around campus until I found Cisco, the head custodian, working on fixing a water fountain. "Mr. Diaz?" I called. "I've got to go home. Can you let me into my homeroom?"

So he followed me back and let me in, and while he waited at the door, I dug up my skateboard, then went over to Mrs. Ambler's desk and left her a I-hope-you-don't-mind-I'll-return-it-tomorrow note where her magnifying glass used to be. Then I went to the office.

Mrs. Tweeter took one look at me over the tops of her reading glasses and said, "Are you sick, dear? You look like you're running a fever."

I nodded. "Can I call home?"

She reached for the phone, saying, "I'll have to do that for you, dear."

I gave her the number, and I could tell when Grams picked up because Mrs. Tweeter's face fluttered into a smile as she said, "Mrs. Keyes? Yes, this is Mrs. Tweeter calling from William Rose? Samantha's ill and needs to come home. Can you pick her up?"

I shook my head and whispered, "She doesn't have a car. I'll just walk. Can I talk to her?"

"Hold on a moment, Mrs. Keyes," Mrs. Tweeter said, and handed me the phone.

So I said, "Hi," into it, and when Grams asked me if I was okay, I just talked right over her, saying, "No . . . no . . . that's okay . . . I can make it."

At this point Grams knows *some*thing's up. And I can practically hear the wheels in her brain coming up to speed as she says, "Are you in trouble again?"

"No, Mom," I tell her, because as far as the school knows, I live with my mother.

"Do you need my help?" Grams asks.

"I'd like that."

"How?"

Mrs. Tweeter's back at her desk, digging something out of it, so I turn my back on the counter and whisper, "Meet me at the Vault."

"The Vault? Now?"

I face the counter again and say in a louder voice, "That's right. And don't worry. I'll be fine . . . bye." Then I hand the phone back to Mrs. Tweeter, saying, "Do you need to talk to her some more?"

"Thank you, dear," she says, and wipes down the whole receiver with a Sani-Wipe before putting it up to her ear. "I have your permission to send her home, then? . . . very well . . . good-bye."

So I left school, and the minute I hit the sidewalk I felt better. Riding my board helped clear my head. And the closer I got to the Vault, the more sure I was that I'd found a tiny opening into something deep and dark and complex. Like a termite hole bored into a windowsill, drilling through two-by-fours and crossbeams, chewing out a maze of destruction. Maybe things looked fine on the outside, but inside was a world full of sawdust. Sawdust and rot.

When I got to the Vault, I popped up my board and pushed through the door thinking I was there to uncover the truth—there to fumigate. But halfway across the Bean Goddess, I knew something was wrong. Jojo had his back up against the Vault gate, looking like a cornered peacock in his green and purple clothes. Austin Zuni was looming over him, his arms crossed, his cowboy hat pulled down hard. And Tess was slashing her claws through the air, hissing at Jojo like an angry cat.

I edged closer and heard Jojo say, "But I *can't*—she's changed the locks!"

"She can't just do that," Austin says. "I know for a fact that renters got rights."

"I told her that exactly, and she said fine, go on and sue her if I want."

"Why don't you just *pay* her!" Tess snaps.

"I don't have the money!"

"Where's the three G's I fronted you?" Austin asks.

Jojo gives him a helpless shrug. "Gone?" Then he punches his hands onto his hips and says to Tess, "I was counting on a *sale* . . . ?"

Tess shoves him. "Well, maybe if you'd quit buying all these tacky clothes and those stupid mirrors for that ridiculous Vespa—"

"Maybe if *you* didn't want a kingdom for cra—"

He buttons his lips. Hard. So Tess puts her hands on her hips and says, "For what?"

"For...creations...creations that moved much better at their former, lower price," Jojo says, cowering away from her.

"Oh, for cryin' out loud," Austin says. "Just call a locksmith and let's be done with this."

Jojo straightens a little. "Don't think for a minute that you can just take your work with you—we have a contract."

All of a sudden Austin's looking about seven feet tall. "You're crazy as an outhouse rat if you think—"

"Down boy, *down* boy!" Jojo says. "As soon as I get some money together, this gate will open and we'll be back in business."

"I want my paintings, and I want them now," Tess tells him.

"So you can what? Cut me out of the equation? Pay Neddy boy another bribe?"

Tess freezes, and after a second of nobody saying anything, Austin nods and says, "Uh-huh. I had my suspicions." He shakes his head. "You went too far with that one, Tessy."

"Me? What about that robbery she staged?"

Austin shrugs. "Seemed like a legit holdup to me."

"Yeah!" Jojo says. "I don't think she had a thing to do with that!"

Tess snaps, "You wouldn't, you dolt!" which makes Jojo gasp and put one hand up to a cheek like he's been slapped. Then he gives her a really prim look and straightens his posture. "Back to the *point,* dumplin', which is that I've got cards to play yet. I'd advise against forcing my hand!"

Tess stares him down a minute, then simply says, "Look. You let Diane have her paintings, so of course you'll let us have ours."

"I let . . . Diane?"

Tess squints at him. "You think I'm blind? Just because the lights are out doesn't mean I can't see."

Jojo whips around, then grabs the bars of the gate like he's stuck in jail. "They're . . . they're gone!"

"Oh, please," Tess says, rolling her eyes. "Call the reporters. There's been another heist." She glances my way, and since I'm not exactly hiding, she sees me and does a double take. "Come to save the day again?" she calls with a sneer.

Jojo looks at me, blinks for a few seconds like he's hallucinating, then looks from Tess to Austin and then back inside the Vault. "But—"

So since they know I'm there, I step forward and say, "Maybe Diane picked them up, you know, earlier? I mean, you did get the pictures taken, right? For the lithographs?"

"Lithographs?" Tess asks Jojo. "She's agreed to lithographs?"

"She signed the contract today if it's any of your business," Jojo snaps. Then his eyes get big like he's suddenly having a horrible thought. "Please, lord. Don't have them be . . . *stolen.*"

"Stolen?" I ask him. "What about the security guard?"

"Mrs. Weiss fired him!"

"But he's *your* security guard."

Jojo gives a helpless shrug. "She said he was eating up the money I owed her."

Austin's eyes narrow down on him. "Something don't smell right here."

Jojo's face flutters around like crazy. "Uh, maybe I'll call Di and—"

Austin grabs him by the arm. "Partner, what you'd better do is call a locksmith. Pronto!"

Jojo makes some little choking sounds, bobs his head a bunch, then scurries off to use the Bean Goddess phone. I shadow him behind the counter like I'm part of the phone-call package, and thirty seconds after he says, "Di, darling?" into the receiver I can tell—his tush is toast.

"She doesn't have them?" I whisper when he gets off the phone.

"No!" he wails. "How can this be?"

He jets off, but I just stand there a minute, thinking. Then I take a quick look around, and since no faux-bos seem to be watching, I grab the phone, dial information, and in no time I've got the number for the Heavenly Hotel.

André picks up on the third ring, saying, "Heavenly," right through his cigar.

"André," I whisper. "It's Sammy."

"Who? Speak up, would ya?"

"Sammy," I whisper louder.

"Oh, hey!" I can practically see him sitting up straighter. "We in trouble?"

"No, but I need to know something—has the Harley guy checked out?"

"Uh, noooooo. He just paid for another night."

"He did?" I charged ahead anyway. "When?"

"Not mor'n ten minutes ago."

"So he's in his room?"

"Believe so."

"Connect me, would you?"

"Yes, ma'am."

A long minute later I hear, "Hello?" in my ear.

"Mr. Reijden?" I whisper.

"What's that?"

"Mr. Reijden? It's Sammy. My grams and I met you in the lobby?"

"Oh, right."

"I know why you stole the paintings."

Silence.

"I understand why you did it, and I don't blame you."

Finally he says, "Miss, look. This is between Lizzy and me."

"So she knows you have them?"

There was a really long pause, and finally he says, "Come again?"

"The paintings—she knows you've got them? Like I said, I don't blame you, I just don't—"

"Are you saying they're not at the gallery?"

My skin felt like it was crawling right off my shoulders. "Uh . . . that's right. The Vault's been shut down because Jojo hasn't paid the rent. All the rest of the paintings are locked inside, but hers are gone. And since Jojo just called your sister and *she* doesn't have them, I figured you took them. I mean, that *was* you the night of the reception, right?"

I could hear him across the line, thinking. And finally he says, "My sister's wrong about a lot of things, but she's right that you're a real smart kid. And I'm sorry about kicking your jaw. That looked like it hurt pretty bad. Didn't mean to harm no one. And I know the whole thing was kinda crazy, but I was afraid she would sell some that night."

"So you do have them?"

"No, ma'am."

"But—"

Just then a bean-brewing bohemian snatches the phone from my ear and says, "What do you think this is? A pay phone?"

"Hey!" I cried, but she slammed the phone down and wagged her pierced tongue at me like some weird lizard or something.

"That's supposed to *scare* me?" I asked her. "Go French a frozen fish, why don'tcha?"

She blinked at me once, then threw me over the counter.

So I was dusting off, collecting my cool, when Grams blows through the Bean Goddess door. And before she can get a single question out, I grab her by the arm and yank her back outside.

"Samantha! What on earth is going on? Where are we going?"

I pull her along, saying, "I'll tell you on the way," because in my heart I know.

I don't have much time.

TWENTY-TWO

Santa Martina's probably got a grand total of two taxis, but when Grams found out what I suspected, she jumped out into Broadway traffic and flagged one down. And when we got dropped off in front of Diane's driveway, I wedged Mrs. Ambler's magnifying glass into my back pocket, then stashed my skateboard and backpack in the same old bushes and said, "Let's go."

About halfway down the driveway, Grams whispers, "My hunch is she won't let us in."

"But she's got to be home. Jojo talked to her just a little while ago."

"Oh, she's home, all right," Grams says, pointing to the sky. "What I'm saying is, she won't answer the door."

What Grams had pointed to was smoke coming up from the chimney, blowing in a thin gray stream over the rooftop. And at first I didn't think anything of it, but then I got this awful, nauseating thought. "Grams!" I gasped.

"What, Samantha? What is it?"

I was staring at the smoke. "Nooooo!" I cried, and took off running.

I pushed the doorbell like crazy.

Nobody came.

I whacked the door with my knuckles.

Nobody came.

I pounded with my fist and my foot and rattled the knob and screamed, "Diane, don't!" but nobody answered the door.

Grams caught up to me, panting, "Samantha, what is wrong?"

"Oh, Grams! Oh, Grams!" I cried. "She doesn't need them anymore. All they are now is evidence."

Grams tried to calm me down. Tried to talk me out of what I was thinking, but it was no use. I beat on the door like I wanted to kill it. "Grams, call the police! Go over to Mr. Moss's and call the police!"

"But—"

I took off around the house, looking for another door. A side door. A back door. An *unlocked* door. And when I came around to the sunroom, to the big, wide window of the sunroom, I could see in, clear to the family room.

There was Diane, sitting on the edge of the fireplace hearth with perfect posture, watching the fire burn. And I couldn't tell what was inside the fireplace—all I could see was a flame in the center and black smoke curling up the sides—but leaning against the hearth was something I would recognize anywhere.

Whispers.

"No!" I screamed as I pounded on the window. "Diane, don't!"

She didn't even look over. She just kept staring at the fire.

I ran around the house, rattling doorknobs, trying windows, yelling, "Help! Help! Somebody, help!" And I was clear around the back side of the house when I heard a loud noise. A *brittle* noise.

At first I froze, trying to figure out what had broken. Then I ran. And I was barreling past the sunroom when I saw it—a six-foot hole in the sunroom window. And lying across the bottom frame on its nonexistent face was that hideous, nursing home statue that had been standing guard outside.

I stepped on it, over it, right into the house. And when I got into the living room, what did I see?

My grams on the ground like a professional wrestler.

Seriously, she's on top of Diane, pulling her head back by the hair with one hand, wrenching a leg back with the other. And Diane's flailing around, trying to hit her, but Grams is bouncing up and down on her back, crying, "You fake! You phony!"

Now, part of me is dying to jump in and help Grams, because Diane looks like she might break free any second, but Grams cries, "Samantha, quick! See if you can save them! She threw them all on!"

There's smoke pouring into the room from underneath the paintings, and as I charge the fireplace, I see *Whispers* on top, still intact.

I grab for the top few frames, but before I can get a grip, flames flare up around my arm and I have to pull back.

So I try from a different angle, but suddenly the hood of my sweatshirt yanks me back, cutting into my throat and choking me.

It's Diane, hanging on, dragging me away, crying, "I . . . am . . . not . . . going to let you . . . ruin this . . . for me!"

And there's Grams, sprawled on the floor behind me, down, but definitely not out.

So I'm twisting and kicking and yanking, trying to get back to the fireplace, when all of a sudden Grams charges Diane with a flying tackle from the side and sets me free.

Black smoke is billowing everywhere now, but *Whispers* is still okay. So right through fire and smoke and heat, I reach inside. The frame is blazing hot, but I hold on anyway. But just as I'm pulling *Whispers* out, fire shoots through the middle and *poof,* the girl in the painting disappears.

I yank it away, crying, "No! Noooo!" and smother the flames on the carpet.

I knew it was ruined, but still, I couldn't bear to believe it. And when I finally did turn it over and look, my eyes spilled over. The whole center was crinkled and melted. All I could make out was the tail of the rocking horse and a little bit of a hand.

I almost gave in and bawled my eyes out. But there in the bottom left corner was what I'd come to Diane's house for in the first place.

Proof.

I checked Grams. She had ol' Purple Eyes in a hammerlock, but Diane was still fighting hard to get to me. So I dried my eyes, pulled out Mrs. Ambler's magnifying glass, and got to work.

She'd done a good job. A very good job. The color

matched almost exactly. And I didn't have to scrape the paint away to know I was right, but I did anyway. I picked at it with my thumbnail until the *i* was back to its original *u,* and the true artist's name was showing.

"Well?" Grams asked me, twisting Diane's arm back extra hard.

I nodded. "Says Duane."

The minute I said her father's name, Diane gave up, crumbling onto the couch. And while Diane's whole body's wrenching up and down, sobbing, Grams dusts her hands off and says, "Told you she was a phony."

I turned back to what was left of *Whispers.* And I couldn't help it—I started to cry again. Partly I was crying because this painting that I loved so much was gone. But with those tears came smaller, harder tears.

Deeper tears.

I mean, I finally, finally understood what it was about this painting.

It was the joy of belonging.

The joy of sharing.

The joy of love.

I shook the painting at Diane and choked out, "Why?"

She flung aside tears and said, "Was it worse than leaving them here for no one to see? Was it worse than—"

"Why couldn't you just have shown them as *his*?"

"Because he's *dead.* No one cares about a contemporary artist whose future is over. I was doing him a favor! I was combining our talents to bring the world his paintings and—"

Grams snorted. "Don't delude yourself, woman. You did what you did for strictly self-serving reasons."

"It's not true!"

I hugged what was left of *Whispers* and choked out, "Then why'd you *burn* them?"

She looked right at me. "Why'd you have to come back? Why'd you have to talk to Pete? Why couldn't you just have left me alone?"

And that's when I noticed it—one of her eyes was . . . *brown.* I looked at her closer and said, "You wear . . ." I turned to Grams and cried, "They're just contacts! Purple contacts!"

Diane turned away, but Grams was in her face in a flash. And when she saw her brown eye, Grams tisked and muttered, "A phony, through and through."

Then all of a sudden Grams stiffens. Just sort of gains two inches and pricks up an ear. And as she hobbles over to a small window and pulls back the curtain, I begin to hear it, too.

One tricked-out Harley-Davidson coming down the drive.

"I have a hunch your brother's not going to be too pleased with you," Grams tells Diane.

"He had no right to show up after all these years!" She flings aside some more tears. "He's a deadbeat! A good-for-nothing bum! At fifty-six, he's still trying to *find* himself!"

"Hrmph," Grams says. "And I suppose you fancy yourself an artist? A deserving member of cultured society? Well, look in the mirror, *Elizabeth.* It's not a pretty sight."

Grams heads for the front door to let Lance in, but she's still hobbling, so I say, "Grams? What's with your foot?"

"My shoe's broken and my ankle's sore. And I don't want to hear about it, okay?"

So while she's gone, I ask Diane, "I don't get why your brother didn't just turn you in."

"I told you! He's a deadbeat! The courts have been after him for ages. He owes fifteen years of child support! Never paid one cent! So no, I wasn't going to give him half the paintings. Why should I? *I'm* the one who's worked so hard to get them noticed, *I'm* the one who's put my life on hold. He didn't move back to take care of Mother like I did. He never called or wrote, and now all of a sudden Daddy's paintings are *special* to him? All of a sudden he develops a *conscience*? I offered him a nice percentage, but no! He doesn't think what I'm doing is *right*. Well, he's nothing but a hypocrite!"

Just then Lance charges into the room, shouting, "How could you burn them?" And when he sees what's left of *Whispers,* his face completely pinches up and he looks like he's about to cry. *"Why?"*

Diane's checking around for her missing contact lens and doesn't even look at him. So I say, "She burned them because she had negatives made for lithographs. They all say Diane, not Duane. And with the originals gone, no one could prove she wasn't the artist."

"You heartless *leech*. These were our father's—"

Diane stops searching and faces him. "Don't you dare talk to me about our father or about being heartless.

Where were you when he died? Where were you when Mom died? And regardless of your banal accusations, the paintings were mine. I inherited them, not you. So don't tell me what I can and cannot do with what's mine."

Lance stood there for a moment, his lips clamped together, air sucking in and out his nose. Finally he says, "Dad could never see you for what you are, but if there's any justice in this world, he knows now. All those years he paid for you to be in New York and Paris—the *fortune* he spent on you dilettantin' and gallivantin' all over the globe." He squints at her. "Even in my darkest days, I've never stooped so low as you."

"You think trying to bring beautiful art into the world is a *crime*? You think—"

"You'll never change, Lizzy. You talk a good game, but that's as far as it goes. You'd rather party than paint. You want the glory, but not the sweat. I'm sure you'll find a way to justify this—if only to yourself."

Grams hobbles over to him and whispers, "Would you like us to call the police?"

He shakes his head. "He left them to her." Then he grumbles, "My own fault for taking a lifetime to sober up."

"Well, you need to talk to Jojo about the negatives," I tell him. "She signed a contract with him for lithographs."

"I will," he says, then turns to his sister. "I'm through running, Lizzy. From my past, from my problems, and from you." He pulls what's left of *Whispers* out of the frame, yanks it off the wood it's stretched over, then rolls it up.

And Diane did try to stop him, but he just shook her

off and told her to shut her two-faced yap. And when he tucked the ruined painting away in his fringed jacket, Diane collapsed onto the couch and started sobbing in her hands.

And that's how we left her. Trapped with herself. Surrounded by beautiful things that weren't hers and some pretty ugly statues that were.

When we got out to the drive, Lance said, "That's a mean limp, Rita. Did you twist your ankle?"

"She did it bringing down your sister," I said. "Grams is the one who broke in and tackled her."

He stopped putting on his helmet. "*You* did?"

Grams shrugged. "Someone had to."

"Well, well," he says with a grin.

"I'm just sorry I wasn't able to do it in time. They really were beautiful paintings."

I started to tell her, Oh, *now* you admit it, but Lance cuts me off, saying, "Well, you managed to do more than I did." He pats his jacket. "And thanks to the two of you, I do have proof." Then he smiles at her and says, "So why don't you let me give you a lift home? It's the least I can do."

Her eyes get all big and she says, "No! No, thank you!"

Now, my board's in the bushes, so getting home is no big deal for me. But really, I don't know how else to get Grams back to the highrise. Calling Hudson doesn't seem like the greatest idea, Mr. Moss probably doesn't own a *lawn* mower, let alone a car. And besides, standing there looking at Lance's Harley, it hits me that this is one pony Grams should have jumped back on years ago.

So I tell her, "Grams, you're going."

"I am not!"

"Yes, you are. You can't walk on that foot, no buses come by here, we already know that a cab's *real* expensive, and he's staying right across from the apartment. Just get on that thing and go."

She just stands there with big ol' owl eyes.

"Unless you want me to get Hudson to come to your rescue?"

"No!" she says, then turns to Lance. "*Promise* me you won't take chances with my life. I have a granddaughter I want to see get married someday, you know."

He grins at me, then says to her, "You have my word, ma'am."

He gives her his helmet, helps snap it in place, then kicks on the Harley, *brummm-bum-bum-bum-bum.*

Then he flips down her foot pegs, and my grams—in her patent-leather pumps and A-line skirt—swings onto the back of the Harley and rolls down the driveway, showing leg like I've never seen.

TWENTY-THREE

I didn't race Grams and the Bandit home or anything. I needed to take a detour to break the news to the "Silver Knight" before he heard it from someone else. I was actually pretty worried about telling him. I mean, being as smart as Hudson and being fooled by a purple-eyed phony, well, it wasn't going to be easy for him to take.

I found him reading a book on his porch. "Hey, Hudson!" I called as I turned up his walkway.

"Sammy?" He put the book down. "I was afraid you might not visit for a while."

I plopped down in the seat next to him. "Abandon my favorite place in the world?" I grinned at him. "Nah."

He looked at me like he was noticing something new about me. Like you do when you've known someone your whole life and never really noticed they have freckles.

So I said, "I'm sorry I called you old. I didn't mean it like that and—"

"I overreacted, Sammy. And I've been feeling bad about it since. You were just trying to help, I know that."

"Hudson?"

"Yes, my friend?"

I cringed a little. "I've got some bad news."

He sat up a little. "Is Rita all right?"

"Yeah, she's fine. She busted a window, pinned a pretender, twisted her ankle, and broke her shoe. But other than that, she's fine."

He sat up even straighter. "Sammy, what on earth are you talking about?"

"Hudson," I said gently, "you're in love with an impostor."

Very carefully, he says, "I never said I was in love."

"You didn't have to."

He could tell something serious had happened. So he sat there and listened as I told him the story. And when I broke it to him that all the paintings were destroyed, his chin quivered and he whispered, "No . . . !"

"I'm sorry, Hudson. I tried to save them, but they're gone."

He was quiet for the longest time. Then finally he said, "How could I have been so blind?" He turned to me. "And how on earth did you manage to see?"

I shrugged. "Thank Tammy Finnial."

"Come again?"

So I told him about picking up Tammy's still life by mistake and how my mind had wandered off about names and about what a big difference a single letter can make. But when I started in about Icky and all of that, he says, "Sammy? Sammy, please. What does Ichabod Regulski have to do with this?"

"Well, Ichabod changed his name when he started school. At least that's what everybody says. But he had a *reason* to change it then. So I started thinking about Diane. I mean, she was born Elizabeth, she went by Lizzy her whole life—why did she switch to Diane? At first I figured it was because she had a reputation as a rejected artist, but Reijden is such an unusual name, so what good would that really do?

"And then I started thinking about her. How she's so, you know, perfect. Her hands, her nails, her hair, her clothes. Remember on the day we went over there how she was wearing that pouffy white blouse with long ruffled cuffs?"

He nods, but then shakes his head. "I'm not making some connection, Sammy, forgive me."

"She didn't have a spot on her! Anywhere! My art teacher gets paint *every*where—in her hair, under her nails, on her clothes—she's like, permanently stained. And then I started thinking about how Diane's house smelled like cinnamon and oranges. Every time I was there, that's what it smelled like. It didn't smell like paint or turpentine or linseed oil—even her studio didn't smell a thing like art class.

"But the big thing was the fence. And the tree."

"What fence? What tree?" he asked.

"Do you remember in *Awakening* how there's a little tree beside a meadow of grass and tiny yellow flowers?"

"Of course."

"And in the background, there's a little picket fence?"

"I suppose . . ."

"It's kinda subtle, because it was an olive green color and it blended with the grass. But the more I looked at that painting, the more I started thinking it was the same fence that was in Diane's yard. So I went over there and scraped through the white paint—"

"And?"

"And it was yellow underneath."

"But under that?"

"Was green."

Very slowly, his head goes up and down. "So it was green a long, long time ago. Long enough that a sapling grew into a giant walnut tree."

"Exactly. And I should have figured it out right then and there, but I didn't. I kept thinking that she must have been remembering her childhood. But the eyes of the girl in *Whispers* were brown, so that threw me. Then I thought maybe she had worked from a photograph, but she said she didn't *do* that, either. It wasn't until I picked up Tammy's paper that things started coming together."

"The spark that finally lit the fuse, huh?"

I cringed, remembering the fire. "Man! Why didn't I put it together sooner? I could have saved the paintings, I could have—"

"Sammy, you did more than the rest of us. At least you managed to save some proof."

I sighed. "Which will help Lance make sure they don't print up lithographs."

"Hmmm." He turned to me. "They can alter the negatives, you know."

"Alter the . . . what good would that do?"

"They can change Diane back into Duane. They can do it pretty easily."

"Really?"

He tried to smile. "Would you like a print of *Whispers*? I could see if I could get you one."

I thought about it a minute, then shook my head. "It wouldn't be the same."

He sighed, then nodded. "I know. It's not. But it would be something, at least."

"No, Hudson, I don't want one. Diane—or I guess, *Elizabeth*—was right about one thing—I was better off not knowing. I mean, now that I've figured all this out, the painting's pretty much ruined for me."

"It doesn't have to be."

I gave a little shrug. "Well, it is. I mean, that's *her* in the painting." A lump was suddenly gathering in my throat. Gathering hard and fast. "How could she do that to someone who loved her so much?"

He studied me as I tried to blink back the tears.

"You're thinking that her father must have loved her enormously, to capture her that way?"

I nodded and choked out, "What would that be like?" I slapped away some tears and sat up a little straighter. "Doesn't matter. I've got to focus on what I *do* have, not on what I'll never know."

"Now, don't say that, Samantha. You can't predict what the future holds."

I let out a choppy laugh. "Right."

"You can't." He looks out over the rooftops, thinking, then finally turns back to me and says, "Well, I'm sorry *Whispers* is ruined for you. The whole situation really is a tragedy."

He looked tired. Older than I'd ever seen him look. So I said, "I'm sorry for you, too, Hudson. And I didn't come here to try and say I told you so or anything. I just didn't want you to hear about this from someone else."

"I know, Sammy."

"And I know you really believed that falling in love with the artist was a logical extension of falling in love with the art, but Grams was right—you fell for her looks." I laughed. "I mean, if it *was* just the art, you'd have to be in love with an old dead guy right now."

He gave me a wry look. "You're right on that count."

"So now you have to decide—is she worth it?"

"Oh, no. If what you say is true—and I have no doubt that it is—then I want nothing more to do with the woman."

He was staring straight ahead, looking sort of hurt, sort of angry, and very tired. So I tried to get him to talk about it. "Well, did you have a good time going out with her?"

He shook his head. "It was very odd, actually."

"How so?"

"For one thing, she refused to talk about painting. Her work or anyone else's. She just moved around the room, being charming and gracious and, of course, beautiful. But it was all just chitchat." He sighed. "It makes a lot more sense to me now."

So we sat there, being quiet. Being friends. And inside I was feeling better again. Feeling happy. My favorite place in the whole wide world, with my favorite seventy-two-year-old, just being us, warts and all.

And then I heard the best sound I'd heard in days—Hudson's chuckle.

"What?" I asked him.

"She threw that statue through the window?"

I grinned. "Uh-huh."

"She *tackled* her?"

I could feel my heart swell with pride. "She may not have Liz Taylor eyes," I told him, "but there's no one like my grams." Then I laughed. "You should have seen her, riding off on the back of that Harley."

He sat bolt upright. "What's that?"

"Oh, didn't I tell you? Lance Reijden gave her a ride home. Sort of rescued her from her dress shoes."

"She's not . . . she's not *interested* in that hooligan, is she?"

I shrugged. "She has a thing about Harleys."

"Your grandmother does?"

I grinned at him, then stood up and grabbed my stuff. "There's a lot about my grandmother you don't know. Shoot, there's a lot about her *I* don't know." I hopped down his steps and said, "But I tell you what—I'm looking forward to finding out more."

On the way home I decided to stop by the mall. I knew that Marissa was probably long gone from playing at the arcade, but I wanted to check in anyway.

And lo and behold, there she was, annihilating electro–bad guys. And, it turns out, one cool and suave eighth grader.

She spots me watching and says, "Sammy!" then

actually gives up the round to talk to me. "They said you went home sick—what's going on?"

Danny was sort of hovering, so I shrugged and said, "I don't want to interrupt. . . ."

"That's okay! Tell me what happened."

"It's kind of a long story."

She looks at Danny, then back at me. "Well, in a nutshell—what's going on?"

"In a nutshell? Well, in a nutshell, I'm fine, but I kinda need your advice."

"About?"

"Clothes."

"Clothes?"

"Yeah. I, um . . . I want to do a little shopping."

"You?" She laughs, "I'm there!" She turns to Danny and says, "Sorry, but I've got to go."

"You want to play tomorrow?" Danny asks her.

"That'd be fun," she says, then gives me a private grin and calls over her shoulder, "Maybe I'll see you here."

We left the arcade and, believe me, my eyes were pretty buggy. "Wow," I whispered. "Was that *you* in there?"

"He may be cute," she says with a grin, "but no way is he my best friend."

It took us almost two hours to find what I was looking for. They had to be just right. Not too trendy, not too frumpy, not too expensive. And because I didn't actually have any money on me, I put what we found on a twenty-four-hour hold and then went home.

When I snuck through the apartment door, I discovered

that Grams had company. Not the Harley dude—that would have been very weird, let me tell you. No, for the first time ever, Hudson Graham was in our living room.

He was sitting in a chair across from the couch, and he was looking very awkward. There were some drooping wildflowers wrapped in wet paper towels and aluminum foil lying on the coffee table, and Grams was reclining on the couch with her foot propped up.

"Well, hi," I whispered as I put down my board and stripped out of my backpack. They just sort of sat there, mum, so I took the flowers, put them in a vase, and placed them on an end table so they wouldn't be dwarfed by the big bouquet Hudson had sent before. Then I whispered, "Should I go to your room, Grams?"

She shook her head and said, "No, Samantha, of course not. Hudson and I have had a very nice conversation—"

He nodded. "Revolving around what a fool I've been."

"Ah," I said, sitting down. "So is the air clear, or are we still filtering?"

Hudson sighed and stood up, saying, "I think it's as clear as it can get."

"For now, anyway," Grams said. "I appreciate the apology, the flowers, and the concern. But as you can see, I'm going to be just fine."

I walked him to the door, and right before I opened it, I did something I'd never done before—I gave Hudson a hug. An enormous hug. And I whispered, "Everything'll be fine, Hudson."

He nodded, then did something *he'd* never done before—he kissed me on the forehead and whispered,

"Thank you, sweetheart. Come by and see me sometime soon."

"Of course!" I said, then let him out the door.

When I went back into the living room, I sighed and said, "So. How do you feel?"

Grams sat up and said, "Good. No, great. Better than I have in decades."

"Tackling bad guys can do that for you."

"That must be it," she said. "It also gives you a big appetite—I'm famished!"

"I'll make dinner. What do you feel like having?"

She thought a minute, then gave me a mischievous grin. "I believe the events of today deserve something, uh, *god*-like."

I laughed, "Mac 'n' salsa, coming up!" and headed for the kitchen thinking it was true—there's nobody on this planet like my grams.

After dinner, I got busy on my homework. Most of it was easy, but the whole time I was doing it, I was sort of dreading the one assignment that I knew would be hard—my art report.

And really, I didn't know where to start. I mean, I had all the beautiful interview answers, but I'd interviewed a fake! Not that Miss Kuzkowski would know about that.

Yet.

No, chances were good she wouldn't hear about anything that had happened until *after* she'd graded the reports. Besides, who said I knew she was a fake before I wrote it?

I *could* get away with it.

Trouble is, I didn't want to. Actually, I kind of wanted to talk to Miss Kuzkowski about things. Not about Diane so much as about art. I wanted to confess that I *didn't* think joy was a psycho pink eye. Wanted to tell her that I *did* think Tess was wearing no clothes. I even wanted to tell her that Merriam-Webster—which has answers to *every*thing—was clueless about art. I mean, ol' Merriam thinks art is "skill acquired by experience, study, or observation," "a branch of learning," or "the conscious use of skill and creative imagination in the production of aesthetic objects."

Please. That's like saying a human being is bones, blood, and muscle.

No, to me art had become much more than an object or a definition. It had become a search. A way to teach me more about myself.

And just thinking about art that way made me realize that I also wanted to thank Miss Kuzkowski. I mean, if she hadn't given us the wacky assignment in the first place, I probably would still think of art as being just, you know, *decoration*.

So I decided, okay—I would at least *try* to explain what I was thinking. First I wrote up my interview with Diane, then I tacked on a note for Miss Kuzkowski that said I needed to talk to her in person about something. And *then* I took out a fresh piece of paper and started writing down all my thoughts about art.

Now, maybe Miss Kuzkowski will understand what I'm

trying to say, and maybe she won't. What I can almost guarantee, though, is that she won't agree.

After all, I'm a seventh grader. And her mentor, Tess? Well, she's got a Ph.D.

You just gotta hope that someday she'll also get some clothes.

TWENTY-FOUR

At school the next day, things were normal—quiet, calm, almost peaceful.

Which is to say, they were completely abnormal.

At least it wasn't weird running in to Casey—we just said hey to each other and kinda grinned. And I didn't even *see* Heather, so I think she was out on another one of her R&R days. They can mean big trouble for me, but you know what? I'm not worrying about it.

And it wasn't until lunch that it hit me that it wasn't just the kids at school that were mellow, it was the whole place. The teachers, the campus, the *trash* . . . I mean, wrappers and papers weren't whipping around campus like they had been all week. They were just lying on the ground, still.

And then I noticed that the trees weren't bending over sideways and the dirt from the fields wasn't tornadoing around. For the first time in weeks, there was absolutely no wind.

It was like the Big Bad Wolf had packed up his big bad lungs and gone home.

After school, Marissa and I rode to the mall together, but instead of hanging out to watch her play video games, I went around and picked up my twenty-four-hour holds and cruised home. And when I snuck through the apartment door and whispered, "Hi, Grams!" she looked up from her book and said, "You've been shopping?"

"Uh-huh. For you."

"For . . . what on earth?"

I made her sit next to me on the couch, the bags right beside me. "Don't say no right away, okay?"

She just looked at me, worried.

"Here," I said, handing over the first bag.

She opened it like it had a cobra inside. "*Blue* jeans?"

"That's right. And they go with . . ." I put the box from the second bag in her lap.

She opened it and blinked at me. "*High*-tops?"

"Very cool high-tops."

"Samantha, they're *red*."

"Exactly. And I've decided, they're *you*."

"They're me."

"Yes, Grams, they're you. Just look at them, will you?"

She held one out like it was a piece of overripe snapper. Then she switched to the jeans and sort of turned them around, back to front, front to back. And I could tell she didn't quite know how to break it to me that she was *not* going to be wearing the jeans *or* the shoes, so I said, "Look, if you're going to go around tackling bad guys, you need better equipment."

"But—"

"Just give them a chance, would you? You'll look great, I promise."

She inspected the tags. "How'd you know what size to buy?"

I laughed. "Like I haven't spent any time stuck in your closet?"

She laughed, too. Then she shook her head and hobbled to her room, muttering, "High-tops. Jeans and high-tops."

Underneath it, though, she was smiling.

So I slouched back on the couch and smiled, too. She was going to look great in blue jeans and high-tops. She'd look cute.

Young.

And if I've learned anything about my grams in the past few days, it's that it probably won't be long before she'll be *needing* those high-tops.

And when she does, believe me, I'm going to tag along.

Have you read
SAMMY KEYES and the PSYCHO KITTY QUEEN
yet?

Here's a sneak peek.

PROLOGUE

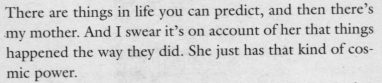

There are things in life you can predict, and then there's my mother. And I swear it's on account of her that things happened the way they did. She just has that kind of cosmic power.

Grams says it's silly to blame her, but I know in her heart my grams has suspicions, too.

Strong suspicions.

I mean, the minute my mother hit town, one thing after another went wrong. I tell you, that woman's the Diva of Disasters.

And then all her little disasters sort of added up to a *big* disaster, which made me go and do something I *swore* I wouldn't do anymore.

Snoop around the seedy side of town.

ONE

I have to admit that it didn't *start* with my mother. It started on Hudson's porch. Hudson Graham is my favorite old guy in the whole wide world because he's got great stories, great advice, and he knows how to listen.

He's also got the coolest porch you'd ever want to hang out on, and when Hudson's home, it's usually equipped with iced tea and cake.

"Sammy!" he said when he saw me turn up his walkway on my skateboard. "How are you?"

"Starved!" I grabbed my board and trotted up the steps, eyeing the crumbs on his plate. In a flash I knew it had been a piece of his mega-maple upside-down cake.

He took one look at my face and laughed. "Your grandmother let you out of the house without breakfast?"

"She was preoccupied. And besides, I wasn't hungry then—now I am!"

"Why don't I fix you some eggs and toast. Then cake."

"Aw, come on, Hudson. It's Saturday." I plopped down in the chair beside him.

He looked doubtful. "Somehow I don't think your grandmother would approve. And you know I've been working hard to get out of her doghouse..."

"Forget the doghouse. If she asks, I'll just tell her it was an early piece of birthday cake."

"Birthday cake? When's your birthday?"

"Tomorrow."

"Tomorrow?" He jumped out of his chair. "Why didn't you mention it before?"

I shrugged. "I don't really like my birthday, that's why."

"You don't *like* it?" He was hovering over me. "Why not? Kids your age love their birthday!"

I kicked my feet up on his railing. "Well, let's see . . . When I turned twelve my mother celebrated by taking me to McDonald's, which is where she broke it to me that she'd be leaving me with Grams while she went off to Hollywood. Then, when I turned thirteen, she didn't even bother to call or send me a card or *any*thing. She finally called two days later gushing excuses, but it was pretty obvious she just forgot."

"Yes, but Sammy, I thought you had gotten past resenting your mother."

"I know, I know," I sighed. "I guess I just have negative associations when it comes to my birthday." I swung my feet down and laughed. "So could you help me get over it? I want some cake!"

He laughed. "Coming right up."

I followed him inside, saying, "Actually, Grams always tries to surprise me with a really nice cake on my birthday. She goes all out and is totally secretive about what she's concocting. I'll bet that's what she's doing right now."

Hudson handed over a giant piece of mega-maple cake. "So you're double dipping, huh?"

I laughed. "I'm entitled, don't you think? I mean, given the circumstances and all."

He chuckled and opened the fridge. "Can I at least insist on milk?"

"Perfect!"

When we were seated back outside, he said, "So catch me up. What's going on at school? And with Heather! You haven't said anything about her in a while."

"That's because there's absolutely nothing going on with Heather." I laughed and took a bite of cake. "Can you believe it?"

Actually, I was finding it hard to believe myself. Ever since my first day of junior high, Heather Acosta has worked hard to make my life miserable. That rabid redhead has done everything from jab me in the butt with a sewing pin to frame me for vandalism. But for the last couple of weeks, there's been nothing.

Well, nothing serious, anyway. I don't count glaring and sneering and catcalls. That's just junior high stuff that everyone goes through. I'm talking diabolical, evil, twisted plots to take over the world. Or at least the school. Elections aren't for another month, but she's already angling to be elected William Rose Junior High's "Most Popular Seventh Grader," or "Class Cutie," or whatever other stupid category she can con the rest of the seventh graders into believing she should win.

Too bad they don't have a "Most Likely to Psycho." I'd vote for her in a hot second.

Hudson shook me from my thoughts, saying, "Two

months until summer vacation. Is that what you're thinking about?"

I laughed. "Actually, I wasn't."

"Aren't all kids in countdown mode by now?"

"It's only the first week of April!"

He gave a knowing nod. "Ah. Maybe I'm confusing the kids with the teachers."

I said, "Huh?" but then he said, "So what else have you been up to?" and I remembered what I had come to tell him about. "Oh!" I said, swigging down some milk. "Holly and I have been checking out Slammin' Dave's. Hudson, I've got a whole new perspective on pro wrestling."

He raised a bushy white eyebrow. "You do, do you?" Then he grumbled, "I still can't believe that Bargain Books is now a pro wrestling shop—"

"Slammin' Dave's is not a *shop*, Hudson, it's a *school*." I almost added that having wrestling dudes across the street from where I lived was a whole lot safer than having a bookstore, seeing how the guy who used to own Bargain Books got hauled off to jail for theft, attempted murder, and arson, but I didn't. I just said, "And Slammin' Dave takes his *school* very seriously."

Hudson grinned. "Can I deduce from your apparent knowledge base that you've been spying on him?"

"I wouldn't call it *spying*," I said through a mouthful of cake. "Just, you know, watching."

"Through binoculars?"

"No! You can't see anything from the apartment. I just go down to the school and look."

6

"Doesn't that place have heavy black curtains covering the windows?"

"Well...yeah."

He grinned at me. "So they let you just stand in the doorway and watch?"

"Hudson, quit it!"

He laughed. "I just want you to be able to admit it, that's all."

"All right, all right," I grumbled, scraping up cake crumbs with the back of my fork. "I've been snooping, okay? You happy?"

"Through cracks in the curtains?"

"Yeah," I muttered. "Or the back door. They prop it open for ventilation."

"Mm-hmm," he said.

"There's nothing illegal about it, it's just interesting."

"Interesting? How so?"

"Well, you've got all these beefy guys in these totally cheesy wrestling suits doing flips and body slams and rope dives. It's like they're catapulting cattle in there."

"And you find catapulting cattle interesting?"

I laughed. "Well, yeah." I leaned toward him and said, "There's this one guy who started showing up last week. He wears an orange-and-black-striped caveman suit and a hooded *cat* mask. It covers his whole face. His whole *head*. I mean, once in a while some of the guys will wrestle in full-on costumes, but this guy wears his mask all the time. He shows up in it, he wrestles in it...he never takes it off."

"So?"

"So does he sleep with it on? Does he eat with it on? Does he take a shower in the thing?" I leaned back. "What *doesn't* he do in his mask, that's what I want to know."

Hudson laughed, then said, "Sammy, it's just part of his character."

"His character?"

"You know, pro wrestlers create personas—the character they play in the ring. Like Mark Calloway was The Undertaker, Robert Remus was Sergeant Slaughter, Terry Bollea was Hulk Hogan—"

"Wait a minute! How do you know these guys' real names?"

He shrugged. "I've been around for seventy-two years. I'm bound to have picked up a thing or two."

Now, when he said that, it hit me that Hudson had been seventy-two for a really long time. So I was about to ask him, "When's *your* birthday?" only just then something catches my eye. Something *pink* off to my left. Behind some bushes. Along the far side of Hudson's porch. So instead I whisper, "What was that?"

"What was what?" Hudson whispers back.

I stand up and tiptoe the length of Hudson's porch. And when I sneak a step down the side stairs and peek around the bushes, I choke out, "Aaarrh!" and jump back. Right on the other side of Hudson's bushes is one of the scariest sights I've ever seen.

A super-sized, batty-eyed Barbie.

She isn't exactly a *doll,* though. She's more like a Barbie gone to seed. She's middle-aged, with super-bleached hair and a mountain of makeup—thick black eyeliner that curves way up at the corners, three-inch fake eyelashes, sparkly gold eye shadow, and pink lipstick. She's wearing a halter top that matches her lips, high heels, and jeans that are so tight they look shrink-wrapped on. And as if that's not enough of a fashion statement right there, on the top of her head is a tiara.

A *tiara*.

"Who are *you?*" she snaps, and her voice sounds really...snotty.

"Who am *I?*" I ask. "Who are *you?*"

Hudson steps around me, saying, "Katherine Brown? Why, to what do we owe this pleasure?"

"Don't play nicey-nice with me, Hudson Graham. And it's no longer Brown. Or Truesdale or Stewart. It's just Kitty. *Miss* Kitty.

Hudson is such a gentleman. In a heartbeat he says, "Well then, Miss Kitty...to what do we owe this pleasure?"

"I *said* don't play nicey-nice. You know exactly why I'm here!" Her gaze shifts from Hudson to me, and back again. "You're harboring a criminal, and I intend to do something about it!"

My life flashed before my eyes: My suspensions. My detentions. My breaking-and-enterings. My run-ins with Officer Borsch. My illegal living situation at the seniors-only apartment complex.

I'd never seen this woman before in my life.

How did she know?

But Hudson says, "A criminal? What on earth are you talking about?" He motions over the back gate to his rental unit. "There's not even anyone living back there at the moment."

"I'm not talking about your renter," she says, all huffy-like. "I'm talking about that vicious *beast* of yours!"

Hudson's eyebrows reach for the sky. "Rommel?"

"I hear him howling at night! Do you think I don't know he's roaming the streets, thirsting for blood? This is the third of my kitties that's disappeared in two weeks, and I intend to get to the bottom of it!"

"But—"

"If your beast got ahold of Snowball, I'll sue you, you hear me, Mr. Graham? I'll have your heinie in court so fast you won't know what bit you!"

Hudson and I look at each other, and although Hudson manages to keep things under control, I can't help it—the thought of Rommel taking on a cat just busts me up.

"You think this is funny?" she says, stepping toward me. "All you dog people are alike. You look down your noses at cats, but you think it's A-okay to let your monsters jump up on people and sniff in their privates and do their business in their yards—"

"Hey!" I said. "I've *got* a cat. I just happen to know that there's no way Hudson's dog attacked *yours.*"

"Oh, is that so?" she says, locking eyes with me. "Well, excuse me if I don't believe you."

Hudson says, "Miss Kitty...," but I'm not about to let her get away with how she's acting. "Watch who you call a liar, lady."

She didn't reply, and she didn't respond to Hudson,

either. She just kept staring me down through those ridiculous eyelashes.

"Miss Kitty?" Hudson tried again.

"Is this sassy brat a relative of yours?" she asks without taking her eyes off me.

"I am *not* a brat," I tell her, still staring her down.

Hudson says, "Kitty—"

"*Miss* Kitty!"

"Miss Kitty, please listen to me. Rommel couldn't possibly have attacked your cat. He's old and arthritic."

"He's a *canine*," she says. Like she's hacking up a fur ball. "It doesn't matter how old they get, a dog's got it in for a cat."

Wow. This woman could stare. My eyes were watering, but no way was I going to blink.

"Miss Kitty!" Hudson says. "If you would please just follow me, I have something to show you." He back-hands me softly and says, "Quit it, will you?" under his breath.

So, okay. For Hudson I let her win the stare-down. Then I turn away and blink a gazillion times to clear my eyes before following along into the house.

Hudson leads Miss Kitty over to a corner of the kitchen, where Rommel's sleeping in a little wicker bed on the floor. "There he is," he says, "my bloodthirsty beast."

A wiener dog is not real ferocious-looking to begin with, but at this stage in his life, Rommel's got more sausage than spice, if you know what I mean. It's a wonder he can walk anywhere at all. Especially without scraping bottom.

She frowns. "That can't be him."

"It's the only dog I've got," Hudson says, putting a piece of mega-maple cake onto a plate. "How long has your cat—you said her name was Snowball, right?"

"*His* name," she snaps, sort of circling Rommel's bed. She was dying to poke him to see if he'd spring into action, you could just tell.

"Ah. Well, how long has Snowball been missing?"

"Since yesterday." She nudges the wicker bed with her shoe. Rommel doesn't budge, so she mutters, "He's playing possum."

"No, he's just old," Hudson says, laying a fork on the plate alongside the cake. "He's thirteen."

"Thirteen? Really?" I ask.

"That's not so old for a dog," ol' Bleachy Brain says. "Especially not a beagle."

"You mean dachshund," Hudson says.

"Same difference," she mutters, frowning at Rommel.

Hudson hands her the slice of cake. "So if a cat happens by, how will we know it's Snowball?"

Her face pinches at the sight of the cake. Like she thinks Hudson's trying to poison her. She waves off the offer and says, "He's black."

"*Black?*" I choke out. "Why'd you name him Snowball if he's black?"

"Because he's mine and I could." She turns to Hudson. "Snowball's fluffy, with green eyes and a long, bushy tail."

"Does he have a collar? Tags?" Hudson asks.

"Just a Zodiac."

"Pardon?"

"A flea collar," I whisper.

"Oh," Hudson says.

"Not that he *has* any of those nasty beasts," she says. "But since there are flea-ridden *dogs* in this neighborhood, you can't be too careful." She scribbles her phone number on a napkin and says, "Call me if you see him." And just like that she clomps out of the house. No, Sorry I accused your dog of mauling my cat. No, Thank you for listening. No nothing.

"Wow," I whispered when she was gone. "She's something." Then I asked, "And what's with the tiara?"

Hudson shrugged. "She was once rodeo queen."

"Her? When? A hundred years ago?"

He pinned her phone number to a small bulletin board by the table. "Don't be cruel, Sammy."

"Cruel? I'm not trying to be cruel. But she must be, like, *fifty*. Are you saying she's still wearing the crown she won when she was a teenager?"

Hudson nodded. "That's what I've heard."

"Hudson, that's crazy. Why would anybody want to go around wearing—"

"Because she's trying to hold on to the past, Sammy." He sighed and shook his head. "I can only feel sorry for her."

"Feel *sorry* for her? Why?"

"Because it's pretty obvious that the high point of her life was that crowning moment at seventeen or eighteen. You can't relive your glory days—and there's no living new ones if you're a prisoner of the past."

I thought about that a minute, then said, "So why haven't I ever seen her before?" I laughed and added, "Believe me, I'd have noticed!"

"It's been a good five years since *I've* seen her. She lives in that orange adobe place down the street."

My eyes bugged out. "*That* place? Every time I go by, there are cats everywhere. On the fences, on the porch, in the yard . . . that place is just creepin' with cats!"

"Very well put," he laughed.

"And she wants to be called *Kitty*?" I shook my head. "I think she's more like *crazy*."

Hudson gave a little nod. "She's definitely someone who could use a little help."

I snorted.

And that, I thought, was the end of that.

TWO

After the Kitty Queen left, Hudson invited me to watch him develop some pictures in his darkroom. Now, if it had been a school day, I might have gone. But it was Saturday, and it was beautiful outside. Flowers were blooming, birds were chirping, there were little puffer-belly clouds all across the sky. And the air smelled sweet—like pine resin and honeysuckle and . . . sawdust. I love the smell of sawdust. Don't ask me why, I just do.

Anyway, the point is, I didn't feel like being cooped up in a dark little room with stinky developer and a bare red safety bulb. I wanted to go *do* something. And normally I would have ridden over to Marissa's house, only Marissa had been kidnapped by her parents for a weekend of "family love and reacquaintance" in Las Vegas, of all places.

So instead I headed over to the Pup Parlor to see if I could get my friend Holly to break away from her chores. But as I was cruising up Broadway, clicking along the sidewalk past the Heavenly Hotel, this lady I know named Gina—or Madame Nashira, as she's called by her clients—steps out of the lobby.

"Sammy," she sings. "How *are* you, girl?"

"Great," I tell her. "How about you?" I size up all her scarves and bracelets and her mountain of shellacked hair. "You going to work?"

"Yup," she says. "The House of Astrology awaits." She grins and adds, "Got a birth chart to finish—some classy lady's paying me double to do a rush job."

"Cool," I tell her, 'cause even though I don't believe in all that stuff, Gina makes it seem interesting. I mean, listening to her talk about the twelve houses of the zodiac, and conversions into sidereal time, and all the other stuff she jabbers on about when she's telling you what she does as a fortune-teller, well, it almost makes you believe that she really is a star scientist.

Anyway, she says, "Don't be a stranger, girlfriend. Stop by and see me sometime." And she's hurrying off, tippy-tap-tapping her way down to Main Street in her spiky high heels, when all of a sudden she turns and says, "You're an Aries, aren't you?"

For a second I just stare, but finally I nod and shrug like, Yeah, so what?

She tippy-tap-taps back to me, then tilts my chin up and looks deep into my eyes. "And you have a birthday coming up real soon, don't you?"

I break free of her and shrug again, saying, "Yeah. Tomorrow," as I toe at microscopic rocks with my high-top.

"Tomorrow! Well, hey. I know you think it's bogus, but you ought to let me do your birth chart. I promised it to you way back in what? September? Let me give it to you for your birthday. All I need is a birth certificate."

She laughs. "You got one of those, right? Everybody's got one of those."

I shake my head. "Well, actually, no."

"Well, your *mom* does, right? She's got to. So get it from her. Then come in and see me." She starts walking down the street, calling, "It'll be fun!"

So I head up to the Pup Parlor, trying to shake off the thought of my birthday. And when I jingle through the door, I call out "Hi, Vera. Hi, Meg!" to Holly's guardians. "Is Holly around?"

Meg was combing out a cairn terrier, and Vera was busy soaping down a golden retriever. Both of them said, "Sammy!" and then Vera added, "Holly's out back, dumping the trash."

"Probably peeking in on that carnival next door," Meg said.

Vera blasted on the water sprayer, calling, "Go on back and see!"

"Thanks!"

I went through the grooming room, turned left at the register, and made my way past pet carriers and stacks of towels to the back door. And sure enough, there was Holly, crouched behind the bumper of a long white van, peeking in Slammin' Dave's back door, a big plastic garbage bag at her side.

"Hey!" I whispered when I got up close.

She jumped a little, then laughed. "You should never have gotten me started on this."

I laughed, too. "I know. But how can you *not* watch?"

17

There were guys pumping iron over to one side and bodies smacking onto mats on another. The guy with the cat hood was there, talking to a man wearing a white T-shirt and jeans. Slammin' Dave was coaching two wrestlers in the ring. One had a good-sized gut hanging over tight black wrestling shorts. The other guy was in skimpy red shorts and had the biggest outie I'd ever seen. I swear, it looked like a little fleshy toilet plunger, without the stick. Both of them were wearing tall black wrestling shoes, knee pads, and elbow pads.

"That's Ronnie Reaper in black and The Blitz in red," Holly whispered.

Ronnie Reaper dragged The Blitz along, spun him around, then lifted him up and dropped him so The Blitz's stomach squashed across his knee.

Holly cringed, "Oowww," as The Blitz collapsed onto the mat.

Slammin' Dave pulled Ronnie Reaper back, and when The Blitz straightened up, I was sure his outie would have been plunged to an innie, but there it was, poking way out.

I whispered, "I always thought pro wrestling was so bogus, but man, they are really hurting each other."

Holly nodded. "Meg and Vera call it a carnival—which it kind of is—but they won't even give it a chance."

Just then Slammin' Dave comes charging toward us, saying, "How many times do I have to tell you? This is not a peep show!"

"Hey!" I call as he's shutting the door in our faces. "I'm thinking about signing up!"

He hesitates, and looks me over. "You?"

"Yeah!" I flex a biceps at him. "I've got potential, don't you think?"

He snickers.

"C'mon!" I flex a little harder and turn from side to side like a body builder. "I may be scrawny, but I'm tough. And Holly here's a real gymnast. She does flips and stuff like you wouldn't believe."

Holly looks at me like, I do? but Dave doesn't seem to notice. Instead, he stops scowling and actually opens the door a little wider.

"Besides," I tell him, "everyone's always saying how bogus pro wrestling is, but I tell them you're for real."

Now he's grinning. "You do, huh?"

"Yeah! So come on. Don't close the door."

All of a sudden the guy in the cat mask is standing behind him. "We're ready," he says to Slammin' Dave. His voice is low and raspy, which is kind of creepy right there. But then he looks at me, and I about freak. He's got *cat* eyes—yellowish gold with long black pupils. And I know he's just wearing a pair of those wacky contact lenses you can buy for parties and stuff, but the whole package of him in his cat hood and those eyes is giving me chills.

"Well," Slammin' Dave says to us. "We do need the ventilation, so as long as you're interested in the sport, and not just gawking . . ."

"We'll be cool," I tell him. "And don't worry, we won't put up bleachers or anything."

He laughs and wags a finger at me. "Start pumping some iron—someday we'll put that spunk of yours to good use." Then he props the door all the way open and heads back inside.

The cat guy, though, doesn't follow him right away. He waits until Dave's out of earshot, then steps toward me and whispers, "Go away!"

"Dave said we could stay."

He glances over his shoulder, then says between his teeth, "Curiosity kills the cat, so scat!"

Now, I'm not big on being bossed around. Especially not by potbellied cat dudes. So I lean forward a little and—just because it seems like a good way to get my point across to this guy—I bare my teeth and let out a low, doggy growl.

He doesn't say a word. He just squints his cat eyes at me, then follows Slammin' Dave back to the ring.

"Wow," Holly whispers. "That guy's got issues."

"No kidding."

Anyway, we keep watching for a little while, and we get totally into the way The Blitz and Ronnie Reaper are going at it in the ring. Holly and I even try a couple of moves that they're practicing on each other. One's a block, and the other's this slick twisteroo–hammer-hold–make-'em-bite-the-mat move. It takes us a couple of tries to get that one, but when we do, Holly and I both go, "Oh, that's cool! Let me try it again."

So we're in the middle of twisting each other around when the guy in the white T-shirt and jeans comes out with some trash.

He sees Holly and says, "Hey, chiquita. What's shakin'?"

"Hey, Tony," she says back. "We're just watching."

"Looks like you girls are preppin' for the big leagues."

Holly and I both kind of blush, but he doesn't make a big deal out of it. He throws the trash bags into Slammin' Dave's bin and says, "So when you gonna get your old ladies to hire me? I'm quick. I'm cheap. Lots of people around here use me." He takes her trash sack and flings it on top of his heap. "Let Tornado Tony do your work— you girls should be at the mall."

Holly laughs. "Thanks, but we do fine on our own."

"Don't you even want to know my rates?"

Holly shakes her head. "It's never gonna happen, Tony."

"Hey, I don't believe in never, so expect me to keep trying." Then he nods and says, "Cha-cha, girls," and goes back inside.

Holly eyes Slammin' Dave's trash bin, which is now overflowing. "I'd better not leave that there," she says, more to herself than to me. "Vera'd have a fit."

I follow her over to the Pup Parlor trash bin, asking, "So, do you think you'll have any time to cruise around today?"

"Maybe." Her trash-bin lid won't stay propped open, so I hold it up while she hefts the sack. And she's in the middle of swinging it into the bin when all of a sudden she stops and moves some papers aside. Then she gasps. It's a weird gasp, too. With a little squeak to it.

So I look inside the trash bin to see what she's so wide-

eyed and gaspy about, and in a heartbeat *my* eyes are popping and *I* let out a little squeak, too.

And in my gut I just know.

We've found Snowball.

Don't miss these other great books by Wendelin Van Draanen:

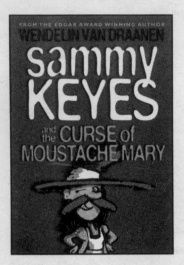

FROM THE EDGAR AWARD WINNING AUTHOR
WENDELIN VAN DRAANEN
sammy
KEYES
and the CURSE of
MOUSTACHE MARY

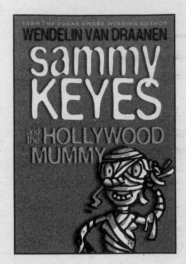

FROM THE EDGAR AWARD WINNING AUTHOR
WENDELIN VAN DRAANEN
sammy
KEYES
and the HOLLYWOOD
MUMMY

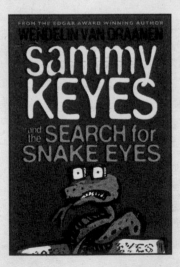

FROM THE EDGAR AWARD WINNING AUTHOR
WENDELIN VAN DRAANEN
sammy
KEYES
and the SEARCH for
SNAKE EYES

FLIPPED

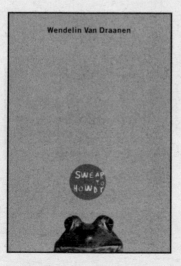

Wendelin Van Draanen

SWEAR TO HOWDY

SHREDDERMAN
1 SECRET IDENTITY
by: Wendelin Van Draanen
Illustrated by: Brian Biggs

SHREDDERMAN
2 ATTACK of the TAGGER
by: Wendelin Van Draanen
Illustrated by: Brian Biggs

SHREDDERMAN
3 meet the GECKO
by: Wendelin Van Draanen
Illustrated by: Brian Biggs

SHREDDERMAN
4 ENEMY SPY
by: Wendelin Van Draanen
Illustrated by: Brian Biggs